Climate Spirit

by Les W Kuzyk

<u>Our Near Future</u>
https://0urnearfuture.wordpress.com/

<u>Novels</u>

Pinatubo II
The shela directive
The Sandbox Theory

Climate Spirit

Les W Kuzyk

**Climate
Reality
Series**

The story Brother's Keeper was originally published in the 2015 anthology Enigma Front by Analemma Books. The story Eco History Exam 2052 was first published under the title A Future History of the Environment in Volume 3:6 (2012) of Solutions (The Solutions Journal) and subsequently as Environmental History Exam 2052: The Last Half Century in the World Scientific anthology Creating A Sustainable and Desirable Future: Insights from 45 global thought leaders.

For my fellow authors

I want to pay tribute to my IFWA writers club, and Imaginative Fiction Writer's Association that keeps a focus on speculative fiction. And I'd like to specifically express my appreciation for Salty Quills, our mini club of aspiring and accomplished writers and their input on these stories. Individual members of SQ are Elizabeth Grotkowski expressly appreciated for her fantastic writing, Justin Acton for his writing techniques evaluations, Shane Heath for his deeply insightful feedback, Tommy Ng for his military expertise, Lise Brassard for her in depth critiques, Philip Vernon for appreciating *Orion Ang0157*, Daniel Wright for his fantasy world creations, and Christa Collett, Kathy Briant, Dee Hahn and Kristine Saretsky for their feedback and reviews. Also, The Solutions Journal first posted a speculative fiction climate theme, shifting my writing focus from science papers to researched stories of fiction. I also want to thank the scientific community for their ongoing published research on the global phenomena of climate change.

How about replacing science fiction, the imagining of fantasy by a single mind, with new worlds of far greater diversity based on real science from many minds?

E. O. Wilson
The Meaning of Human Existence

I could perhaps like others have astonished you with strange improbable tales; but I rather chose to relate plain matter of fact in the simplest manner and styles' because my principle design was to inform you, and not to amuse you.

Jonathan Swift,
Gulliver's Travels

Table of Contents

Climate Spirit

CLIMATE REALITY SERIES

Green Sahara

Vince sat back in the meeting room chair. "So we speak only to the Niger national scenario," he said.

"Yes."

"Any other side effects?" Here in Africa. Or god-forbid back home in Calgary.

"Oh yes," Tamanna said. "The scariest thing is, we don't know all the side effects. We know the ozone layer will take some beating. But politically, we use this project and any predicted side effects to negotiate."

"What about the military?" Vince leaned forward. "Our Nissan got blasted by that Hellfire missile–say they start zapping at the balloons. Now that could affect our release."

She glanced up from her visiscreen.

"You're the engineer. You tell me."

"Well, we've designed a mostly nocturnal release. Reduced night-time visibility keeps us hidden. No doubt they have night detection capabilities, but we count on our distribution–we have release points spread all over the Ayăr Mountains. For any military, I'd speculate a statistical nightmare."

This contract was a poles-apart design project, nothing like the oilfield back in Alberta. His contingency plan could replace a fifty percent loss. The sulphur supply line had that restored in a week and same for any balloon damage.

He felt queasy. What if they took him out as a drone target? And just hearing his voice talk this way, full of fear yet excited. Like eco-blackmail strategy...

"Good." She smiled. "They'll worry about media too. Politics."

"What about who's financing? Can we talk about that?"

"Short answer, no."

"So Tami, who is financing? I mean, so many payments are Asian. The Chinese have a high climate change risk index, and other countries bordering China too. India was high, Bangladesh the highest. So it fits."

"Open trust fund. Any country, or individual for that matter, can make anonymous contribution. I tell you the truth, Vince. Any country can leverage any financing towards its own political agenda. Nobody knows who contributes, but everyone knows the outcome. One exception to that short answer; we can emphasize the budget size." She beamed. "This project has no wealthy-nation-only restriction–a country like Bangladesh now has equal say."

He nodded. He knew the cost was low, very low, from his sulphur tonnage calculations. He had liquid sulphur dioxide trucked in from local oilfields of Nigeria and balloons and helium shipped in from Asia didn't add much price.

"And why did we pick my country again? Why Canada to deliver this message?" He knew, but he needed to hear it again. Out loud. He'd had so many wild thoughts circling around his head lately.

"Take it from a global business outlook. Say Her Excellency was choosing from the five northern countries claiming Arctic rights, as the polar ice recedes. Maybe take military into account, and say environmental record as well. Who dropped out of Kyoto?"

"Yeah, OK. You know North Americans are pretty attached to their lifestyle, carbon based or not."

"Well, you know what you tell a child in a sweets shop. You can't have it all."

"I feel like a rat." He had grown up in an Alberta oil town, played hockey as a kid and listened to his grandfather's stories of pioneering. Everyone did better in Canada, that was always the story.

"Think of future generations."

"Eco-terrorism, that's what they'll call this."

"Your daughter."

"Yeah ..."

"Ready?"

He didn't answer.

#

Vince stared along the bridge at the dim twinkles spread along the south shore. How much had changed since he first saw the dirty Niger River. Only weeks back he'd stepped off the plane into the African heat. People, Tami's gawkers, global attention so focused on the Martian pioneering drama. Most people could put name to face of the eight Martians, especially the Jackie and Haydon romance story. Like an afternoon soap. The fantasy of escaping from the crib while their own planet overheated.

This low budget contract...his device buzzed and he pulled his eyes from reverie to Jeenyus, reading. Daddy I saw my furst star I see tonite. His face softened. I made a wish but I'm not telling it. He thumbed in his reply. OK baby, your secret. But tell me, what color was the sky?

He pushed send. No, he'd never carried out such a low cost, high impact project. All due to the sulphur leveraging factor–he'd now learned the basics of geoengineering science. Straight out of Harvard, that research professor had published the leveraging power of sulphur: a near million-to-one advantage. What you got ton for ton when it came to carbon gas warming versus sulphur aerosol cooling. He reread that more than once, but yeah, the chemistry was solid. That professor from Calgary left to the better support of Boston. Would he end up doing something like that?

He liked the measure Tami and the climatologists used for heating, watts per square meter. And the Space Agency climate scientist drew an eye catching image; a Christmas card picture of a tree. With a 240 watt light bulb shining energy on each square meter of the Earth, you had an energy balanced planet. But you add in a few extra watts and the impact should scare anybody. Scariest thing, it didn't. If you double the carbon load in the atmosphere, a happening fact, you only have 4 watts extra. That's less than 2 percent.

How do you talk up these dry numbers so the story gets heard?

Take the science of the Fifth Assessment report Tami handed out. Right there in the title, 8.5 meant watts per square meter. So you snuggle in an extra little 8.5 watt bulb beside each 240. An added decoration for Merry Christmas tree Earth. The average Joe might say whatever, but really, that whatever now scared Vince the most.

The Christmas tree was a good start, but the hardly noticed global warming was more challenging. Say you switch light bulbs to degrees Celsius. Easy math, you take three quarters–the latest climate sensitivity estimate–of the 8.5 watts and you get just under six and a half degrees. Much scarier now. That much warmer by the year 2100!

You should be hearing a deep rising scream.

The danger line was anything over 2 degrees, or the Space Agency scientist said over 1 degree; way too hot. But people weren't getting it, distracted by their house and their car and the latest Martian romance. You have to get in with a better story, something Tami kept telling him he could do. Another skill set, storytelling, besides engineering.

And you have to switch your audience to politicians, the ones who hold the strings on real change. And how would you ever make a story like this fly for voters, let alone consumers?

These politicians would arrive any minute. He'd never engaged a federal minister before, and these were high end global politics.

The next thought stabbed his fear deeper, with knife blade anxiety. Geoengineering science was likened to the Manhattan Project. He wasn't totally sure what to believe yet, but Harvard said any nation could play politics like North Korea. Right beside nuclear arms, geoengineering was there for any country. You didn't need any high cost bombers or fighter jets either, no intercontinental missiles, just a few balloons and a guy like him to estimate the sulphur tonnage. Then you dictate your back off terms to the world. The calculations were simple; the cost quite low. This story will catch attention, but the scariest thing was how people would react. Countries weren't exactly friendly when it came to global cooperation. But, his heart shivered, his daughter needed a friendly future. She truly did.

The buzz. The sky was bluey darc. But Daddy, my star wuz whit. The times he picked her up from grade 2...he could hear her happy laughter. He struggled to keep it together, blinking hard. How would he tell her, one day, what her Daddy's time in Africa really meant? Physics explained the change of sky color, but this was the sky of her future too. The why-of-it-all raged at him, with his little daughter's life hanging out in the storm. He felt torn...what he did now either way, no question, would be consequential. He had to choose to be called an eco-terrorist, or to claim ignorance, an engineer following contract specs. To take the right side and be labelled, or to take the do-nothing side. One day he'd explain his choice, somehow.

He turned back to the room.

Tamanna sat in one posh chair, focused on her visiscreen. She looked up to smile, giving a reassuring nod. They'd been waiting patiently, with pitch rehearsal after discussion. The door clicked opened, and they both looked up. Vince watched the three men file in, evaluating each face as they took their seats.

"Good evening gentlemen." Tamanna spoke. "As you have been informed, we represent Her Excellency Nishat Jabbar, the High Impact Climate Change Countries Minister of Negotiations. My name is Tamanna Meacham, this is Vincent Patel. Any issues with an audio record?" She glanced around, finger poised.

With no disapproval, she left it recording.

"Alright, let's begin. Both Vince and I are consultants; as a paleoclimatologist I consult on climate change issues and Mr. Patel is a chemical engineer. Thus, you will find us speaking in a very pragmatic tone."

She returned smile to their man in the middle. "I should think you are the Canadian Minister then?" Her light accent, British, rang with that colonial hint Vince knew.

The man leaned forward slightly, his polished look expressing empathy and regret. "Unfortunately, the Honorable Minister was unable to attend. However, my name is Harry MacLean, and these are my assistants; we are political negotiators, consultants like yourselves. We are fully commissioned to represent the Minister."

Tamanna's face twitched.

"Right."

She glanced at the assistants, then at Harry. "Her Excellency deferred on meeting your Prime Minister, but insisted we speak to your Environment Minister. She was specific."

"With all due respect to the High Impact Countries." Harry seemed to pick his words. "The Minister conveys his deepest apology."

"Our message was absolutely clear."

"Our apologies."

A shrewd look came over Tamanna as she slowly released her breath. Vince glanced at her eyes of ice as she spoke in the calmest voice.

"Your Minister may have just made the political clanger of his career."

The air conditioning fan hummed through the silence. Harry sat back, his face twitching, almost bristling. But he said nothing.

She spoke again. "We require a recess–to consult with Her Excellency." She touched audio pause and rose to her feet.

"Absolutely, no problem." Harry's eyes bored into her, his face now like stone.

Vince followed Tamanna out.

#

"Pretty dramatic." Vince glanced at Tamanna as they sat in the next room.

"We negotiate. Nishat insisted on a mature conversation, with someone able to comprehend when and where cooperation becomes an absolute necessity. With at least a national minister. She does not want more bickering amongst playground school boys over who wins." She slapped her fingers on the table edge. "She wants us speaking on the truth, about where responsibility lies, and about the real impact of climate change. Based on non-politicized science."

She leaned forward, eyebrows furrowed.

"Despite our best intentions, that was rubbish Vince. I twig now why Nishat didn't attend; she has more than one strategy. She now depends on her messengers, and she needs our message to be crystal clear." Her look hardened more. "If she decides to proceed, your presentation will be absolutely important."

Vince nodded.

Tamanna raised her device to select a number, holding her forefinger up as it buzzed.

Vince stood, drifting back to the starlit evening framed by the window. Was he responsible? The furst star, the one his daughter waited on as the sky darkened before bedtime. If he could find that same twinkling brightness...he had a wish for Annalise. Amidst the back and forth arguments in his head, among the swirl of terror and tension, the political drama had triggered an inner eagerness, a pervading elation. To play the game for what's real. To act as negotiator, sure storyteller, brought that on. He could take on the role of an ex oilfield engineer–or eco-terrorist depending who was talking.

His eyes scanned the edge of the horizon, but in the dark he could only imagine their erupting bunch of balloons. The all night release rose, he knew, even if not visible. Out on the streets that afternoon amidst cheering crowds, he'd supervising the ascent of the couple hundred around Niamey. Each emblazoned with Green Sahara, for the president's campaign and his vision for Niger. Horns had blared all day, bicycles flew green flags high, and the pedestrian masses wore green armbands. These people didn't know most of the soaring release would rise camouflaged over the next three weeks, up north around Agadez at the edge of the Sahara. Several thousand balloons loaded with their sulphur release systems.

The afternoon urban bunch had drifted south; they'd been lucky on the daytime wind, getting an 80% retrieval with the crews driving up the wadis. Recycling, same balloons, same tank, new sulphur load, they cut project costs even lower. He'd be flying to Agadez tomorrow or the day after, depending.

Each balloon was designed to lift just over a ton up to the specified 15 kilometers in the stratosphere. Vince had first gone up in the platform balloon for the Phase I Preliminary, to watch as the smaller test balloon emitted its sulphur load. A pressure sensitive valve opened before his eyes at 3 kilometers, down in the troposphere as he couldn't go higher without oxygen. As it lost sulphur weight, the balloon and tank accelerated upward like a volcano erupting to finally empty kilometers higher. An invisible eruption. Until the sulphur dioxide mixed with atmospheric water to form aerosol. Acid rain in the troposphere, but a blue-haze reflecting aerosol up in the final target stratosphere. Eruption over, another sensor released the helium and the balloon descended back to the ground. The GPS showed it on visiscreen map, and he followed down to retrieve and reuse both balloon and sulphur tank. The contract could have ended right then, or even with the next local assessment.

But now he had Agadez, Phase II. And extra danger pay.

From high in the next balloon flight, he'd watched his driver race from the Nissan to dash behind a rock, the targeted detection app blaring siren warning. The Nissan disappeared in an explosion of sand and he learned then about Hellfire missiles. Launched from a Predator drone invisible in the high above sky, he learned the hard way his project made him a select drone target. For someone's interests.

Invisible was a big problem when telling a story. Harvard said for every ton of trash going to landfill, 40 tons of carbon got dumped into the atmosphere. If carbon was a stinky jumbled mass, people would have cleaned it up right away. But you didn't see carbon. Unlucky or unfair.

But a lot in life wasn't fair.

How many tons each in Niger? How many back home? Way below a single ton here–Sahel countries emit a fifth of a ton each person. Back home depends, rich countries in the OECD average over 10 tons. Canadians over 15, Calgary higher, like Americans, over 20. So really, North Americans had caused it, Nigeriens hadn't.

He quick-crunched more math. He, living in Calgary dumped over a hundred times the carbon as the green armband Nigeriens. He drove an SUV, they lost their rice harvest. Was he one of those kids in the candy shop?

Over the next three weeks they'd reach their 5000 ton target. Then every autumn for a decade, pending political decisions. The liquid sulphur dioxide now in storage could supply the mid-Atlantic release they had before only talked about. To boost the West African monsoon by cooling the Atlantic. Watch and attack drones would be everywhere over the Atlantic...that was open seas airspace. They would use modified business aircraft to deliver there, not balloons. Shooting down a plane in international airspace, however, that would scream political. The Atlantic release was but a reference calculation anyway, and their 5000 tons would cool the Nigerien climate only. Yeah, right! No way that could be so simple, not globally, not with a fluid atmosphere encircling the planet.

That was just the engineering and the climate science. The impacts of a successful launch brought in politics, where the real game got played. The laws of physics couldn't care less about national borders, and as the sulphur thinned it would drift north towards the pole, over Algeria and Libya to start, and it would spread east and west too, over Chad and Mali. There'd be some kind of impact everywhere, all around the globe. Niger would affect his daughter's life, even back in Calgary. His heart sank, fear dragging him to depth. But fear hit bottom and drove him forward too, tinged by hope.

#

Back in the conference room Tamanna restarted audio record. Nishat had suggested tactics on ensuring the Canadian Minister was best informed and ways to go forward with this negotiator. She tried one. "Her Excellency has decided you may represent the Minister for the Dominion of Canada at this time."

Harry lifted his head, catching the tone. His lip twitched, the slightest smirk running over his face, but he covered the tremor with his winning smile.

Tamanna, however, had noticed.

She stared at him. "Was there something I said?"

He knew, and she knew.

The smile held. "Oh, nothing really. Look, just to be up front, we refer to our country as Canada. The Dominion of was dropped some time ago."

Tamanna nodded slowly, "Perhaps Her Excellency refers to an earlier name to set a time context. One more appropriate. Back when your country's lack of knowledge then, could explain its dated climate change policy now."

Harry's eyes narrowed. "Oh, I see." But his smile widened. He looked at Tamanna and then Vince, emphasizing compliance. "We remain willing to represent the Minister."

The sound of shuffling in chairs pervaded the room.

Tamanna began again. "The first point of business, then. Your Minister must realize that negotiations between our consortium and yours, the Organization for Economic Co-operation and Development–the OECD will no longer continue as per previous. The situation has changed. Significantly."

Harry settled back like a practised listener.

"The Minister must realize that the HICCC decision to act came about due to OECD non-response to repeated requests. Our appeals to basic human interests and a globally focused solution have not received adequate response. Further to this non-response, we decided on a project we expect will be noticed."

"You realize that while Canada does hold OECD membership, our country does not represent the OECD as a whole," Harry said softly.

"That may be the official status, however, we will reveal a unique opportunity for your country. With your membership, Canada will carry a message directly to the OECD as a whole." Tamanna looked Harry's way calmly.

He said nothing.

"So we can speak in metaphor or stick with scientific terminology, what would be your preference?"

"We can be flexible."

"Brilliant." She looked to her visiscreen. "We will touch on both then."

She stood, straightening her skirt.

"First, let us point out that we all share one planet and that to a certain degree, we have a common interest in our mutual wellbeing. Her Excellency wants to truly emphasize those two words, mutual and wellbeing." Tamanna paused, looking directly at Harry. "With wellbeing in mind, we must all understand the true value of nature, that being our mutual life support system. We inhabit only one planet."

She paused, touching her visiscreen. "Any comment?"

Harry shook his head absently.

"Although there was a time when nature was big and society was small, today those circumstances have reversed. A basic fact. While nature may still seem ample in northern latitudes, when we measure our planet globally we find significant carbon footprint overshoot. Led by industrialized countries like the OECD. These measurements, with repeated scientific confirmation, speak to our wellbeing."

She paused again, waiting. The Canadian team remained silent.

"Not to beleaguer the point but simply put this sets our context. Like all countries, members of the HICCC have specific interests in the wellbeing of their citizens. What we emphasize here are the effects our mutual atmosphere has on climate change–also mutual. Our project we believe will help move negotiations along."

Harry appeared cordial.

"Now, our engineer."

She nodded towards Vince as she sat and he rose.

"OK, so once upon a time there was a volcano." He gauged first reaction. "The first volcano in our story goes by the name Pinatubo–a naturally active volcano." He detected interest, the human ear connecting to story. "Now, you may have heard of Pinatubo due to a recent eruption. What you may not have heard of are the atmospheric effects some of which jump out on any global temperature graph. Volcanic eruption can, in fact, have a cooling effect on our planet albeit short-term. So from Pinatubo we get our project name, Pinatubo II."

Vince's felt that excited shiver run up his spine.

"What we have going here, really, is a make-your-own-volcano project. And our HICCC client has defined five different volcanoes of interest. Each has an increasing size and by default a greater effect."

He held a hand up five fingers extended.

"We can classify each volcano geographically. We have local, regional, national." He held his hands close together, moving them wider as he went down the list. "Then major regional and even a hypothetical global." He stretched his hands wide.

"Major regional would be a group of countries." He moved his hands back in a notch. "An area like the Sahel in North Africa."

The Canadians watched attentively.

"At this time our client's Minister has directed we carry out sulphur release tests for both the local." He returned his hands quite close. "And the regional." He spread them a step wider.

"We have already created both of those volcanoes."

He opened his hands to the middle size.

"And, we now have a green light on a Niger national release. The first country to create its very own volcano." He grinned. "I'll let my colleague speak more to this but I believe this is happening with solid political support." Tami nodded confirmation. "Just to give you a little project engineer insight, the Niger national sulphur release has an expected completion date three weeks from now."

"OK, wait, wait, sulphur release? Create a volcano? " Harry's pen now tapped on the table. "Can you please clarify."

His assistant leaned towards Harry's ear pointing to his visiscreen and speaking quietly. "Geoengineering. We have been trying to tell you, Harry, high or low, this has always been a risk. With increasing probability." Harry stared at his assistant, then back at Vince. He turned his pen sideways, tapping now in staccato bursts.

"Vince, can you explain sulphur release as you summarize the Nigerien national," Tamanna said.

"Sure, no problem. So back in school we all learned how a volcano works. Maybe later, any earth science class would teach a little on plate tectonics. Now, our Pinatubo eruption occurred geographically in the Philippines in 1991. A dormant volcano covered with dense forest erupts unexpectedly. Our first volcano importantly sits geologically on the edge of a subducting oceanic plate. Now we bring in a second volcano into our story named Krakatoa. This bigger volcano erupted in 1883 in Indonesia also on a subducting ocean plate."

He paused, eyes on Harry's bouncing pen.

"While Pinatubo adds importance to our story because she blew recently, giving us better records, Krakatoa gave us significant data due to her size. Now to the sulphur question. One volcanic emissive substance when eruption occurs on an ocean plate edge is sulphur dioxide. And this sulphur gas can be blown up into the stratosphere; that portion of our atmosphere situated way up above our weather zone. Skipping all the chemistry, once up there sulphur gas turns into a haze or aerosol. And that haze blocks a certain portion of the sun's rays. Again, all natural."

He looked for any glazed over eyes, detecting none.

"So our Pinatubo II project replicates that process." He spoke slowly now. "We produce a haze in the stratosphere that blocks a certain portion of the sun's heat. We engineer a cooling effect. We can design-a-volcano for any client, for anyone actually, anyone who wants one." He held up a finger. "When I say replicates, well, there are differences. Unlike natural volcanoes exploding, artificials are silent. Rising in the night time too when everyone's fast asleep. And mysteriously invisible. So they go unnoticed, kinda like no one notices the global-average climate change."

Vince looked at Harry.

"So that's the sulphur release we're talking about."

Harry stared at his now motionless pen. "What you are talking about will screw up our entire climate." His voice rose. "Completely."

"You're screwing it up right now." Vince matched tone. He had practised.

Harry glared, but caught himself. "We could talk specific to this."

"Sounds like you've already been talking. A lot. Minus any real action."

Harry began tapping.

"One more fact." Vince went on. "In spite of our two story volcanoes being local, that is a one mountain location, they had significant global consequences. People in Europe felt the Krakatoa cooling, but what they noticed most was a different colored sky. So, our project design, at this point our Niger volcano, will impact our global climate due to aerosols blocking out sunshine."

Vince felt like a spin-around, like his daughter after ballet class. But he forced a professional saunter over to the window.

"If you can bear with me, just a couple baseline numbers."

He turned to face them hands behind his back.

"For Krakatoa, global thermometers recorded a drop of over one degree, precisely 1.2 degrees. Celsius." He paused, looking around. "Good, we all speak Celsius here. For Pinatubo, the cooling effect was less than half a degree, 0.4 degrees. So now we need to offset the global warming effect of current greenhouse gases emissions." He grinned. "And we can do that with Pinatubo II." He raised a paper report to show a title. "Or Pinatubo 2.0."

"OK, hold on." Harry cut in. "Just how much warmer are we now?"

"Now? Triple Pinatubo or 1.2 degrees so far. Same as Krakatoa."

"And really." Harry followed with his suggestive look. "How much difference would one or two degrees ever make?"

Vince looked at this man of politics. A negotiations opponent to spar with, could this be? He came up on his toes against the wall and spoke slowly. "Most trend estimates agree the carbon already released into the atmosphere will double that temperature increase. So we are committed to 2.4 degrees. When that happens, we'll need Pinatubo 2.0 even more."

"But I mean...give me a break. That kind of temperature change happens all the time." Harry spread his palms wide. "I'm no engineer, but I would guess the heat changes that much here in this room at the touch of a button." He pointed towards the air controls. "Or much more outside in this African heat. We all know that. Right?"

Vince looked at Harry again. He heard his wife's voice telling him of the new Bow River valley after the Calgary floods. Freshly formed channels with gravel bars shifted to new places...quite pretty actually she had said. He spoke patiently, precisely, keeping it simple. "Look, like I said, no one feels the global-average climate. You have to be smart enough to know it's there. Are you familiar with two degrees? What impact a global two degree increase would have?"

Harry looked to his assistant, who slowly shook his head. He resumed tapping, not speaking.

Vince took a deep breath and began his now practiced spiel on the Intergovernmental Panel on Climate Change defined two degree danger line. He made direct reference to the global game being played by humanity and the many feedback loops waiting to be triggered just past two degrees. Or before, that being a Russian roulette game of chance. There were severe weather events, rising sea levels, the drought end of the hydrological cycle, the new normal floods in places like southern Alberta.

Harry kept glancing at his assistant but holding silent.

Vince ended with the socio-political turmoil likely to come about not just globally but locally too, wincing inwardly when he thought of Annalise. His assistant leaned into Harry's ear again. "Sulphur gases are cheap commodities." He tightened his lips. "So any rogue nation could do this, just what he is saying."

Harry stopped tapping, speaking back. "We budget for an improved media campaign." He tossed his pen on the table. His assistant shook his head slightly. "Our believability to be honest is already stretched." Harry shook his head. "Well there's no flooding in Ottawa. Let Alberta deal with their own problems." His assistant leaned back, silent.

Vince watched them with interest.

"So, our Nigerien artificial volcano replicates Pinatubo aerosol creation only a lot less conspicuously," he said. "Two last items. First, we design the long term impact through continual sulphur release with a ten year timeframe now proposed for Niger. Second, we have strategic release locations spread all across this country. So up north here would be up beside the Sahara."

He walked back to the table and pulled his chair out. "And as you would have deduced from Pinatubo, or Krakatoa, any local sulphur release has a global impact. As will the Nigerien national. Assuming cooling would impact the Nigerien landmass only is a grossly incorrect supposition. But that's where engineering becomes politics." He waved a hand towards Tamanna. "So at this point I step out and Ms. Meacham steps in."

As Vince sat the room fell into silence, but for the air conditioning fan squealing faintly.

"Lovely. What Mr. Patel stated is correct," Tamanna said. "Niger has an initial ten year plan. While the president wants one release close to Niamey for citizens to see, other release points will not be disclosed." Tamanna rose, looking at Harry. "This plan, however, is available for adjustment into the foreseeable future as climatic and political conditions warrant. With your minister now informed Her Excellency proposes further talks on a global climate change agreement."

"OK OK, just a minute here," Harry said. "To start, I find it difficult to accept you represent the country of Niger. You are nothing but technical support. But just assuming you do, is Niger familiar with international agreements? Does Niger realize how irresponsible this action will be seen by the international community?"

Tamanna looked at him.

"We can review the responsibility of other national actions, say those of your country," she said. "We could discuss the carbon pollution your country has chosen to release into our atmosphere, our mutual atmosphere, the carbon now causing direct climate change impacts. Missing monsoon rains dry up Nigerien rice fields, bring on the Ganges delta exodus in Bangladesh, and flood your own Alberta south. In fact, we would like to compare notes as we negotiate. Carbon emissions per capita for Canada versus say, Niger. So please, yes, bring that topic to the table."

Harry retrieved his pen, squeezing it tight now. She went on.

"Might I also mention that at this time there is talk in Niger as well as in other high impact countries, of temperature reduction. Below that of pre global warming. As citizens here learn cooling is possible, they rally around their own volcano's potential."

"Below? Why would anyone want a colder planet?"

"National interests." Vince put in. "Like hungry people."

"Politicians want happy citizens," Tamanna added. "Political points, you know. The Canadian or Russian citizen may be happier on a nice warm day, however the Nigerien people cheer on a cooler day. And let your minister know this outlook is not unique to Niger."

"Not unique." Harry parodied, chin dropping. "But only Niger now. Correct?"

Tamanna smiled and went on. "Did you know that during the last ice age when Canada was covered by a kilometer of ice, the Sahel was not? Not long after that time of ice sheets, the Sahel became wetter and much greener. So now, the president of Niger gains a lot of political traction when he reminds citizens of the Green Sahara. Especially when he talks of how he will bring it back."

"Are you threatening us? What, are you threatening to throw Canada back into another Ice Age?" He glared at her. "So you can have more rain here?"

"Modifying our mutual climate can bring about unpredictable results," she replied evenly. "And rain is good for crops, is it not?"

"Canada's not just an OECD member, we're a NATO member." Harry scowled. "We'll easily put a stop to this pitiful African president."

Vince recalled the drone attempt on his life. But, he could play by other rules. "As one Canadian to another," Vince said. "I'm telling you we've got to look at what we're doing. To our children's future, to our own future."

"Canada has an extensive carbon capture research program with many Alberta energy companies on board. We have ongoing breakthroughs from our research teams–there's a new lab under construction in Edmonton." Harry spread his hands. "We'll have a market solution any day."

"How many tons?" Tamanna's voice was loud and clear. "How many have you captured so far?"

Harry stared.

"Listen, I've spent most of my career as an oilfield engineer." Vince matched Tami's volume. "So don't try telling me about Alberta. Moving all that liquid carbon dioxide would need a pipeline system as extensive as the entire Alberta oilfield production and transmission lines we have now. Carbon capture is out of synch with reality. Typical symbolic action!" Vince took a breath. "I've learned a few things from this non-oilfield project. Another perspective on the politics of climate change being one of them. The first world lifestyle, Canadian like mine, like yours, is highly subsidized by a free dumping ground for hydrocarbon emissions. In this situation, what we're gonna do doesn't count anymore." Vince could almost hear his daughter's not fair voice. "These countries may not be doing the best thing for our mutual planet, but they never caused climate change in the first place. And now they're doing something."

"Hydrocarbon energy drives near all of our civilization." Tamanna kept her tone. "We need energy and we want cheap energy. We've got a dodgy situation, with a lot of inertia in both the carbon cycle and the human economy. That has to stop."

"Everyone wants that lifestyle." Harry demanded, shrugging back and forth between them. Then, confidently subdued, he repeated. "Everyone."

"Yeah, well, at what cost?" Vince asked. "There are people dying here in Niger because of that lifestyle, not that we ever cared much before. But I, for one, am thinking about back home too. I've got my daughter's future to think about."

"I have two boys," Harry said.

"Good. So take it from me, you're raising them on a lifestyle they can't have."

"My boys play hockey–now that's Canadian. We'll never let that be taken away." He glared. "Not from my country, not from me, not from my boys."

A pin might have sounded as loud as a pounding fist.

Harry spoke again, now strategically. "So just how big is this Pinatubo II project?" He looked from Tamanna to Vince, with a show-nothing face.

"At this time we're authorized to speak of Nigerien national." Tamanna dropped her voice. "But a little political insight. There are other high impact national interests. Take what we have told you to your minister."

The air conditioning fan wound down into off cycle.

Harry took a breath. "I'd like to request a recess to contact the Minister."

"By all means." Tamanna lifted her hand in a small flourish.

Harry rose and followed as his team filed out.

#

With the room cleared Tamanna spoke one word. "Nishat." Finger in the air she attended to her buzzing device.

Vince looked out again at the middle of the night bridge traffic flowing lightly now. Tami had first told him of her own vision, a modified global discussion. The Bangladeshi canary would screech from its coal mine, she said, no longer signaling via sacrificial death. And no more farce negotiations dominated by the historical essence of colonialism.

The truth was starting to sink in. The numbers were plain enough, but maybe he actually got it now. Not just in his head, but in his gut, maybe even in his heart. Acceptance, Tami said. The Canadian lifestyle, his lifestyle, that was the real carbon dumping issue. A deep dragging guilt swirled within. His own time in the candy store left the shelves bare for Annalise. Just like these Africans, his daughter loses. So what about her and other kids? She gets to pay for his party...unless he does something.

Vince told Tami of southern Alberta tradition, the pioneer focus on rebuilding after the first flood. Little change came after the second one eight years later in spite of triple Calgary over-the-dam flow rates. Prioritize repairs, build bigger berms, dig a diversion channel around High River. And then the third flood. Yet even after another downtown soaking, many argued normal forces of nature. Her stories of Bay of Bengal cousins resonated with similarity, just other waters forcing other peoples from their homes. All effects of this mutual problem.

He listened to the story of Her Excellency's shopping trip for a fall guy. Selection came down to Canada and Russia, Tami said, Nishat's primary candidates. A proposition arose—why not bring a new guy on stage and how about the little guy with the puffy chest? An easier pickings bad guy. Free advertising helped, with global media focused on Alberta tar sands. Nishat had called for a scapegoat, and now that goat was right here, entangled. Negotiating, that could be his new career—his oilfield enthusiasm long subsided anyway. But with that an eco-terrorist label no doubt.

Tamanna pushed end on her device, letting her breath out slowly.

"So?" Vince came over. "We expand our story?"

"No, well maybe." Her eyebrows creased. "Remember I told you I'd never walk through the doors of any totally shit COP meeting again? Ever? Well, we may be flying out with these gentlemen tonight. So if that happens and only outside Nigerien airspace." She looked at him. "If all that comes, then let's have another look."

"Look at what?"

She took a breath. "Piss it!" She looked directly into his eyes. "Right, look Vince we never told any HICCC contractor, so you're the first to know. Niger is not the only artificial volcano. Sulphur balloons are releasing across four other Sahel countries. Tonight."

Vince's jaw dropped, a deep hollow swirling into place. Back and forth in his head, car crashes resonated to the rhythm of a cuckoo clock—this couldn't be real—they were so fucked. He had known, he should have known. Oh Christ. They were going major regional, and what was left between that and the mid-ocean monsoon enhancing release? Tami had been clear; the only way to get a Green Sahara. Fuck! What had he gotten himself into?

He dug deep through the internal churn, OK, decide! He took a deep breath...fuck it, forget the Alberta oilfield. He had a new career, he would bring real voice to Alberta, he would tell the world–he would do anything he could for this HICCC. And for his daughter Annalise.

#

The other Canadian's returned, and Vince stared as the opposition sat at the table.

Harry began. "The Minister wishes to speak to Her Excellency Nishat Jabbar."

"No." Tamanna shook her head. "Her Excellency is not available." She paused. "However, she has suggested we accompany you back to COP. Due to time constraints and as we have more to disclose, we propose reconvening this meeting on your plane."

"More to disclose." Harry stared.

"Yes."

"The two of you."

"Vince for logistics, myself for contact with Her Excellency."

Harry looked at his team, his eyes falling. He glared sideways at Tamanna, but spoke evenly. "Yes, follow us to the airport. Here are my contacts. We need speak car to car." He loosened his tie and removed his suit jacket, exposing his wet sticky shirt. But a determined look remained on his face.

"Brilliant. Her Excellency assumes your Minister will be communicating with your Prime Minister...we must speak to that."

Vince rode beside the climatologist in one presidential car listening. She expanded on the politics; the fact that five Sahel nations could synchronize national volcanoes together would send a clear signal, a powerful signal. And that those volcanoes all released then, in the early morning hours of influence, must be revealed most strategically. He could push further the mid-Atlantic topic, allude to the special design business jets being ready. But what would she say now? For reference only, they had officially been told. Shit!

"On the plane, Vince, when you talk." Tami's voice was soft. "Create if you can a picture in their minds. So when we land, what they remember seeing out the plane window was a string of volcanic explosions down there all across the Sahara. We want the color of fire, of conflict, of challenge imprinted vivid in their minds."

Vince looked at her, nodding, then away. He couldn't tell thrill from terror–what was a terrorist anyway? He stared from the limo at that horizon, knowing the string of invisible-fire volcanoes blasting off must grab world attention. So to start, the line of fire was not just here on the Niamey outskirts, not just in Niger, but on the urban edges of Bamako in next door Mali. Had the president there been out in the streets, hearing cheers? And others would be souring high across the western deserts of Mauritania, then the sands of Chad to the east, and throughout the mountains of the Sudan.

His mind raced, forming all into a storybook picture. Tell it as you would a seven year old, but twist it into political pitch. Not one, but five, smoking holes in the planet, like gunshot wounds. Five blossoming North Koreans, fire-bursting volcanoes, and a lineup of other High Impact Countries waiting eagerly in line. But, those five were not North Koreas–not dictatorships with some archaic obsession, but democratically popular with their people, cooperating hand in hand...this had to be his daughter's best chance for a friendly future.

He sat in silence beside Tami with her secret political directives from Nishat. Vince had to learn how to play this new game career. He could almost feel his daughter sitting there next to him, her tiny hand in his.

African Monsoon

Brad heard the wakeup tone, and blinked his tired eyes open to the dull roar of jet engines. Glancing over at the Nigerien pilot, he turned his attention to fellow engineer Vince in the HoloCube. Tomorrow remained distant.

"You pass into international air space in ten minutes." Vince spoke from the Niamey office.

"Copy that," Brad said, glancing at the icons on the flight screen map. No more national sovereignty ahead—their airspace would match jurisdiction of the high seas below. "Both carrier fleets are holding course in the direction of our dispersal point."

"They gonna force you down?" Vince asked.

"The British base on Ascension maybe," Brad said. "Better forced than shot down."

The American strike fleet upholding North Atlantic naval security sent a carrier task force south towards equatorial waters. The Asian Alliance carrier fleet rounded the Africa cape from the Indian Ocean to the South Atlantic two days ago. Behind the Chinese carrier, the Alliance doubled their naval presence in the west Indian Ocean.

"They'd never go that far, right?" Vince said.

Amidst all this, Brad's demeanour remained calm, too calm he knew. After weeks in the Nigerien drone zone, he felt indifferent at times. Like a seasoned tour-of-duty vet, in firefight after drone strike untouched, believing he'd never be taken out. That was crap. Reality dragged him back to the facts—he'd only ever taken on civilian engineering for the Seattle air force base. Before this combat zone contract.

"A military commander will be talking to a high end politician in a war room on that," Brad said. "Our Chirpfeed broadcast could make all the difference."

He could still feel the hot African dust in his teeth that time they tumbled out and raced from their Nissan. With surface drone detector blaring, they ducked around the wall just as their SUV blasted into a missile smoke hole. His false courage built on that. He stood to volunteer for this flight caught between rational thought and feeling invincible. That belief did help ignore any drone likely tracking this flight as far as the coast. Whose drones on the African continent, they'd never been sure.

"Tamanna's standing by in London," Vince said.

Brad would coordinate Chirpfeed transmission from the plane, while the British climate scientist and Canadian chemical engineer explained the stratospheric aerosol effect. Or parasol effect, whatever word better built a voice badly needing attention. The standoff could come to a head when the carriers passed within strike distance, and that would happen this flight. Escalation then depended on captains' initial launch commands.

The flight screen showed their unarmed jet leaving the African coast. Over the open ocean of the mid-Atlantic, outside any territorial waters the laws of the high seas prevailed—what had once been pirate waters little changed to this day. Less than four hours remained in the flight time to release target half way between the equator and Ascension Island.

"We transmit in thirty minutes," Brad said.

"Anyone with Chirpfeed can resend," Vince said. "We've got quite a few feed links connecting, Brad."

"Yeah copy," Brad said. "That..." He took a deep breath. Shooting down an unarmed plane in international airspace would scream political—they had to play on that.

#

Brad had taken that first flight from Niamey to supervise sulphur dispersal over the mid-Atlantic, and then on to Rio je Janeiro. A long uncommon flight path, but international airport to airport at least. The Brazilian aeronautical company, designer of the business jet to liquid dispersal modification had required a manufacturer's check. Vince supervised the second dispersal and Brad the third, but the mid-ocean turnaround then glared abnormal. Return flights from mid-ocean to central Africa were detected as anomalous blips by both Chinese and American military satellites.

The American carrier task force and the Alliance fleet protecting a Chinese carrier both changed course the same day, less than a week ago.

He leaned back, resting in the redesigned co-pilot seat—the cockpit had been repurposed in Brazil for a load release operator. Business seats and cocktail bar removed, the fuselage had been converted to maximize storage of his liquid sulphur dioxide load. Though an aeronautical engineer, his predilection for heights ended with rock climbing and flying paragliders. All co-pilot controls had been removed anyway.

On top of his invincible rationale turmoil, he flew for God and country. As an American, yet as a father too he took this fifth flight for his kids back home. Especially after this contract he knew too much about the looming crisis not to act. The British citizen and the engineer from the tar sands province, also father of young children, would join via HoloCube. Their international representation was a calculated risk, most on Chirpfeed not knowing the other two sat across a virtual interview table.

Could invincible be what it felt like for those driven by delusional religious belief? He could only guess. Here, they wanted but to provide a deterrent presence, nothing impractical, only with a high risk level. Old school thinking worked away out there at maintaining military control, with a drive to secure national interests at all costs. Those strategizing an alternate future wanted peace too, but with transition to a climate change solution.

Brad knew their global cooling design to be imperfect, and the old school outlook would pounce on that. The monsoon experiment would be tipped by any natural volcanic eruption. Solar radiation management accomplished nothing to mitigate ocean acidification—algae blooms continued replacing nature's marine wonders. Any regional change like this Green Sahara effort could throw a loop into any global initiative. Better to have a calmer more reliable method, something organic like extensive biochar, or the seaweed forest alternative. But when did people ever make the best choice? With this atmospheric chemical venture on the go, they could sure use some calculated global negotiating.

The two countries either side of Niger east and west had joined in on synchronized sulphur balloon releases. Weeks ago one backup option had been Niger's extra release capacity, and as the centrally located country potentially the only balloon release point. Niger's solitary discharge technically worked, knowing stratospheric sulphur would spread east and west across the Sahara on its way towards the Mediterranean. As it turned out, the Sahel countries had not only common mid-desert geography like Niger, but strong political interests in a Green Sahara.

Lifting one eyelid, he glanced at the time digits floating in the cube. Fifteen minutes to go.

Days after their arrival in Niamey Brad took Vince up on that first balloon ride. The smaller test balloon had rocketed skyward spewing sulphur and helium, finally emptying two miles higher like a mini-volcanic eruption. But with both gases colorless, the eruption had been just as invisible as any green house gas. Brad had joked around with Vince about adding color to mark a true chemtrail, bringing truth to the conspiracy theory some imagined in any visible jet trail. That aside, being visible remained a primary climate change issue—would the world pay attention to this atmospheric drama?

Brad could picture the Niamey bridge lined with presidential campaign posters, a smiling face beside those stone giraffes. They'd been sent up to Agadez on the edge of the Sahara, where nocturnal releases lifted most sulphur by balloon. Their Harvard science million-to-one leveraging advantage spoke wonders— every ton of sulphur cooling offset a million tons of carbon warming. Other Green emblazoned balloons went up in the daytime close to Niamey for the Nigerien president and his citizens to see. Background action had to support any front stage show.

The Atlantic release option floated up in conversation with the British climate woman as an add-on when their project shifted to Phase III balloon release, the Sahel regional. Continental balloons were not enough. Officially for reference calculation only, yet even back then they tactically put together a plan to store liquid sulphur for the mid-Atlantic, roughly calculating to compensate for any loss to the ever present drones. According to the official stance at Phase II stage before, desert balloon-released tons cooled the Nigerien climate only. Ridiculous to think a political border contained atmosphere, though climate did have its own regional geography. That ever changing official outlook.

Brad had unofficially talked that time to Vince, with the Brit joining via HoloCube. Sitting around that paper map hanging on the Niamey meeting room wall, they had pointed at arrows sketched in over the ocean. Stratospheric drift over lower wind zones and ocean current directions defined weather patterns. There and then, they roughly engineered a significant cooling effect over the mid-Atlantic.

He told them right away 'no way' on balloons out over the ocean. Nor in global airspace. A little research told him best to use a small fleet of high flying modified business jets with dispersal technology. Next unofficial meeting he told them that. Business jets were not much higher tech than desert balloons, really, just extra susceptible to drone or fighter jet interference. Requests for proposal got them a Brazilian aeronautical design that beat out the Hindu quote with a shorter turnover time and identical quality.

Strategically, they would seasonally stop balloons to leave the Sahara summer sands hot and cool the summer Atlantic. They could keep the winter continental Sahel release going and introduce this into Phase III regional—that fit. Brad became aware that heat didn't have influence so much as the temperature difference between the Sahara and the equatorial Atlantic to bring in more monsoon. Cooling one was the same as heating the other. Most effective to cool the ocean when the Sahara was naturally at its hottest, during summer.

Assuming engineering only, the British woman pointed out, released sulphur drifting south towards Antarctica would spread, but never east and west enough to influence southern Africa or South America. All effects would remain over the ocean. Minimal impact on anything else, still pretty regional. Easy to talk engineering assuming non-politicized engineering interests. Benefits and risks considered, the plan became official.

Of course the reality of politics rolled out dicier. How do you explain all this to the guys at the top? They knew even then if they went poking a sulphur release out over mid ocean many airspace interests would scream global. That assumption turned out totally correct, with military interests now poking back.

#

Brad touched the HoloCube to connect Niamey and London. The other two faces formed in the cube, joining him across the virtual meeting table for Chirpfeed transmission.

"What's our status please?" Tamanna asked. She'd need a military technical update for the High Impact Minister.

"Our American carrier is three hundred miles past Cape Verde coming south," Brad said. "The Chinese carrier passed within fifty miles of Saint Helena territorial waters approximately ten hours ago bearing north towards Ascension Island."

"They're both close?"

"They'll be within fighter jet launch range within two hours."

As Tamanna filed her ministerial report, and Vince rose to shift pins on the Niamey paper map, Brad went over one last time his take on what best to say.

Asia showed an ever growing interest in a Green Sahara, with active Chinese land speculation deals going down on the sand dunes around Agadez. The Chinese may have subsidized biochar for agriculture, that looking good in the public eye, but a bigger monsoon in the background would surely boost biochar soil creation. The Chinese would be keeping a close eye on enhanced food production in a place like the sulphur-cooled Sahara. How many Asians could be planning to emigrate to the newly greened Sahara to set up shop? Which political negotiators signed long term trade deals on a potentially huge food export market?

Tamanna returned attention to the cube.

"We want to send the Chinese incentive," Brad said. "To call back their carrier."

"Brilliant, however the Chinese monsoon back home for them, Brad, has reduced in size due to carbon-warming," Tamanna said. "China has serious incentive to seek alternatives to their rice growing loss."

"That's about food," Brad said. "We've got military involved."

"Food's one thing people bicker over," Tamanna said. "With armies."

"America standing with NATO allies is not a question," Brad said.

"American and NATO may condemn the High Impact Countries' incursion into atmospheric space with sulphur emissions," the British scientist said. "But HIC rightfully holds them responsible for historic dumping of carbon emissions into the same airspace."

"So that's our situation." Vince returned to cube, listening. "We speak to that, Brad."

"Right. Let's finalize the points you guys are gonna make," Brad said. "Our broadcast has to send a strong statement, to the carriers, and to the people of the world."

"We build story around your science, Tamanna," Vince said. "We bring in the Dabous Giraffes, for sure."

"The Vostok ice core?" Tamanna asked.

"No," Brad said. "Science overload there."

The naturally caused historical Green Sahara, Tamanna had explained, also known as the Neolithic Subpluvial, had actually been caused by a variation in the planet's tilt and the effect that had on African monsoons. But that story was a hard sell like analyzing annual ice deposition in that Vostok core.

"I apologize for my own country," Vince said. "Canada's inaction for so long."

"We can't voice national regret," Brad said. "Nor any personal heart throb."

The looked at each other for a moment.

"The High Impact case for extra climate cooling." Tamanna said. "Knowing they can extra cool the planet."

"Below pre-industrial—that's real. If we need to." Brad said. "Military pays attention to any threat."

"No climate transition goes smooth," Tamanna reminded them of a Vostok core detail on climate history. "The Sahara grew larger during the Younger Drydas, when climate shifted to colder globally."

"If colder made for bigger desert then, why not now?" Brad shook his head. "Our message has to be clear."

"That historical event was naturally incurred in association with the global climate of an Ice Age ending," Tamanna said. "Our efforts will be human planned, and regionally we know we will reduce the desert."

"Yeah, okay," Brad said. "How do we start?"

"We weave the tilted earth axis in with the Dabous Giraffes," Vince said. "More story than science. Remember, talk parasol along with aerosol, and atmosphere or upper air to help with stratosphere."

"You tell story," Brad said. "Tamanna does science."

When they told the six Sahel presidents how to best spend the Asian billions, Tamanna said they could increase their balloon release of sulphur dioxide into the continental stratosphere. But, she made it scientifically clear, the benefits of a mid-Atlantic release would be huge. Worth a certain risk. Recreating the Green Sahara based on the Nigerien balloon release was more political hype than science, and the best the Nigerien president could hope for there had been more rain. Maybe like decades ago. When Vince came in with the story of the historical green Sahara, the presidents perked up. That could be returned by cool breezes and refreshing Sahel rains, and the giraffe mystique of the millennial African past. All with the awe yet real world task of a mid-Atlantic high altitude direct release from a jet. The presidents nodded, having chatted about arriving in their own jets.

Brad eyed the others as he counted down from ten, and touched Chirpfeed.

"Hello. My name is Brad Moore and I'm an aeronautical engineer." He opened his arms towards the other two as if a practiced TV host. Keeping face focused on HoloCube, he projected the feeling of experts gathered at a distinct moment.

"I want to introduce you to Dr. Tamanna Meacham, a scientist and paleoclimatologist, and Vince Patel here is a chemical engineer. We are speaking to you from an unarmed jet now leaving the west coast of Africa, and we will, in about three hours, arrive at a point just below the equator in the middle of the Atlantic ocean."

"If you've been following COP 33 in the news," Tamanna spoke up. "You may have heard of the mainland African balloon initiative in the national airspace of Niger and other Sahel countries."

Brad nodded as Vince brought a globe into the hover space, running a finger across the Sahara, and the Sahel just below.

"So that balloon release contains a climate cooling substance," Vince said. "A sun shade that will mirror back a little of the extra sunshine to cool us off a bit."

"Sulphur dioxide aerosol can cool our planet," Brad said. Seeing Vince wince, he slowed. "Or, a part of the planet, like North Africa. We're sending mini parasols up into the high atmosphere to cool the Sahara desert."

Brad waved towards Vince.

Vince picked up on the parasols that rhymed with aerosols, shifting tone to talk as if telling story to a child. Not so long ago...but well before the Europeans came, the people of Dabous, where the Sahara desert is now, carved giraffes into stone. Beautiful giraffes, one male and one female, he said, pointing to a spot on the globe. The Dabous Giraffes tell us of a time when the Sahara was green enough for the African animals we all know. And, giraffes eat tree leaves, so back then enough rain fell for trees to grow. Back then, science tells us, a wobble in the Earth's axis pointed our little planet a little more towards the sun. The extra sunshine we got then warmed up the Sahara even more.

"No way we can tilt our planet." Brad said.

"Absolutely not," Vince chimed in. "But we have another plan."

"Still, c'mon." Brad said. "You said the tilt warmed up the Sahara. We want cooler."

"Science tells us..." Vince looked to Tamanna.

"Bizarre, truly, but amazingly, extra heat reduces the desert," the British scientist explained. "Our climate doesn't always work as you might think. What happens in this case is, extra heat rises drawing air in off the ocean. That's the basic monsoon effect. For the Sahara, more heat stimulates the West African monsoon drawing more humid air in off the Atlantic. And all that humid ocean air dumps a lot of extra rain."

"Yes."

"Rain."

"Like a big vacuum sucking in rain clouds," Vince said. "That's what makes a Green Sahara. The Dabous people back then would have cheered on all that extra green desert. Today, we can cheer on our little aerosol parasols."

"To stimulate the West African monsoon today," Tamanna said, looking to Vince. "And to recreate what the Dabous people had, we need a regional cooling out over the mid-Atlantic. To enhance a Green Sahara plan, we gain extra ocean impact on stimulating the monsoon."

"A hot desert beside a cold ocean makes a bigger monsoon," Vince said. "And that pulls rain up into the Sahara."

"And," Tamanna said. "We propose this Green Sahara will bring harm to no one. The bonus will be a slight cooling to offset global warming."

"No harm at all?" Vince asked. "No risk?"

Brad caught sight of new icons appearing on the screen map. He glanced away from Holocube to see jet fighter squadrons launching off the aircraft carriers. Looking back at the others, he kept silent estimating flight times.

All factors considered, this proposal made for their best compromise for regional cooling, Tamanna had said. She argued that any acid rain or stratospheric ozone depletion would be minimal over an extremely arid and relatively uninhabited desert. Same over the Atlantic.

"Actually, we have an overall bright outlook," Tamanna said. Brad let her explain how their parasol would drift south down the middle of the Atlantic towards Antarctica, maybe disrupting mid-ocean weather patterns, but impacting very few citizens. Vince followed her story running a finger down the globe. Stratospheric drift was polewards, like north of the Sahel over the Sahara desert where so few people lived so far. No one gets disturbed cause no one lives there. She couldn't say where the sulphur spread was based on high elevation winds and risk analysis.

"The stratosphere's way up high," Vince put in. "Many miles above us. You might one day soon come on vacation to see live giraffes around the Dabous rocks."

"How're we tracking the sulphur, post release?" Brad asked, watching the fighter jet blimps line up on an intercept course. They needed switch to a science focus.

"Satellite imagery partially," Tamanna said. "Partly our climate model. We have weather happening at the bottom of the stratosphere, so at mid-Atlantic we go higher, and the process goes smoother."

"Unfortunately," Brad looked directly into the cube, at the world out there. "Any operation carried out in international airspace holds political risk. At this moment we have aircraft carriers approaching our jet from two directions, and we're really hoping they'll talk to each other."

They all looked at each other.

"This isn't a two way standoff, but a three way," Brad spoke carefully. He was in a fighter jet of a different type. America and NATO wanted status quo, the Asian Alliance wanted to experiment and Africa wanted to roll the dice on a desert replaced by forest with a shot at a cooler planet. "What else do the High Impact countries say on global cooling?" Brad asked, looking to the scientist.

"The presidents of the Sahel countries are growing quite popular," Tamanna said, equally cautiously. "When they talk about the Green Sahara, when they bring up the idea of a planet cooler than pre-industrial, they're hearing cheers. They've got a popular conversation going around a negative 1C degree world."

"That would be like," Brad said, "a mini Ice Age."

"Only in high latitude regions like Europe or North America," Tamanna said. "A cooler day in Africa rings as appealing as a warm day in the north."

"Not good for everyone," Brad said.

"Climate inaction hasn't been either," Tamanna said.

Brad sensed a moment to close the conversation; just as well on those notes of dramatic doom.

"There you have it folks," Brad said. "Reporting from our unarmed jet."

Signing off Chirpfeed transmit, Brad took a deep breath. "Okay guys."

"Alright bud," Vince said.

"I've got the minister on," Tamanna said.

The powers that be need talk directly to diffuse any military standoff. Lifting hand to eyebrow, Brad saluted whatever decision was to be made in the war room, and the world out there. A tear rolled down his cheek.

#

The information transmitted, Brad could do nothing but watch the screen icons. The race against time showed the NATO jets slightly ahead as they approached on the screen. Brad glanced at his Nigerien pilot, reading fear in his eyes, but equal resolution. Nothing would change their flight track, not by their choice.

Dark dots appeared on the horizon on the north side.

Staring out the windshield into the cloud cover rushing past, Brad watched the shadows of two fighters edging in along either side. They matched the speed of their jet so close Brad could pick out one NATO pilot speaking into his intercom. The conversation went on, as if in the fighter pilot was receiving conflicting commands.

Asian Alliance fighters approached from the south.

"You watching?" Brad asked.

"Yeah," Vince said.

Then, had Brad seen or just imagined that fighter pilot saluting his way. Just as he had.

"Vince, I think..." Brad said.

"What?"

The wing dip next was distinct, and both escort fighters shot out ahead. Brad shifted his look to the map screen, struggling to suppress another invincible moment. But the receding fighters weren't circling back, as the Asian jets also veered off on a return course.

"The North Atlantic strike fleet appears to be shifting their naval presence." Brad reported to Tamanna for her minister. "Asian Alliance too."

"Are we sure?" Tamanna asked. "Before I tell the minister."

Brad stared at the screen, as the two escorts rejoined their squadrons.

"Confirmed," Brad said. "At this time."

All fighters appeared on altered tracks towards their carriers. Staring in amazement, Brad watched the Chinese carrier changing course as well. The NATO commander would have eyes glued to that.

"What happened?" Brad said. He thought of his wife and two boys back home. For a moment he could hear the children's laughter, his kids, like the gurgle of a mountain stream. He risked all for them, and their climate tomorrow.

"They've opened diplomatic channels," Tamanna said. "New political proposals on alternate methods of climate cooling will be tabled."

"Yeah, well they sure need coordinated intentions," Brad said. "And a defined course of action if they want to avoid another firestorm."

They looked at each other, nodding.

"What went down?" Vince asked. "Really."

"The Minister says one commander totally broke the strategic discussion," Tamanna said. "He started talking of his granddaughter's fuzzy giraffe."

Brad pumped a fist up and down into the air.

"The extra global cooling's trending on social media," she added. "We've deescalated complications, at least for our African monsoon release."

"What chance the extra cooling gets trade off space," Brad mused. "And we target the climate we had?"

"Yeah," Vince said. "Let's hope."

International recognition the atmosphere belongs to everyone. No pirates allowed, Brad could tell his kids. Everyone who breaths, and everyone who looks up at the sky. The sky covers international waters, and all nations need keep in line. Like at the playground, certain things, not allowed.

Brad could again think of tomorrow. They'd release another load of sun parasols to cool the planet, and give people extra breathing room to tone back on carbon emissions.

Blown Bridge Valley

He voice activated Answer and his American friend Brad spoke fast.

"Vince. Listen Bud, I just got word your BC province is fielding no response. So that south highway closes real soon. Julia says maybe even tonight."

"What? Where?" Brad's wife Julia sat on the Valley Council. His fingers tightened on the j phone as he paced his Calgary townhouse kitchen floor.

"We don't know—maybe at that ski hill town. I'd say decide now, you wanna be in or out. Like I told you, each valley will be autonomous."

He knew no response from the old British Columbia government meant the province would not be interfering. He'd struggled with this choice before. Stay or leave. Live and work in the chaos of Calgary or chance an idealized life in a rural valley straddling BC and America. He shook off his inner trepidations as his anger rose.

"Christ! What about the Trans-Canada?"

"You should be on top of that. You live up there."

"Yeah right." The latest news Vince heard reported Ottawa so disconnected from the West the federal government was out of the picture. In the real world it was Greater Vancouver about to snip another connection with Alberta. Another move in the drama dividing the prairies and the coastal western mountains.

"C'mon Vince, you gotta decide." He could picture the relentless beam on Brad's face. "Your Thanksgiving was last weekend, right? So our One Valley joint committee voted for this low traffic moment. We take over choke points on the highways— river bridges, mountain passes. Come spring, the Pacific NW Valleys project will be official."

"You talking to Council?" He knew an established border would mean an application to immigrate. And that could mean a years-long wait or a flat out application denial. Who knew what Calgary would look like by then? This might be his last chance to choose the valley. Staying meant an ongoing struggle adapting to climate change disruption.

"Julia's on our South Valley Council, and you know how we really want the One Valley to go through. She's talking to your guys all the time."

"Yeah...shit," he said softly. "Annalise just started grade 12."

"Josh and Jimmy have high school too, Vince. I dunno about there but public education here is a joke. Hey man, school will be a lot better through our new network. Think community, real community. Now's the time."

Vince's daughter was already on optional distance learning to keep away from the turmoil in her Calgary high school. Distance learning was technically there, still, he often questioned the teaching value. And there was a real choice to be made here on her face-to-face social needs. Not only his daughter's career future was on the line but her total life. His career was a mess having dropped oilfield contracts for environmental work.

The gangs Annalise talked of, the ones infiltrating her school were now organizing swarms right out of the classroom. That fit with media coverage of the growing waves of urban delinquency. The latest were gangs of young men, some girls too, in home-armoured vehicles roaming out of the city to hit the wealthy countryside. Those first caught ended up in Young Offenders but they were quickly replaced. Thieving and drugging, not caring, they tested defiance against the latest City Police mini-drones. Annalise carried pepper spray—all girls at school did she said—and she had four years of street-smarts martial arts. She could name two boys from her school now dead. When a once wealthy Canadian city like Calgary becomes so unstable it must be time to try something new. Like Brad's valley—better go now.

"Alright Brad. Can we stay in touch texting?"

"Sure. We cross the state line early morning, so we'll be there by sunrise. C'mon Vince. The longer you wait, the harder it'll be to get in. Maybe harder to get anywhere."

Vince had returned from that geoengineering project exhausted yet excited. He met Brad there in the African Sahel. Maybe out of different engineering schools but it turned out they had a lot in common. In their late thirties then, here they were a decade later still in contact. Brad was the only one he knew who looked knowingly at the climate change crisis with such a grin. Many others simply lived in denial. That same grin had been on Brad's face in any test balloon back in Niger when he'd talk on his plan for a worst case climate change scenario.

#

Vince took a deep breath, and then knocked on his daughter's door.

"Come in." Annalise looked up from her study screen, waving PauseAll.

He wrapped his arm around her shoulders. "The Valley," he sighed. "We gotta go."

"But dad...now?"

"I know, I know. We knew this might come, remember?"

Annalise looked at her father, then out her window. The tears began streaming as he knew they would.

"The good thing is we are prepped," he said giving her shoulders a squeeze. "So it's nine o'clock. Let's give ourselves two hours to load and then we make a night time leave. Just like we've done."

"I have an exam Monday." Her face was angry. "I have a life here...my friend Kara anyway. No way dad!"

"Annalise..." He paused. "Look, we're going." He walked out, giving her space.

They would bring bicycles, yes, especially if the road was blocked at the ski resort town. Best option would get them all the way to the valley by car. If a bridge was out, they would continue on bicycle. From resort town to valley would be an exhausting long cycle trip better ridden in two days with an overnight. That would mean living out of backpacks, and cycling through the swarm gang turf. So hopefully not; they really needed to be driving all the way. Backpacks, car camping extras, emergency bags—it all had to go in. He fitted the shotgun into the back seat floor rack he had rigged. What else?

He paused. That second flood flushing Calgary's downtown twenty years ago caught some attention—but not the right kind. Frigging adaptation. Why could people not wake up to the need for mitigation? Berm up the river banks. Shit!

He yanked the door of their hybrid open, touching Induce to ensure full charge.

The goddam Alberta advantage—hail net installation grew into a thriving business as insurance companies adjusted their rates. And droughts created a demand for expanded irrigation systems—the deep water well business boomed. Of course that massive prairies crop failure four years ago had something of a reverse impact, shooting market food prices through the global roof. One real bonus of the Valley would be local food production.

Nothing else was working, not around Calgary. The faraway yet global impact geoengineering project got bombed. His years working for Pembina never panned out to anything. No one was doing anything; they were all stuck in the decades old mindset of his father. So why not, why not give this Brad idea a shot? A model of civilization designed to traverse the transition to low carbon, and not only that designed to just work better. So people might have an improved future. A friendly future.

He slap-checked the two jerry cans strapped in the back corners of the vehicle, verifying the refill dates on the sloshing biodiesel. Hoisting their bicycles down from garage ceiling hangers, he strapped them onto the NearE rack. That 2028 had been a good hybrid design year...long range electric combined with a liquid fuel engine. This one was five years old with almost no maintenance. Importantly now, they had a range of eight hours at highway speed.

Annalise came down with her backpack, dry eyed, and he threw both their packs into the rooftop carrier. Vince had always kept the Valley option in back of his mind since hearing Brad talk. Prepared had been their pivotal word, so this was kind of routine. They had spent their summer 'vacations' in the Valley, even staying in their little cabin until Christmas that once just for rehearsal. They called the cabin their survival cell, like Brad's, their S cell. Trial runs helped but accepting this reality would take a lifetime.

"OK, just like August. I drive to the corner an hour south, you drive to BC border. We get as far as we can by car."

"Yeah but dad." Her lips were pressed firm; her arms squeezed in tight. "This is our home, our only home...you know." As if in her sunken heart she wanted to hug the place goodbye. He could see her doing that. "And what about Kara?"

They backed out down the driveway, and stopped in the street glancing back at their townhouse. This time it was real, no return. "You can keep in touch with your friend remote." He waited until she bumped fists, silently knowing they were committing to a pioneer life. He had listened to Brad and Julia enough to be a little excited about the better lifestyle promise in One Valley.

#

They accelerated to highway speed coming off the ramp onto Deerfoot south. A few other cars jostled along as late night traffic.

He had reviewed this trip in his mind dozens of times, eventually believing it might actually happen. A night time departure was best—get out when things are calm. The best place to be when shit really hit the fan was, no matter what the destination, already there. He listened to Brad too much, idealizing, when the fact was this trip was in front of them. The range of the city's influence was as a distinct worry. Amidst others. Lots of what-if scenarios, but the farther they got from Calgary the better.

As they passed McKnight Boulevard an orange glow appeared as a flicker on the horizon. He felt his heart speed as he stared. That must be near downtown.

"Inner City boys party on the hill," Annalise said. "Kara went once."

He didn't say anything, wondering if she had gone too.

The fire burned high on the riverbank hill overlooking the inner city. As they drove closer two City Police patrols drones appeared hovering in formation on the next interchange ramp. The drones entered the freeway lanes not far behind their hybrid. To keep things under control Vince thought but whose control?

"Kara says the drones take down some guys in wrap straps," Annalise said pursing her lips. "The cops in cars better show up fast though. 'Cause the guys got those low-tech drones figured out pretty good."

"No shit."

Vince caught sight of another glow reflecting off the glass of buildings right downtown. Could there be a fire at the Olympic Plaza across from City Hall?

The mini-drones pulled up beside them on either side cutting into their talk with a short siren blast. Vince watched his dash flash telling him the drone had confirmed their vehicle ID and taken a licence plate photo. They had been investigate tagged. The drone voice came through his smart phone demanding a voice response.

"Provide purpose of trip. Provide destination."

"Vacation. Ski Resort." He kept his voice as calm as he could. The drones followed them further, and then moved on to the next vehicle."

"Shit," he said. "Tagged! Just what we need."

"Kara said gang guys blast those drones out of the air," Annalise said. "They use shotgun buckshot just like cowboys used to."

Vince glanced over jaw clenched.

"So the police load drones with real bullets now," she said.

"Jesus," he breathed. He could feel sweat building on his brow.

As they finally crossed the Bow River to leave the city's south limits he wiped at his forehead. The smell of patient hay growing in the fields and the hum of the tires on the highway helped him calm. The RCMP officially policed the regional roads out here using surveillance and control mini-drones. Whatever that meant. The road block gang swarms worked the countryside—he did not want to know Kara's insights on that. Focusing on the divided pavement ahead he was unable to keep their back seat shotgun from his mind.

The military checks he and Brad had bribed their way through in Africa were more civilized than this. And that was a decade back. If only that damn HICCC project in the Sahel had made the difference in climate change. But High Impact Climate Change Countries or not, those countries' geoengineering challenge to the West did not sit well with global politics. Not then. A few select targeted NATO bombs later Brad and Vince's project design ended up in a closed file with a bad public name. No matter how useful the engineering that option closed politically for the planet.

Vince had concocted his version of risk analysis back then. Brad smiled but few others really heard. The traditional game the Russian's play with a revolver. One loaded shell his calculating mind estimated fit for each global degree C. Now two chambers of the six were loaded with climate change shells. Click, click, bang—if you were sequence lucky. The ensuing brains-on-the-wall scene was not pretty. Better to deny. Better to pretend your life away.

He looked out to where High River once was. Beyond the abandoned interchange the now defunct town with its provincial diversion channel had been flush-formed into new gravel bar territory by flood number four. Displaced residents had never become climate refugees. The media reserved that term for faraway places the first time water flooded the town and still now. All part of the politically touted adaptation strategy. Tough hard working frontiersmen worked everything out with a gunfight at the corral.

What corral?

We build a new community, a real community, with this regionally supported One Valley project Brad spoke with his incessant grin. The guy was born to smile. Maybe optimism could help form a more resistant community.

The night turned darker as the divided highway lanes merged into one. Roadblock swarms happened more in the summertime and usually closer to the city on lower speed roads. Still, he reached behind to check the safety on the shotgun.

They switched drivers under a town streetlight at their first turnoff.

Vince noticed his daughter's new tears. "What are you thinking?"

"Mom."

"Yeah."

Annalise' mother was stuck in the go shopping mode—Vince got the updates from Annalise. His ex-wife Natasha now lived out her dream with John behind a wall in that Rocky View mansion with private guards watching security cameras. The latest was a solar panel install as a backup power security feature. Winter trips south were not to gun patrolled beach resorts. Her SUV had been armoured for the shopping trips.

Vince had consoled his daughter telling her there was nothing he could really do to change another person's—her mother's— outlook.

Annalise slowed for the first right angle corner on the narrow secondary highway. Vince watched another set of headlights ahead make the turn. They followed the curving asphalt up through the foothills under the starlight. The night almost held a peace and Vince relaxed for a moment.

"Kara says the country gangs work intersections," Annalise said. "They park trucks in the ditch with headlights off until someone pulls up to stop. That's when they swarm."

Vince tensed. Their next turn would be at a T-intersection with a stop sign. "Right. Look Annalise, don't stop when we get to the corner ahead." Vince wondered if he should be driving—this was not exactly a vacation. "Slow down just as much as you need to."

"I know how to drive dad."

He glanced her way. She had grown up in a world so different than his.

They came down the slopes of the last hill and around the bend. As the car ahead slowed to a stop at the corner headlights flashed on from four points. Vince stared in disbelief as Kara's warning played out before their eyes. Annalise hit the brakes and they skidded to a stop. A kilometer back from the intersection. But their lights had been spotted and one of the vehicles roared out of the ditch heading directly their way.

"Dad," she said determined. "The Porcupine Hills road. Remember?"

"Yeah, yes," Vince heard himself say. He couldn't think. "Yeah." Nor believe the calm in his daughter.

Annalise hit the gas cranking the steering into a tight U-turn. Their outside wheels dipped deep into the ditch as they spun wildly around and bounced speeding back the other way. "We need to get the right corner."

Vince looked at his daughter's fixed determination. She truly was part of another world. He snapped back. He had always held back on another thing too, maybe his decades old world but now he needed to think like a cowboy. They had a scene at the corral. He reached back and grabbed the shotgun from the rack clicking the safety off.

The vehicle behind turned into a 4 wheeler truck as it gained on them.

"Top of that next rise—the two white barbwire fence posts. Turn."

Annalise braked just enough to skid the car hard around the corner and as she straightened their swerve he leaned out the open window. Hard faces leered through the truck's windshield. Young faces—his advantage he knew. Waiting 'til the truck just started its corner, he aimed at two lined up front mud-grabber tires and pumped all three shells through the chamber blasting ball shot out the barrel. The truck with two blown tires swerved crazy and skidded on gravel into the ditch. Last he saw as he swung back into his seat the truck was tipping over slow. He was breathing hard.

They tore up the gravel road following the ridge into the pine forest, alone now in the dark.

"Sorry baby," he placed his hand on Annalise' shoulder.

His daughter nodded. Her face was maybe tear-streaked but set firm. They checked GPS on the dash map. Previous trial runs told them there was a turnoff ahead back down the ridge to rejoin their highway—should have had GPS on all along. At least he knew they would come out far south of that swarm corner.

And better than being on bicycle so far was all Vince could think. He stared out from the heights at the distant lights.

#

"So you want bridges on the dash map?"

He was driving again.

"You can hack that into our vehicle chip?"

Annalise uncrumpled her pocket screen. "Everyone's got HakChoir."

He'd been counting river bridges through the window and they were approaching a BC highway hotel before a river crossing. Strategic chokepoint there, on a wide river. One thing was noticeable; rivers flowed full this side of the mountains, while semi-arid Southern Alberta on the other side dried up even more.

The question of the moment—was the ski resort valley separating too? Or would they keep connected to the wide open valley ahead? And the last small BC city.

They passed the Hoz Hotel, and crossed over the bridge.

"Check it dad. You see bridges now?"

"Yeah, cool." The two bridges ahead in the ski resort town now showed dash map icons.

They rounded a corner, and slowed. A downhill ski resort town, but with no airport. One reason to stay connected to the BC city ahead.

Thinking, he gave Annalise a light shoulder punch. "A girl should get a pilot's license." He had gone up in that first test balloon with Brad over the southern Sahara. The contract called for a release design of sulphur dioxide up into the stratosphere. To cool the planet, to offset the warming. He had designed the sulphur supply on the ground, while Brad took care of lifting the load into the air. The guy loved any kind of air time and up in the air he would talk about the valley survival plan.

"Whatever," she looked out the window.

He could make suggestions no more. She did think things through, Vince knew. He had to just support her, and trust her decisions. Her future would be longer than his.

They passed the ski hostels and hotels, both bridges intact. Yes!

The small city ahead would have a trickier time sealing off their part of the mountain valley. But where the river reversed directions and wound back north from America to form their Valley was even deeper in the mountains. So this south flowing river valley would be a natural buffer. He couldn't help but think strategically.

"So what else besides bridges, dad?"

"Railway overpasses if you can...there's that one little tunnel, ah, never mind that. You know, what we really need to think about now is that border crossing in our Valley." The small BC city might have issues, but they would have their own. A valley half in BC, half in America, with a gate-guarded international line dividing. What kind of choke point would that be? A lot depended on those One Valley negotiations.

"Julia helped me with my school project last year, remember? What women say, especially on a council. Those old country borders are pretty silly sometimes."

"Yeah, true." Vince knew Brad's wife got Annalise some Valley data. He would vote for more truly feminine voice in their future community model. Brad had talked a lot about the Taureg back in Africa. Maybe tribal, and maybe Moslem, they still had women with a strong voice. And a lot of good choices came through in their community.

They passed through the little tunnel. The resort town might seal the tunnel later but that would be their choice. Their own Valley deep in the mountains ahead had good geographic logistics, a high pass to the west and a now-rarely-operating lake ferry crossing to the north. Assuming the American border crossing was tight. The question was how to control the highway east, the one they were coming in on.

Brad said some bright people were being attracted to the future community design concept. A valley in British Columbia had a low climate change impact risk, and was one of the best places to wait out what some called the transition. The overall Pacific North West regional agreement had a lot of promise. The plan was to stay under the radar of climate change turmoil, to wait out the international chaos phase, while at the same time developing an improved model of civilization. A design team out of the University of British Columbia with some pragmatic human nature specialists were getting involved. Brad loved to talk with those guys.

After a few tight curves along this river's windings Vince settled in for the long flat drive across the wide valley. They were getting closer. Maybe he could find engineering work on valley energy. Maybe electric or biofuels. Worry about that later—he was exhausted. Annalise had crashed right out.

He slowed under the railroad underpass, coming into the small city.

At the old gas station a mini-drone fell in beside them. Clearly marked RCMP. If they crosschecked their Calgary tag, they would confirm his destination.

He had other priorities now. He gave Annalise a nudge.

"Pass me the shotgun. Keep it low on the floor, out of sight."

She was awake in an instant and he could feel the gun barrel sliding past his legs on the floor.

The dash flash confirmed a tag. The drone signalled a pull over with a short siren blast and incessant flashing neon yellow. The drone would await whatever local police they now had here. He had to play an appeasing role to the last moment he knew as he pulled the car over to the side of the street. The drone hovered up beside the window as he rolled it down. Another cowboy moment.

He staring into the camera he lifted the gun from his lap and blasted three buckshot shells through the drone. Pieces of mini-drone flew in all directions scattering across the asphalt.

"Cool dad," Annalise said. "Those drones are so low-tech. They're bullshit—that video eye might not even be real time. They're pathetic engaging people."

Vince sped away. He didn't stop at any middle-of-the-night red light, slowing only to clear intersections and hitting the gas. They passed two 4x4 trucks and each driver stared down at their car. As if these were patrolling the streets. A police car with blaring siren raced past them the other way. To the blasted drone site no doubt. What would Vince have done facing a uniformed police—he hoped never to know. As they left the small city behind he kept their speed as fast as the highway allowed.

Hugging the road curves along a resort lake, they approached the RV village at lake's end. One of the last holdouts of the baby boomer summer vacation mind set; their last vacation had now come and gone. This lost lifestyle was strewn out among abandoned motor homes in once campgrounds. Some remains had become permanent housing.

Past the village, the river draining the lake led them along its valley towards the last corner. They were getting real close now.

#

As they swung around a curve, and lifted over a rise, a glimmer ahead grew steadily into flashing blue and red lights stabbing out into the night. Vince felt his adrenalin resurge as he pulled his foot from the accelerator, coasting, staring ahead and touching high, then low beams to penetrate the morning mist. The clock showed minutes before 4 AM. Details stood out as freeze frames now, a battered blue Rest Area 400m sign, with a 4 Axle Limit hanging below. Angular patterns within taillights reflected, and ahead the curves of neon roadblocks glared. They eased up slow motion before the overhead beams of a dark orange metal bridge looming dark in the mist.

Just as Vince felt the tiny jerk of a final stop, it seemed the mountains trembled.

Lightning flashed ground up and the shock of an explosion rocked their hybrid. Annalise sat up with a start as an eruption of concrete dust and rubble flew skyward casting twisted shadows into the hazy air. Then a sprinkling of shatter tinkled down on the hood of their car.

Vince sat up straight, rigid, staring. Then he relaxed and almost laughed. Christ, he just couldn't help it.

"Hey, don't worry." He shook his head. "It's just the bridge." Annalise looked out through her tears. She'd been through so much. "We caught the closing scene, that's all. We're almost there, close enough." Vince glanced at the dash map; this blown bridge had crossed its river a few kilometers short of their last corner. Still forty five to get to their S cell but good. "OK, we make like this is a border crossing." If Brad was right, this would be an official Pacific North West controlled crossing. By spring their Valley Council would have the real decision-making authority.

His heartbeat slowed. They could trace the flashing blue and red to the outline of what might once have been an RCMP chase-car. The car, now painted with another design was parked across the middle of the highway.

A walking shadow turned into a uniformed officer holding flashlight and shotgun. He walked towards their window, pistol hanging in holster. His finger jabbed back the way they had come. "Highway's closed. No one gets through."

"We live in the valley."

He ducked down to look through the window. "I'll need driver's licenses...both of you." He shone the flashlight on their license cards.

"You live in Calgary." He looked at them.

"We own land in the valley. We qualify as One Valley residents."

"Wait here."

They looked at each other. "Can we even trust this guy, dad?"

"We have no choice." One risk Brad said the Valley took was on the Pacific NW regional agreement. Three American states and BC had been talking. The BC effort was their biggest interest especially in a regional police force. "These guys are gonna be our new police. We'll need regulation, so police can be good when they're on the right side. We have to be careful though; we have to keep them responsible."

With the wait-out-the-global-climate chaos strategy, the biggest problem might be the refugees, Julia said, the others on their way there. Who gets in, who stays out. That would have to be policed. His choice to leave when he finally made it was good Vince decided.

"We've got quite a few hours by car between us and Calgary now." He looked at his daughter. "That's good, Annalise, real good. We just have to get to our S cell, our new home. Forget about Calgary. We'll wait for daylight and cycle the rest of the way. Down a nice paved highway; shouldn't be bad. We'll be there by midday."

Vince read the latest email message from Brad. All outside vehicles would now wait on Council approval, based on a qualifications list. They will have to go through the new vehicle entry process. All inside vehicles would get the same review this winter.

"And hey, we got past the ski resort. That would have been a good two day cycle ride."

The officer came back to their car.

"Look, no vehicles enter, not today. You can park down by the Station bridge. That's a walk across only for now. That will be your entry point once you get a vehicle entry permit."

"Any more choke points ahead?" Vince asked.

The officer looked at him directly, as if confirming him to be of the in-crowd. "The next bridge up ahead is gonna have a welded gate. All vehicle entry will be double checked there."

"We have bicycles."

"Restricted. You can get a cycle permit at Valley office."

"We don't want to be camping here."

"Look," the officer looked at him again, and at his daughter. "Walking in is an option. We advise daylight hours only." He walked away towards the flashing lights.

"Check out the map, dad." Annalise seemed excited now. "See that little train station bridge."

"Right. There's nothing but a trail along that side of the river."

Vince turned the car around, pulling over on the side road leading down to the Train Station bridge. A scatter of vehicle silhouettes poked out from the ditch on either side. Council could control traffic coming in via this smaller bridge and the trail, the only way around the blown bridge. And then a second control point at the welded next bridge. He found a place to park.

"OK, Annalise," he shrugged. "We walk in then, with light loads. We sort things out. We adjust."

Annalise nodded like she'd heard it before. She had Vince knew.

"So, best right now if we take our time, eat, rest and wait for sunrise. A couple more hours."

Vince sent a message to Brad. Kind of like getting on an Ark, Bud.

Annalise tucked back into her jacket, hands up sleeves, eyes closed with head resting on her backpack. He looked at her amazed. How this kid was dealing with this...there had always been something else going on in her he could never put his finger on.

#

They walked across the second last bridge, that afternoon. "Map says nine more kilometers to the S cell." By all rights, they were now in the Valley.

A smile had been creeping in on Annalise' face through the day, and he could feel a lightness in his own exhausted step. Almost like an afternoon hike up a mountain. Great to get to the peak, but anticipating the relief of taking boots off at the bottom.

Still, Vince had been not just counting as they walked, but carefully evaluating the barrier value of river bridges and railroad overpasses along the highway. Three river bridges right in and around that last highway corner, and two railroad overpasses there too. The third bridge back from the valley was just a creek and wouldn't do much, but just out of the valley the last two bridges had potential. This road between the Valley and the last corner will make an excellent eastern buffer, with any point to be closed as required. BC highways were well laid out to isolate the Valley, one blown bridge at a time.

"We'll be there before dark, easy."

Tribe 5 Girl

"Watch what this little one does." Annalise gestured towards the hologram floating above the end of the meeting room table. Before their eyes two aggressive mini-drones manoeuvred around each other, sizing up weaponry. She watched the faces for reactions when a small girl jumped in, stopping directly between, a hand raised towards each.

"Ignoring self-preservation," Annalise stated, "Kiki positions herself to negotiate. She now has the full attention of both remote pilots." As they listened, the girl in a firm voice instructed each pilot to talk, taking turns. From her PhD research Annalise knew that Kiki spontaneously set conditions without any instruction. This T5 voice allowed both parties to get what they needed without any hitting, or in this case weapons discharge.

"We need to seriously consider this proposal," Julia told the other Councillors.

Marta, who was chairing, crumpled her screen and sat back. A sign Annalise knew meant she had lots to say. Their One Valley home security was not a joke, with so many climate refugees, so many movers pushing north. Dark dreams of desperate hordes kept Annalise awake at night while she knew all wasn't right. There shouldn't be an emptying California surging in their direction but there was, leaving the threat of total invasion hanging out in a storm.

Annalise pressed at the tiny creases in her suit jacket, as she judged the tone of the meeting. She had braided her long brown hair that morning and fastened it up into a tight bundle swirl on top. Light makeup added to her natural look.

"As one of the five-to-seven-year-old girls, Kiki's tribal cohort coded as the most community oriented," Annalise emphasized. "What I'm proposing here is a two-pronged approach. First, we use the tribe 5 mindset loaded in surveillance drones as our first engagement with movers. And second, we make this response package available as an advisor to each of you Valley Councillors." While only two percent of the broader population fit into this T5 level from tribal analysis studies, an amazing twenty-three percent fit at Kiki's age and gender. Annalise was proposing the voice of psychologically type-selected girls to be the official voice of both defence and Council advisor.

Annalise had taken a chance when she selected Community Security for her dissertation research. God, not the risk of a generation ago. In her father's time, that would have meant risking her professional career choice. In her lifetime community security wasn't so much about protecting the rights of life, liberty and the pursuit of happiness. Having a life was a lot more about not being dead. And she had her father to consider and any future family of her own. Meanwhile, the Pacific NW needed to risk dropping the archaic shoot to kill mentality. Wrap strapping had to go too and not just due to bears and cougars. On patrol she had twice witnessed the inhumanity of a drone incapacitated person and she could just imagine being strapped. Their valley cultural model had to survive and do that by growing up.

At twenty seven and after years of study she knew the science. But her supervising professor kept saying her challenge was messaging to everyday people. Data existed—thousands of girls in multicultural cohorts had logged responses to typical human situations. The fearless six-year-old female cohort came to be known as Kiki's group. Yet, with all the extra potential the feminine outlook had on community decisions, the challenge remained of getting authorities to listen to this young girl voice. In spite of all the analytics showing a reduced fear factor, who would submit to the directives of a kindergarten girl?

She held her breath until she could hear her heart beat inside her ears. If home Council rejected her, well, there was that lakeside community in Idaho. But her home valley had such potential and she knew the people here! No one moved if they didn't have to—way too risky. She had to make a hero out of this little girl mindset, this digital composite of the girls who came together as Kiki. She exhaled slowly. She knew much depended on perception. Of her model, of her and what she said. Or didn't say.

Although they inherited this chaotic social environment from those ignoring climate warnings a few saw the situation as opportunity. Annalise had high hopes of carrying on the struggle for brotherly love, always feeling her heart soar with that T5 life is great outlook. The trick now was to hold out a friendly hand without being stomped on or conquered or raided and raped. Destruction and assimilation back into the older ways that had caused this mess in the first place was not an option. Most movers, she emphasized, though in the degraded state of refugees, still pursued the inherent human desire for a better life.

This topic was not new to Council. In a region least devastated by a planet in the throes of accelerating adaptation to new normal climate, they had to respond to cultural ambience knocking on their valley door. She was offering Council a way to peacefully engage movers. No bullets, no wrap straps.

"Nothing but child talk," Marta voiced the expected pushback. "With no experience, no education, she offers nothing but naivety. Childish foolishness explains her action."

Some Councillors, many men, nodded. Others remained silent.

Anthony coughed. "A strong defense comes from good offense," he intoned. "We automate ground weaponry at well-marked border points. True some will die, but the message will be clear and consistent. If no one enters our valley we retain our homeland security."

Many in Kiki's group coaxed to respond would immediately sense Boys would do that. Data trends reveled most but not all boys would, some girls would too—all depended on tribal outlook. As people see the world—so they behave. This girl cohort typically responded to imminent conflict saying: Let's try to make friends. A more advanced might phrase it, Welcome to our garden. Consensus revolved around cooperation; Our sandbox, ours together. Many girls, the future thinkers, wondered: How will this make our tomorrow? Sexist though it may seem, Annalise knew from her graduate study boys and girls were measurably different.

"An improved model of civilization, I'm quoting our prime directive," Julia spoke. "Would killing for nothing but survival be acceptable to keep our model alive? Or does that destroy what makes us better?" Julia had grown up in Switzerland.

Anthony shook his head and spoke in even tones. "To lay down all arms would be an ideologically based decision. To put it in a polite nutshell, foolish."

Annalise, feeling a tremor rise within, recalled that prime directive established but a decade ago when the Pacific NW region first gained official recognition. These days their valley contested with other regional communities to create a desired model of civilization replicable planet wide as that old save the world expression merged with the times. Reality required they avoid hostile invasion. Disruption of their model would just as effectively destroy any chance of success. A massive incursion by movers in the take-anything-mindset would be devastating.

With not just her life, but the existence of her home valley at risk, Annalise needed focus on her proposal's acceptance. Not in a theory but in the real world.

#

Annalise threw her backpack over her shoulders as she mounted her scooter. Julia had walked her to the door, telling her to check back for a decision. Later...there was other pressing Council business.

The pristine valley air relaxed her, hues revealed more each day as sparkling mountain snows receded. The aroma of a sprouting springtime green pervaded her nostrils, the earthy smell of a world almost in dream.

As she pulled out of the parking lot, a town patrol-drone circled in with a friendly greeting. Hi. What's your name? She shook her head at the wonder, yet scientifically evaluated the feeling of security engulfing her. Like a character from a fairy story hologram, touching the semi-magic safe feeling of home castle. What one side, maybe all sides, of the human struggle inherently desired.

At Kiki's age, she had listened attentively while her father Vince talked of the latest Calgary flood. As an engineer he encouraged math, three plus one is the fourth, she calculated then. And she entered high school before they made that night-time move. She felt so lucky to be here in this valley. Yet all girls, everybody really, should have this lifestyle.

The drone tagged along as she rode through the village streets. As their primary security technology, mini-drones patrolled One Valley on both BC and America sides, at times scouting beyond. But perimeter patrol drones carried more than happy voices; infrared nightcams, many with live ammunition firearms and laser burners...almost all had wrap strap capacity. The remote eyes and hands of the people, as ongoing Council discussion decided how they engage. When encountering a mover once simple detection was ascertained and an observation routine established, the question at issue asked how best to further interact. A boundary set with a threat, or, now she offered a way to allow what many wanted—an extended friendly hand.

As she reached the town's edge the drone dropped behind and she sped south on the local highway past bright green leaves of huge black poplars. The bridge over the river lay ahead.

She thought of opposing views. Damn it, the theory was almost intuitive. Girls did lose community spirit as they grew, yet everyone knew the personhood they developed depended on social context. Puberty transition destroyed the most spirit, socializing with peers from other tribal stages. Much drag-back came from the T1 life sucks tribe. Many girls regained portions of their truer nature later as elders, but many didn't, and much was lost. Unless they could design an improved social future.

Crossing the bridge, she glanced upriver towards the distant middle-of-the-valley hill. She had finished grade 12 living up on that hill, in that tiny house. Their Survival cell, her father always called it.

#

She rode the switchbacks up the hill, and pulled over the rise into the yard. Her father waved from the lower terrace where he was working on something down by the garden.

"Hey sunshine."

"Hey dad. What'cha up to?"

"Come look."

She walked down the stepping-stone stairway, the one he had dug into the earth bank. He built the Survival cell on weekends those year he came out from the city anticipating what might come. Even then he thought of her fading childhood.

He stood between the lower terrace edge and those nut trees he had planted, outside the garden proper.

"They call this plant a RockOil. Genetically designed with a lichen splice to grow in rocky soil. Biggest problem is growth rate, so they want test plots on this latest splice. Potential biofuel."

"Cool dad. No more hydro installations?"

"Every perennial stream has potential. There's still lots of room for run-of-the-river installs. Especially deeper in the mountains, up north either side of the big lake where the snow pack lasts longer. Keeps the power supply more seasonally even. We need maintenance people living out there. Modern pioneers."

"Kinda like us."

"Yeah, we made our move." He looked at her. "We need more like you."

She never forgets that night they left Calgary for good. That swarm gang at the highway corner, her dad blasting their tires out with his shotgun—that had been the freakiest. After that they were lucky to drive unhindered nearly all the way. The anticlimactic blown bridge ended their drive but they were close enough—they walked the last forty kilometers of highway to the valley. They rode back three days later with Valley permits for their hybrid, both squashed onto that scooter. The social and political chaos of Calgary brought out gangs, what out here kinda matched the movers. In this new model of the world no longer to be ignored.

"How's your Girl proposal? What's Council saying?"

"Oh dad!" She frowned. "I'm freaking out. They're deciding right now."

"Yeah, well be brave, remember." He gazed at her smiling. "Hey, I saw potential in you when you were little so you got me. You were always trying to get others connected."

"What else would anyone want?" She gave him a look.

"Yeah," he took a breath. "You are right."

"I know."

He nodded. "So the T5 Girl makes first contact. Wonder what we would have said at the blown bridge...talking to a little girl instead of who-knows-whose police."

"Not so scary as that swarm gang chasing us in trucks. But those police blew that bridge up right in front of us. We were lucky."

"Coulda been worst. Good planning makes for good luck. Anyway, we dealt with that situation, right? We adapted, just like you're doing right now. You are the best Annalise, I've always told you that, and it's still true."

"M'not a child, dad."

"Yeah...so what's Julia saying?"

"She's helping me, with Council."

"Sit for a bit?"

"Sure." They turned up towards the survival cell together. "But—well, there's Anthony."

"Yeah, old school thinking. Like back in Alberta."

They walked up the stepping stones, and into the tiny house. She took her favorite seat at the scrounged camper table. Her father lit the methane burner to boil water for tea.

"So tell me more about the T5 Girl."

"Here's some numbers for you, dad. Typical tribal populations were always between twenty and a hundred'n fifty."

"Cool. I'll have to remember that."

"But all people, everyone, fits into five tribal classifications," she said. The middle T3 was the largest, the I'm great and you are not tribe contained near half of all people. So in any truth and reconciliation situation how could Kiki's little group implement T3 views? There was a limitation problem anyway—connection could only be made one level up or down. Resultant theory held that introduction of the middle T3s to the T4 we are great people would be optimal. The T4s may seem a bit weird, but that's what gels the group and they were a tribe aware of their own existence. This helped if the overall objective was influencing what the whole world thinks.

He set the tea on the table and sat, sliding a window opened to let the afternoon cool circulate.

"So what does the T5 Girl tell the mover? And how would that help our model?"

She set her face firm. "OK, to start the drone is completely unarmed. So the confrontation level is low, very low. The girl's voice tones reach deep into any sub conscience as non-threatening by default and the conversation she carries touches a deep inner desire in many, even most. Even the enemy for someone like Anthony."

Each first encounter would involve a chat with the Tribe 5 mindset, programmed into the drone. The voice tone analyzer would carry out its acceptability classification. The Girl speaks to the basics of food, clothing, and shelter, then health and education to determine how each individual would fit into the community. No excess wealth, no hoarding, no extra-large houses, a specific contribution to the community would all be covered. Based on the talk, a decision would be made on the client's invitation-to-proceed status.

Vince looked at his daughter, letting out a deep sigh. "Yeah."

"True not all, but many desire to live with Kiki's outlook." She beamed. "Some call it the purity of heart model."

Vince nodded.

With reports of all those movers coming north, she told him, this might be their best chance. Call it a better drone design maybe, but something in their valley model had to change.

#

Council seemed in session when Annalise opened the door, but Julia waved her in. All feelings she had of relaxation vanished.

"Annalise," Marta with screen uncrumpled said. "We have just been discussing eusocial insects. Are you familiar?"

She knew a bit, but shook her head respectfully.

"In an ants' nest the queen is the centre of the community to be protected at any cost. Older females are designated to the most perilous jobs; they patrol the edges of the nest territory. As such, those closest to death carry out the most dangerous activity which makes sense from a rational viewpoint as a very efficient way to run a community."

"Maximizes security," Anthony stated. "Defence must remain top priority."

"The self-sacrificing nature of older women—people not insects—can as effectively be used to teach their experiential wisdom to their grandchildren," Julia said. "Maximizes knowledge."

Annalise didn't say a word.

"So Anthony wants to thin us out," Julia scoffed. "He wants old women out on patrol dealing with invaders that our drones have wrap strapped."

"I never said that."

"Well, what of wrap straps?" Julia challenged. "Recall the Sanders family. Resourceful enough to make it into our valley on the old forestry service road. And what do we do? Our drone wrap straps them and by the time our ground squad gets there we've lost all that resourcefulness. Did they die of exposure or did the grizzlies get there first. What model do we want to create here?"

"To Annalise's proposal then." Marta said. "We did not get consensus so we voted."

Annalise felt her insides quiver.

"We have decided to take on some but not all of your proposal risks." Marta looked directly at her. "Under certain considerations."

She listened.

"You will be reporting to committee, Julia, Anthony and myself."

She nodded.

"And, after reviewing the details of your proposal, we hold this project to three specific restrictions."

"First, a one year pilot. We discussed the old border crossing model. A guard well versed in cross questioning attests to trust or lack thereof. As your proposal suggests our guard will be the voice of your T5 Kiki Girl."

"Second, if invitation is extended the client will agree to our community training program," Marta said. "Julia will take care of that."

The third condition was a three month probation period for each client admitted and agreement to the One Valley resettlement restriction. Depending on how they integrate they may be pioneering a perimeter valley. Remote hydroelectric installations Annalise thought, she'd have to tell her father.

"There's gonna be infiltration. Swarm gangs will trick their way in." Anthony shook his head. "We risk not only damage but a total invasion. We're gonna be wiped out. Maybe completely."

"Everything has risk," Julia said. "And we will not maintain a guns blazing attitude where we live to survive and survive only to eat and reproduce. Our model of the future must look to the wellbeing of all."

Anthony stared at the table.

"We have left the advisors up to each Councillor's discretion," Marta said. She sat back, looking at Annalise and then around at the rest. "After watching my two granddaughters last night, I for one want to take on a new advisor."

Annalise saw the smile grow on Julia's face and she felt her own forming. She knew there would be more than one Kiki advisor for her to prepare.

VALUES

Brother's Keeper

His eyes shot open, his twitching body in a cold, sticky sweat. As always. Through the blurriness, Staphan strained for a vision from the promised above, a glimpse of his other world reward, yet slowly came to focus on the reality of painted steel pipes snaking across the high ceiling.

"Oh God, please help me," he barely heard his own voice, a voice that veered sharply back on itself, transforming into a snarl...

You bastard Creator. Why me? You lame fuck!

Oh...whatever. Who cared, who gave the slightest shit? "I should have taken myself out," he growled, then whispered, "if I only had the courage.

He felt a scream coming on, yet his ears perked, and he listened.

The building creaked a hollow groan, reverberating murmurs sidling up the elevator shaft from the corners of lower floors. Creaks, perhaps carrying insight to the greater plan. That grand plan of someone or something out there in the broad universe.

He didn't move, counting his breaths as they gradually slowed. Disgust wracked his being. He could sense the night's hollow middle, when any half normal person would be in their deepest moments of slumber.

He rolled over in the cot, feeling for the edges of his small world, pushing himself slowly up to sit. From behind closed eyelids, caked with the crystals of half-dried tears, he forced a glance. There on the table the bottle loomed, waiting patiently alongside the flask of water and the loaf of bread.

From deep down his inner fissure the scream sprang forth, engulfing him, driving him to lunge for the liquor. Clenching the bottle's neck, he wrenched off the cap, whipping it to the side. Shivers wracked him as a smile crept onto his face. But, as he drew the release to his lips, his mind's other side shrieked a warning, unbelievably louder. He groaned. Wrath surged out with full force from his being's center, and he hurled the bottle with a new-born's angry howl up against the brick wall. He watched in slow motion as the vessel shattered into a million shards, leaving behind a dripping splatter and the strung out sonatas of tinkling glass.

The scream tucked tail, retreating to its more familiar lair, underground and deep inside, echoing in the confines of his hollow heart. A blissful numbness settled in. For who would hear him anyway? Who ever had...he laughed? His head sank into his hands to finally rest and he heaved a deep quivering sigh.

After a long moment, he sensed a calm. With trembling hand, he reached out to grasp the cross, pressing it softly to his lips, then crushing it to his chest. I'm so sorry, please forgive me. He rocked himself, the infant within, slowly humming his being into a mantric rhythm. Righteous thoughts, breath in; all fear, breath out. The pace took over, encouraging the moment once again to pass.

Acceptance.

The four noble truths.

The way, the new way.

He rose and walked to the window, lifting the pane, seeking a breath of the dreamed-of freshness. Foul air slammed into his face, but cool at least. Disturbing music from across the way forced an entrance. Far below a group of the intoxicated shouted at each other, staggering in unsteady cadence with and against the beat.

A familiar thought flashed to mind. Maybe, just maybe, he could step right out, right now to crash down through their laughter and end it all broken on the concrete. A blood stain on the street, as a final mark. There was creation, and then there were adjustments, the elimination of poor design. He stared down at the electrobikes parked around the entrance. The last stragglers to leave Grio's Grab. Oh, that I could be one of them. If, well, if only...a quivering sigh.

That oh-so-foolish promise, that archaic code of honor.

Shela, who guided the revolutionary movement to take wealth back from the toorich., she would see right through him, of course, but that was why she took that messy VirtuALL track. He pictured the white-haired man in the tailor-made suit outside the Patriot, and the dimmer image of Staphan's brother in the backseat, her illustrative instance of the toorich. He shuddered at his emotional track then. The man who sat at the head of the dinner table, on those occasions he ate at home, the man who had such influence or lack thereof on Staphan's formative years. The stories of struggle, out there in the world of energy business. To make a hero of nuclear power, to bring misdirected solar, wind and geothermal to their knees. The long drawn-out war of competition. His progenitor, his father.

There was shela's action proposal too. "For those of you who qualify, of course." Her Virtual avatar shimmered. The female human super-conscience, revealed as many women at once, a shifting pattern, an endless series of female faces with that multidimensional voice. Their guide to a better world. "Each of you to assist with what ability you bring." Yet shela had a problem with that better world idea: what to do with those special cases having no conscience. Especially, those powerful, and strongly committed to no change. With penetrating gaze, she had probed his inner channels, looking deep into his eyes and even deeper.

He had tried to please his father. He had tried to think and act like him, to be a good son in his father's eyes. As the Son had to His Father. Once in a while, he saw the depths of human fear in those eyes, and in those moments he wished only to reach out a hand of compassion. The well-dressed businessman, adept at facing hard questions with decision, persecuted by those trailing behind, but well protected by his own ruthlessness. A ruthless nature, but nowhere near that of Paul, Staphan's brother. All this lifelong influence for shela to interpret.

Shela, oh shela. From #tags and pages sprouting up just after President Asha's assassination. Anger, and grief, postings that kept her alive formed the Shared Holistic Equity Leveraging Alliance. SHELA...or shela. She loved them all, even those with impure intent. "Check within—

seek the truth," she urged. Her earthly warmth shone through her universal smile. "Set your telecell to VirtuALL, please, for a reverse feed. We will log your inner reactions." Each shela follower had special interests and special talents, they were told. To pit against deeply held traditional beliefs, the greatest barrier to re-education of ones like his father. "Thank you my children." Shela faded into a woman who is all women, waiting patiently.

She'd never pick him, he thought then…he'd be weeded out right off the top. Why did it have to bother him anyway? Why couldn't he just be like Paul? Paul, who stayed safely in the backseat while the city men, vagabonds and tramps, smashed a brick into the Patriot, before the chauffeur got them out of there.

He and his brother had had good times, true. Pulling speed controls from golf carts, careening in and out of the trees to harass gentlemen players. There were his own ventures too, past the golf course by the river with Joshua and Jeira, where Paul would never go. Later, he made honest effort to be just like his brother, picking out a sports car, and following him to the gel tub parties. Then that damn on-the-road-to-Damascus moment. Why him? Why couldn't that have been his brother's epiphany? His brother, with both name and disposition to match that long ago pre-conversion Paul. He pestered his brother time after time, didn't you ever feel like this? What? Like what? You're on something, you little shit.

The closest his brother Paul ever came to Damascus was sneaking into the Crystal Church to pilfer from the collection – just for fun, he said, as he surely didn't need the money. Even better was sneaking girls in through the back, and hearing their wine giggles under the nighttime altar. One screamed, he boasted once, like she was being touched-down on by the All Mighty. Perhaps more truthfully, by the weight of Paul on her no-longer-consenting body.

The beat below picked a new rhythm.

Okay. Think. When shela showed the city men, he did feel true compassion for them, he could recognize their plight. But his father's tone cut in with its calm logical edge. His father's voice simply stepped past them, they with their hands out—they are, after all, simply beggars. For Christ's sake. Look, my business model supplies anyone with a job, get a good education and come see one of my managers. That I can give you. Opportunity, in this land of the same. Our status is God-given; we are the ones He smiles upon. In the Crystal Church the minister approved the blessed, and those who have, certainly have been blessed. In Buddha's Hindu old testament, the city men had bad Karma, simply paying for their past misdeeds. Buddha walked away from the blessing of wealth to sit under a tree for four years.

Shit. His VirtuALL track would be nothing but a jumble. Like his life.

Staphan held the crucifix to the window, staring through its crystal facets at the yin yang symbol floating at its crux. Jesus and Buddha combined, east and west bound tight forever, heaven and nirvana. As they talked of endlessly at SonofmaNirvana, the best of both could be had. They met in the Christian church basement, three times a week. Paul came once, and left halfway through, never to return. Paul fit in so much better with the regular Sunday morning services, where he could smile unruffled, perhaps recalling his own middle of the night attendance. Forgiven.

Yet, Staphan was to pay their brotherly debt.

Why—no longer mattered. To sleep in peace someday had oh, such appeal. Yet there must be a way to bypass suffering, certainly Buddha said so, and Jesus in his own way too. The will of God, known through meditation; to accept circumstances as they were, yet do what He requested. Crucifixion though? All that blood, and hanging nailed in excruciating pain, waiting to die with no companion but prayer. Too extreme. But what to do about Paul…the endlessly trying question.

With his own peace in mind, he decided to do whatever it took. He pressed the cross to his lips again. If those voices inside, gave him a cross to bear, well, he could carry it…for a while anyway. Up the hill at least, but not to hang from spikes with crows pecking his eyes out. God. To at least find release from the wrack of guilt, to someday hear the inner bell ring the tones of tranquility. That, yes.

He carefully lowered the window and turned back to the cot and table. Folding his legs carefully into lotus position, he breathed in, all peace, breathed out, all fear, slowly starting to hum the Ohum mantra. Oh, that shela would invite him to a task.

#

And she did.

He had joined those on the shela mission of picking up flower petals. Full screen map uncrumpled, they had followed their icon-guide across the city. On return, the gangland Blades in long loose red shirts blocked their e-trucks and Eli's ancient motorbike. Arms folded before an old SUV barricade, exposed whip-wires and a loaded shotgun holster. With hand clutching crucifix, he listened to Eli's voice talk their way through. "You men have good cause. You want to wire your brother? The man on the Hill be our hit. Come join us, on the side of truth. Real truth, man."

The lowest thing one could do, run a whip-wire through another.

#

At a shela meeting one voice spoke of the Savior, as that moral Lecturer of two thousand years past, admonishing those who live by the sword—making it clear they will die by the sword. A different tone was set for all shela action—no violence. That they not live by that proverbial sword, however, neither to turn the other cheek.

Then after that meeting, he followed Joshua out into the alley to meet again after so many years. Josh gradually recognized him. "The Bullet Train," he said. "The transition car, you were in black and white. That shirt with the cross."

"Shine out in the dark, surround the dusk with light," Staphan said. "Earlier times too, Josh, you, me and your sister down by the river. When we were children."

"Sas! Jesus, Sas, that's you. God, you look different."

"The Saviour's name is not to be taken lightly. I was Sas, in that more untainted time."

"Wow, and now…hey, you're here, you must know shela."

"Shela, oh yes. She is my guide and my light, testing my purity," He watched his friend's enthusiasm. "It is you who bear news of my next task, she has informed me."

Shela had just confirmed passive submission would bring nothing. That the reek of their flower petals over the toorich Parade Day was but a first message. The toorich reacted, planning to fully enclose the Hill, to control all helihover traffic, to suspend the economy Bullet Trains. Shela's other messages then came forth, one the social underground initiative. We have a potential candidate, shela said, and Staphan's prayer for task was extended. What she wanted he could do, but the others wanted even more.

"So you are the social underground?" Josh said.

He nodded.

"Meet me at the tunnel."

He and Josh found each other later at the tunnel excavation, the hole being bored under the Hill's wall. Shela's second toorich message was to arrive underground, from beneath the Hill. And her third message, her social communiqué, through him.

"Strength and honor," Josh greeted him. "You participate, my friend."

Staphan was straining under the weight of a dirt bag on each shoulder.

"Bread work," Staphan uttered. "Always good for the soul. Something my father never did, not once in his life. Nor my brother."

"Well, labor's not the only type of work," Josh said.

Staphan stared.

"Shela has another task, for you and those like you."

"No one's like me."

"Many are, Staphan, all across the city."

He let the bags slide to the damp clay floor.

Joshua told him of the virtual tour idea. Shela wanted them to bring the toorich down from their Hill. To truly live as they did for a time. "Maybe just in Virtual. Or maybe in VirtuALL. Someone you know from the Hill ... can you think of anyone? This brother ... how about him?"

"Oh, yes, my brother Paul," Staphan shook his head. "Perchance eons from now."

"Shela says whoever we pick, well, it will be doing them a big favor," Josh said. "Say, your brother."

Staphan retrieved one dirt bag, heaving it up on the pile. He turned to Josh.

"I have learned that it is my soul I must attend to," he stared forlornly into his friend's eyes, seeking solace. "For am I my brother's keeper?"

Josh shrugged, speaking lightly. "You know I only have a sister."

He turned away, face to the stack of bagged clay. From behind he felt Josh's hand on his shoulder. "Someone else? Your father works hard, does he not? Maybe a little selfish, but we are out to educate him. And others like him."

He stooped for the second bag, and then spun back, jaw set.

"My father." He stared at Josh. "Oh yes, he fits well into that highly praised hard work ethic. Covetousness brings glorified liberation from the deadly sin of sloth. But, you must know, his culturally ascribed success has been so dependent on his phenomenal advantages."

Josh looked at him quizzically.

"First, my family has been well-to-do for six generations.

"So … the toorich beget the toorich."

"My father's rich kid advantage was not just large, it was huge."

Staphan heaved the second bag onto the stack. "Also," he caught his breath, "to be extra successful, you need a certain disposition. You must have an aggressive character for commerce, uncompromising business acumen."

"Your father?"

"Oh yes, aggressive he is, or has at least learned to be."

A trickle of sweat dripped down his forehead. But not near as ruthless as Paul who comes by that naturally, no learning necessary.

"Look, Sas, the ideas is, we bring your father on a VirtuALL tour off the Hill. So through Virtual emotive feed, he truly experiences life down here." Staphan felt Josh's eyes settle on his cross. "You know, so he might really hear what Jesus told the young rich man. Really, meaning he might not turn away."

"Well, he does use BusinessDream to work through the night," Staphan sighed.

· #

That night he awoke to a subliminal roar. Oh for pure simple emptiness, he wished, oh for nothing at all. The encounter with Jeira awaited, with no choice; the alternatives looming ever more dire. The voices of the others, not shela, supplied him this brother directive.

He found a seat in a wooden booth at the teahouse, and sat to await.

His mind raced, his life flashing. The ups and downs, his struggles for an up and then collapsing into the next down. Why? Nirvana, Creator, maybe human created concepts. The Savior certainly had his ups and downs. What it must have been like out in that desert for forty days and nights, or hanging on a wooden stick for how many hours. What loving Creator would allow such things? To prove faith in tasks assigned? Is that the only reason?

She arrived in her Helihover Air urban police uniform, and they fumbled through a chat on childhood. The ideals of youth, sworn to in blood by river's edge. Their games of knights and ladies, imaginings of medieval honor. But after that, childhood now past, to that he needed speak.

"Look, Jeira, there is something I really need to tell you."

Her smile was bright.

"I've been straightening out recently." He pulled out the yin yang crucifix, placing it before them on the table. "We had our code of honor then, and I still seek to follow a code. You must now know I am with SonofMaNirvana. We meditate; we seek to improve. We must make direct amends for all past deeds."

He bit his lip. "I never told you I have a brother." He paused. "His name is Paul. That night, at a gel tub party, I saw you there. But I was too shy to come over and talk."

Her smile dimmed. "You are a great guy, Sas. We were all unsure of ourselves at times."

He strained to look towards her eyes, going on.

"And I knew what Paul and his friends were up to. It wasn't the first time. He brags about after parties, after the drinks they teased into whoever she was and who knows whatever else they slipped in. Anyway, that night I knew, and I did nothing—my cardinal sin of omission. I am sorry, Jeira, so sorry."

Her silent face sank, and he could stare only at the table now. He knew of the one to three days each young woman would have awakened to, shackled inside the abandoned SUV. Her time as slave dominated by the scheduled gang sex of his brother and friends depended how willingly she submitted. And to what. Cigarette burns to encourage would scar her body now.

An inner urge arose too slam his fist hard, but he held back.

"My brother has engaged in many acts of deviant behavior. All his life. It's not deviation for him, it's the way he is and the way he will always be. And he was born extremely clever, and focused on covering up, no concept of honor. You would know more than I, but our legal system has certainly not caught his deviance."

He forced a glance at her eyes, now laced with stabbing pain. A tear, and then torrents rolled down her cheeks.

"Words without action are meaningless—my amends must be direct." Through deeds he will make retribution, to accompany this pitiful voice of regret. God's creation can be perfect only by His willing some creation pieces to clean up others. The mistakes.

He rose from the table.

"I have a task on the Hill, I must tarry no longer."

#

Staphan touched his telecell to the doorbar, his breathing shallow. The electromag pins whispered out, and as the door swung in, he stepped quickly through, abandoning the middle of the night air. Back slumped against the resealed entrance, he sensed a trace of stone floor polish. Family trust, and his father's pass had gained him entrance…to his brother's home. His eyes strained at the double stairways wrapping up through the dimness above the foyer. He stood, trembling, in the darkness. A memory struggled to surface, what Josh said, those shela messengers all across the metropolis. He was not alone, one of many this night.

He climbed the curving staircase on the left, finger sliding along polished banister. The faintest creak, and he froze again, wary. His brother, so attentive to protecting his secrecy. He listened to the lonely dust particles settle, waiting on the morning maid. One who cleaned up for others, like shela. Shela, who gave such wholesome directives.

He found the Civil War swords hung crossed in shadows back of the balcony columns. As he edged one double-edged blade from its velvet scabbard, he stopped, again unable to still his mind. Surely his brother needed special treatment. Very special, they said. Grow up, he told that thought. Happiness was for the playground, nothing but a frivolous state of mind. He had to find the truly righteous, through action, no matter what the cost.

What would the Master have done? With His love?

He pulled the sword fully from its scabbard, letting the cold steel point drop to the floor. Leaning forward, the sharp tip sunk deep into the Persian rug, he sank slowly to his knees, both hands clasping the ivory handle, staring at the door to his brother's room. His head dropped.

Honorable execution…but medieval times reside in the so-distant past. What would shela have said at this moment? The voices, the Others' request, what they wanted rang clear. And that promise of ever elusive peace.

His mind churned. After the flower petal run, there had been that lightness in his step. Thank you, Jesus, and you too, Buddha, for the strength you give…feeling just a little smoother in Your Hands he had even hummed, rubbing the cross oh so gently. At that moment, he clearly saw the bread and water as on this table. Difficult maybe, perhaps the most critical test 'til then, but shela really had given him a chance. She seemed truly interested in helping him with what he actually needed, oh so badly. Trusting the voices might bring even more.

Real sleep perchance, through the night even, well, at least he'd be a tiny bit calmer when he first woke in the late darkness. That darkness…without the screaming inside, what could be better? That first middle of the night awakening. Nothing had happened. Nothing out of the ordinary. He woke up, and was unable to fall back. He focused on his breathing, release your mind to the universe. Maybe that was the mistake—his mind to the universe. For it was then the voices began.

At times he wondered if time and place of his whole life had been randomly selected. Good luck or bad, a crap shoot at the tables. These Others, these voices now giving unsolicited direction, often unwanted. Though he does understand, at times, after a while. Not always. In times when crotch-to-eyeball was the norm, the act of honorable execution was reserved only for those not able to conceptualize honor. Kind of like putting a dog to sleep with a modern needle, a dog unable to overcome its child-biting habit. Completely justifiable.

When I do what I really need to, he chanted under his breath, my road-to-Damascus friend gets a little happier and smiling Buddha grins a little wider. Believing in guiding voices was a risk, but what choice? Through meditating, if the Buddha was right, the answers were within where these Others seemed to be. God was nirvana, God was within. God's will?

He raised the sword in one hand, the other wrapped tightly about the crucifix and rose up to step through the bedroom door.

His brother lay before him snoring lightly – completely at peace with all things. As he had always been.

With crucifix dangling above both hands, he held the tip of the sword before him, lowering it to a point just below his brother's gently rising ribcage. He watched the exhale. Can one truly be his brother's keeper? The smell of stone, mixed with his brother's sleeping quarters swirled about. Would he reincarnate, for punishment? Or be improved? Freedom, brother, from this world, from yourself. He dropped the sword point to his brother's chest and lunged forward, thrusting deep, and then deeper. Paul's eyes twitched, but never opened, as his final snore ended with a gurgle.

Amy's Jessica

The whole thing had been Bryan's idea. Try it, he persuaded, go see for yourself Amy, what's there. Maybe he had tired of hearing her talk about the television show, or maybe he just knew what she really needed. He put in overtime at the warehouse to pay for the trip, yet he insisted she go for just one day. To be truly frivolous.

Tension hung thick that morning. Vying forces tore at her from all directions as Amy rode the bus to the airport. She pulled her ticket from her purse a couple times, Delta Airlines – Flight 483, that's what it read.

She carried her one small bag, looking straight ahead as she navigated her way through the light crowds, shivering with excitement, yet nervous as scenes of her hero Jessica ran and reran through her head. Jessica, so confident, and with all her money, she could do just whatever she wanted, whenever she wanted.

Sitting by the boarding gate, she listened to others chatting of faraway places. An airport worker, in a blue and gold uniform, released the red cloth strap from a metal post, allowing a line-up to form to check in luggage. The clips of Jessica waiting for her flight ran a close overlap with her own reality now.

Still, she felt a little awkward as she pulled a sandwich from a crumpled paper bag. She glanced around as she ate, careful to brush a crumb from her skirt. Maybe her food wasn't the most refined, but she could see grubbiness among others; she certainly dressed better than some, and she sighed with satisfaction at that.

As she ate her lunch, Amy's discomfort grew. She wanted to be somewhere else. But she sat tight. Thoughts of home, husband and children kept coming to her, and she swallowed deep. She was happy, she tried to tell herself. But she couldn't help feel her hand move to her belly, her aching emptiness.

Finishing the sandwich, she stuffed its plastic wrap back into the bag, pulling out a banana and a pop bottle of trailer water. Exotic soda soon. Finished eating, she slid the paper bag and bottle onto the next seat. This was her life so far, she thought, looking at the refuse, and she pursing her lips, rose up and walked away.

"Any luggage?"

"I need my bag with me." Her brow creased.

"Carry on, OK. Passport please."

She got her boarding pass – she knew what that was for.

"Thank you." She brightened, mimicking Jessica's smile she had seen a thousand times. Her smile came with her through customs into the air-conditioned hallway leading to the boarding gate. Nicer décor than her trailer. But such line-ups. She sat anticipating, looking around. A mother alone kept her children close, and Amy's heart thumped. She looked the other way – this was her time – she rose and walked to a far window, humming, then back to board. A scanned pass in hand, she followed the hallway that surprisingly ended. A set of stairs. This wasn't right. She descended, astonished to find herself outside in the breeze.

"I'm looking for a Delta flight." Her voice quivered. The attendant pointed out across the tarmac. Wow, Jessica always had a boarding gate extension.

She climbed the stairs up to the jet; only four seats wide. On well, a jet at least. The stewardess dressed well, as she demonstrated emergency doors to exit. Amy listened attentively, feeling more uneasy. She put her bag under the seat in front of her, as the stewardess instructed. No one sat beside her when the door closed, but the children's voices were close.

The jet pulled beeping out on the runway and as it accelerated, Amy whooshed back to the Carnival ride in town one summer. The bumpiness disappeared abruptly when the wheels lifted. She watched her city diminish, becoming a bunch of toy houses and cars. She strained to see her trailer, wanting to wave for a moment. The city fell behind, replaced by grain fields, bush and sloughs. She spotted an old church at a grid road corner.

Carnival that Saturday, then church that Sunday. She was ten years old. The neighbours pulled up beside her family's car in their new Cadillac. She watched the neighbour girl push the shiny door opened, as the rust fell off her own door. She waved, and Tina waved back, smiling in a strange way. Later that day she first felt the knot. She asked her mother about Tina's shining car, but she never really got an answer. Just a seed of emptiness.

She forgot about that day, but the seed, now planted like a secret weed, lay dormant, waiting, but not long. She saw other cars, and houses, and the ways of people, fertilizer for the feeling over the years, all while she was busy just trying to live. She only wanted to be happy – to live a full life. She knew that. Now she had her own children, but the seed had matured in the background. Could she ever snip it off, or better yet dig it right out?

Well, she settled back, now thanks to her husband, she was on her way to discover the wonders of Jessica at the Marriot. There would be the shear for the nasty weed.

She had to focus; she wished there were no children on the plane. Their freedom pushed as a fresh flower up beside her weed of emptiness, beside herself as she had been, until that day at church. Not a care in the world, just like her own kids.

The stewardess came by with the drinks cart. She couldn't remember, a list of free items had been mentioned. She would refuse, no matter what they offered, just to be sure. Tomorrow, for lunch at the Marriot Hotel, then she would drink whatever caught her fancy.

"A glass of water please."

"Snack mix?"

"How much are they?"

"Complimentary."

"Oh, sure."

She opened the little package, eating it all except for the pretzels – she hated pretzels. Don't waste, her mother told her what she herself was told by Grandma. Eat everything on your plate she told her kids too – and then she slowly drank the bottle of cool water. The deep hum of the engines droned in the background, punctuated with that children's laughter.

She sighed, glancing out the window as the plane passed through a bank of fluffy white mist. Like the clouds of heaven from church, a church that gave so much to her sister and mother, why not her? Where was Peter at the Gates, right here, right now?

She looked down again, at the bare hilly land and scattered trees. Tiny clouds floated below, how strange. A creek meandering along a valley took her to teenage years. The boys at school pulling up in shiny new trucks, others with old junkers. She went for rides with new truck boys and she kind of liked the plush seats. When she met Bryan though, his kindness touched her in spite of his rusty old truck, and his became the one. Plush seats or not, only with her future husband had she gone for a ride down by the creek. No one else.

Excitement began battle with droopy eyelids, until the jet lurched slightly. Salt Lake City announced the pilot. Below, a big lake came into view with low mountains poking out from the surface, forming islands along its shores.

Ahead, the city spread out to the mountains in the distance and the green grass and trees lay softly between industrial warehouses. Bryan must be at work now. Green highway signs became readable and the dry land around the airport melded into pavement as she watched the jet's shadow touch the jet with a jerk. The children resonated their vocal cords in tune with the engines, as the plane slowed down to automobile speed.

Amy gently picked up her bag, fitting well as a jet set woman, traveling light. The signs guided her well, like a barbwire fence the cattle follow, to the next departure gate. A couple hours wait here. The sun set gently over the lake.

She watched the planes take off and land, just for practice, but this wasn't the right view, not yet. She just wanted to get on with the trip. Finding a seat close to her departure gate, she tried to relax.

The new plane, this time with a boarding gate, was a real jet, six seats wide and twice as long. From another window seat, she glanced quickly out into the dark Utah night.

One of the stewardesses, her hair up, had cute earrings and a little sapphire kerchief around her neck. Now she dressed like Jessica in a way. The jet was almost empty, except for first class. First class people are late night travelers with loose schedules and exciting lives, just like Jessica.

The big jet backed away from the boarding gate, smoothly. Amy half listened now to the instructions on life-vests and oxygen masks. The lights went out as the jet taxied; this take-off would be in the dark. Her ears grew accustomed to the higher pitched whine of this real airliner. Finally the jets roared, a Carnival moment, a little bump and they were off; she felt like a night bird looking down on city lights. A freeway with tiny headlights flowing past each other. Yes, the jet set life, she thought, looking up the dimly lit aisle at her mysterious fellow travelers. On the way to San Francisco, the California city on the sea. And no children.

Amy diverted her gaze upward, seeing romance in the constellation laden sky, the reflection of a flashing light bouncing along the jet's wing to the white light shining at its tip. The jets roared with a power that brought the smiling face of Jessica to mind. Her dreamy silence was broken.

"Something to drink?" The stewardess flashed a radiant smile.

"Water?"

Another bottle and a bag of pretzels. All pretzels. She left them.

How young, beautiful and popular Jessica was, how she had everything, everything money could buy. Jessica, for sure, was happy. Always. She put her hand on her stomach. Jessica would have no knot for sure. Amy felt a tingle of anticipation. Then, so rested, or exhausted, she dozed off.

Popping ears made her swallow, and groggily she looked out at small town lights. But the lights multiplied as rapidly as her heart beat faster. The city revealed itself, looking so mysterious, with low clouds obscuring patches of streetlights. An ocean front city spread out over hills, like an endless ant colony.

A new smell permeated the jet. Whether from the ocean or the city, she didn't know. As her jet pulled up to dock, she saw jets from Singapore, Thailand and Italy; from all over the world.

Amy disembarked slowly, savouring every moment as she walked out into the cool humid air. Asking an attendant, she found her way to the shuttle bus – now Jessica would have had a chauffeur pick her up or at least a taxi – but Amy hopped the evening bus to Jessica's favourite hotel.

Time stood still as she walked through the front doors, every tassel on the doormen's suits waved her in as they elegantly held the door for her entry. Like walking in on the Cinderella party of her life. Everyone there was dressed to the nines, her long sought world opening arms of welcome. A receptionist found her reservation, and she slowly found her way up to the fifth floor. Enthralled, but exhausted, she threw her bag on the bed, washed her face in the bathroom and crawled under the warmth of the covers, a little clammy in the ocean air, and drifted off into a dream filled sleep.

#

Come morning, she gradually awoke from not just pleasant dreams, but knot-free dreams, filled to the brim with cheerfulness. And with the humidity in the air still there, confirming the reality of wonderland, she played the role of Jessica on an ordinary day when the sun always shone, when a strong thread of wonder consistently wove together the fabric of life.

She had arrived.

She peeked through the curtains for a view of the ocean, and its magical shimmer. San Francisco Bay, she just knew it. But thick foggy clouds blocked out the sun, and missing were the rolling ocean waves, the Bay instead lay totally still … covered with some kind of seaweed or floating mire. Her smile dimmed, but only slightly, her inner enthusiasm holding. This was the place; she had seen it a thousand times.

She stepped from the morning shower, wrapping a towel around her hair and pulled out her hair dryer. She lay back on the bed, to rest for a moment. She would look for her cousin Andrew, he said on the phone he would be there.

Amy smiled through mistiness on the elevator down. With her own eyes, she now saw the Bay, through each and every window, where Jessica gazed with her recovered gleam of delight. At one window, Amy gasped lightly, knowing at the moment she herself was really there, the place where she had seen it happen. She strolled slowly along under a lofty ceiling, through the open-air social space, then turned through the doors to the walkway along the Bay. She leaned lightly against a modest sea wall, breathing in the sea air, lifting her arms to invite the sky to cut her knot free. Beyond the sea wall, a tidal mud flat stretched out to meet the lapping wavelets.

Walking along the seaside path, she thought of lunch, pestered by Grandma's voice telling her to find a cheaper place – the food would be just as good. She passed a burger salad walk-in. No Grandma, not this time. She strolled back to the Marriot, determined, circling to the front door to replay the arrival, allowing the doormen to once again greet her entry. She almost melted this time.

Again, she walked gracefully, slowly, down the spiral staircase, looking out over the casual seating where Jessica sometimes met a friend. People lounged casually on couches, chatting with their companions about events in their wondrous lives. She focused for a second, glancing at the wall clock. Half way down the stairs she spotted Andrew, slouched back with his feet kicked on a stool.

Amy waved, calling his name. But the din of the chatter under the vaulted ceiling muffled her voice. Not until she walked right up on him did he push his sunglasses up to greet her.

"Hi Andrew. It's me, Amy." They had last seen each other at the family reunion in Saskatchewan.

"Amy. I was hoping I would find you." Andrew sprang to his feet, smiling through glassy eyes. He wore a classy suit, like Jessica's friends, but when he rose, the scuffs and wrinkles stood out, Amy noticed. "Where's the restaurant? I'm famished."

A sign hung over the entrance to Jessica's restaurant. The American Grill; they must have changed the name for Jessica's show. Amy was delighted when they found a table looking out the window over the Bay. The window's edge blocked out the mud flats, creating a view of life the way it should be.

As the two cousins settled in, Amy looked around, noticing families and a couple of businessmen. They all seemed to be eating the same thing, some kind of buffet. Children scurried about under one table. Amy ignored the buffet, she would have lunch from the bill of fare and she asked for two lunch menus from the Latin waitress. With the noon hour sunshine beaming, she inquired after her cousin.

"A little tired today, but hey, this should revive me." He seemed nervous. "I drove up the coastal freeway last night."

The waitress returned.

"Yes, I'll have an Allie's Shrimp Louis Salad," said Amy.

"Yes Miss. Anything to drink?"

"A Banana Daiquiri, please"

"And you sir?"

"Steak and fries. And a whiskey on the rocks. Canadian whiskey." Andrew calmed noticeably.

Amy relaxed more herself when he asked of Saskatchewan. She listened to his talk of California, but couldn't help catching a few words from the businessmen. The inner workings of the business world Amy supposed. Jessica had some friends that were in business, always high-ended business where deals were exciting and fulfilling; ones that financed their exquisite lifestyles. These ones talked quite softly, in hoarse voices, that in a lull somehow echoed over so Andrew noticed too.

" ... he was driving pissed, man. The cops busted him for that, then they found out what he was carrying. He got six years ..." She heard the words clearly now.

Andrew's eyebrows shot up, like he understood more. Must be a more casual part of their lives, Amy decided, not their real business. Then a pair of well-dressed women, classy, walked over to the men's table. They chatted about club Monaco. Yes, that's more like what happened for Jessica; she knew a lot of men. A cell phone rang, and one of the men excused himself.

Amy focused back on Andrew, still seeking to feel Jessica's secrets. As she nodded at her cousin, she saw past Andrew swirling ice around in his glass. The mud flats shrank as the tide advanced. Gentle turquoise waves lapped up on a white sand shore. Tiny ripples with a tinge of magic. Jessica's world, right there.

Andrew relaxed more when the businessmen left. But then Amy couldn't help but hear the family, and she realized what Jessica's life never included. Amy's enchanted forest threatened to topple as she wondered how Jessica could be happy without children's laughter.

When she finished her Allie's Louis salad, she felt delightfully content, even full. Could it be the feeling she sought, or just the feeling of a good healthy meal like Grandma made for Grandpa Paulo. The wailing and chatter of the children filled in as background noise with little musical songs, she listened closely –

Christmas songs. In August! Andrew chatted on. Then quite abruptly, he pushed his chair out.

"I have to get back to LA today, sorry Amy, it was really nice to see you."

"Remember the next reunion." Amy reminded him. "It would be great to see you at Sahiya Lake again."

Andy's hazy eyes struggled to clear. "Yes, that sure was one cool weekend. You guys were really great to be around." He stood up, putting his third glass to his lips to drain the last of it. "Take care, Amy."

"Goodbye, Andrew. Thanks for meeting me."

Amy turned back to the window, the jet airliners coming into San Francisco International. They flew straight up the long pier, the same pier in Jessica's picturesque background. For a moment Amy felt an inner tingling peace she couldn't describe. It all came together for that one moment. She settled back, watching people strolling along on the walkway in the now bright sun. A beautiful white jet flew in over the pier gracefully seeking its place to land. She saw a flock of seabirds skimming over the surface of the Bay. Then the sunshine faded behind a cloud's shadow. How could the wondrous feeling be so fleeting? She couldn't help thinking of her family now, her refuge. She needed a breath of fresh air.

Wandering outside again, she strolled slowly back down the seaside boardwalk, stopping to sit for a moment, breathing deep. She listened, this time to a couple of young women, well dressed, talking.

"… you want to give as much as you take …" One said straight into the eyes of the other.

The earlier tingle ran reverse, as she somehow realized those words were part of her Marriot message as well. She sat in the sun, musing, as three jet airliners lined up for take-off. The first jet had come down the runway while the other two waited. The airplane circled completely around and began its take off, headed out from the city. Back towards home.

After the jets took off, one by one, she turned, and came face to face with her reflection in the glass wall. Who was this woman? The Golden Gate Bridge loomed in the distance, the bridge that closed each half hour session with Jessica.

Amy walked slowly back to her room. Glancing out the window, she saw once more the cycle of jets taking off and landing while another jet roared high overhead. Everything was right there, why couldn't she connect? She fell back on the bed, a tear rolling down her cheek, praying for an answer, any answer.

Packing her things in her bag, she took one last look around, feeling the moist air, sniffing the aromas it brought out. She closed the door behind her, walking past the cleanup people, playing the role most familiar to her back in her house trailer. The people behind the scenes, the ones who made the front seat view of Jessi's life possible.

Waiting for the airport bus, the voices around spoke of the everyday things. She sat relishing the California view of ocean, concrete and traffic, pondering over what she had seen. Lunch in San Francisco, all the children, the young women on the boardwalk, Andrew's glassy eyes and the businessmen in Jessica's restaurant.

The bus took her through the concrete maze of on-ramps, off-ramps and freeway pieces suspended high in the ocean air. The San Francisco International sign appeared in all its sunshine glory and she stepped off the bus to catch her flight.

On the plane, she settled in. San Francisco, how bitter sweet. Excitement around her children and husband now began to build, yet confusion on leaving the Jessica world behind. What would she do with the stomach knot now?

Amy looked across the plane through the windows on the far side. Who might be at the Marriott now watching planes taking off, who might be watching her plane as she had watched them? As they taxied, she could see the hotel, red letters writing Marriot on the sandstone collared building, like a glance over the past few hours … over the past many years.

The trip back passed with a blur of clouds, clear spaces, the great salty lake, more airport gates, walking out to a smaller jet and a drowsy, dreamy time that ended with a final de-boarding. She felt the embrace of the dry prairie air.

Bryan met her at the airport late that night. They didn't talk much as they drove through familiar streets.

"How are the kids?" Amy asked quietly.

"They're sleeping."

"Thanks." She softly touched his arm. "Thanks, Bryan, for everything."

They parked in front of the trailer. Looking at each other, knowing they had done something, not exactly hand in hand, but kind of.

Amy slept well, very well, and she remembered her dream in the morning. A bird, one that flew freely through the air; a bird that became a jet; a jet that became part of a cycle of endless takeoffs and landings; a cycle that then turned into a hamster running in its wheel.

She told Bryan about the dream, when he was getting ready for work. He told her of the hamster he had when he was a kid. He said hamsters only live for two years, and he had watched that one in its wheel, for two years, running round and round. Nothing more.

Bryan was gone to work when the kids came running in, and she looked around the trailer – the dishes, the vacuum cleaner, the lunches to make, the clothes to wash she just felt different. She never forgot that *give at least as much as you take*. And that knot still came and went.

San Francisco was far away now, far from the trailer she lived in, and Amy didn't watch that show any more. She smiled broadly.

CLIMATE SCENARIOS

AlberTa's Gift

Albert felt the gravel slide under his e-bike tires as he turned into this out-in-the-country parking lot. Pulling off his helmet, he stared up at the wisp of steam rising from the power plant chimney pillaring above. He unzipped his riding jacket. A midterm waited for him back at the University that afternoon but the Minister's invitation had been enough to bring him out. He knew his story to be useful to Minister Teslo yet also that giving his social license helped the guy take sincere action. The Minister had the reputation of a man out to make a difference, and not just in his political career.

As he brushed nervously at the front of his summer office job suit, his eye caught an Energy of Tomorrow - 2025 - government logo fluttering on a banner. He could make out two mini-drones hovering at each end in the autumn breeze and a group gathered over at the power plant entrance. Popping open his cargo carrier he tossed his jacket in and pulled out his device satchel. Bag over shoulder, he crunched his way through the dry autumn leaves towards the crowd.

Good thing the ceremony was this year, he thought grinning as he walked. He would've looked kinda ratty in last summer's work clothes. That summer on the drilling rig and then the office work on surface facilities design this summer had helped him chose his engineering option. As he made his way up the steps the Minister's assistant shook his hand and guided him over to stand at one side of the podium. The news media were setting up their camera equipment in front and two older fellows he recognized stood on the other side of the podium. He lifted a hand to wave and they nodded. He knew Minister Teslo would be profiling more than just his engineering program. He slipped his jPad into a pocket down in his satchel so he could see the screen by glancing down. As the jPad searched for a wireless connection he remembered that other Minister who came to the hospital ten years ago...

#

He had been cooped up in his room again—school holidays had started a day early that Christmas. Tired of the video game he'd played a thousand times his eyes drifted to a paper book on his shelf. He'd read that one so many times that when he skimmed the pages he knew he could rattle off the story by heart. Just that he never did what the boy in the book had. He tossed the paperback on the bed and flopped sitting into his chair. Why not he wondered? He glanced again at the cover image. That Polynesian boy had set off alone in an outrigger canoe to face all his fears. The courage word in the title dug at him that day so much that he made a decision right then. He would call it his courage. That boy killed a shark with a bone knife! All boys could be brave he decided that morning. Duke would be out playing the morning street hockey game with the boys on the block. He'd just do it he thought.

The murmur of Mom's voice on the phone had hummed through the hall all morning. She'd come up the stairs once and ducked her head in to tell him of the air quality warning that day. He'd backed down on that one before. This time…whatever. He had to sneak past quiet and careful and first a distraction. He climbed down the stairs and wandered over to the Christmas tree to fool around with his gift. He knew she'd come out to check. As soon as Mom wandered out and then walked back into the kitchen deep in the middle of something with one of her friends he made his move. Quietly snatching his parka off the coat hook he slid his feet into snow boots and slipped out, easing the door closed behind.

Blowing puffs of white into the cold air he treaded through the backyard snow to grab a hockey stick from the shed. Carefully opening the side gate he walked around the front of the house. Duke sang out his way right off, "Hey Ta." His brother could be such an asshole doing his little girly dance. But what do you do when your older brother's the coolest kid around? The in-crowd at school even called him Le Duke. "You comin' out to play yay?" Another boy snickered but luckily the puck in play distracted him. Mom was always harsh with Duke on teasing especially with the Ta name. But she wasn't here right now.

That time when they were little—like he was five and Duke had been seven—they had listened around the corner when Mom and Dad were talking. They heard mom talked about back in the old house when Mom was going to have Albert. The medical lab mistook Albert for a girl in their sonic scan and Mom at the time had her heart set on a boy and girl family. She had picked out Alberta for a name after Queen Victoria's fourth princess daughter. The next scan changed everything. But Duke poked Albert hard in the ribs that time smirking and never forgot. He endlessly used that final princess syllable to taunt his little brother. Even Ta Ta at times to make it babyish.

He wouldn't let Le Duke phase on him that day. No eleven-year-old, especially a boy who wheezed in the cold air too much to learn to skate wanted any girly name floating around. Not even if Duke had always been taller and heavier and better at any sport. Albert stiffened up and building a haughty scoff onto his face he ignored his brother. He strode into the game between the nets and took a stance pounding his stick on the street right opposite Duke. He would show the whole world his courage.

"Hey, hey to me." He felt so carefree.

Focusing on play patterns, Albert used his wits to strategize moves. So that asthmatic wheeze built up somewhere behind his concentration. As his lungs tightened in the cold air—he had fought for hours so many times before for the next breath—he decided this time no matter what he'd face it and slug his way through. He didn't know how extra bad the air was that day, much worst due to upwind coal burning.

His team began setting up a play. Strategizing, he picked his moment and raced in a loop around behind the net to the other side.

A high warning day. He hadn't heard Mom say the AHQI was out of whack. He learned the four words of that acronym later— Air Health Quality Index. He even came later to appreciate indices as the coolest of measurement tools. He knew now that PM or particulate matter and ground level ozone significantly influenced the AHQI. He learned about weather related temperature inversions that kept coal burning pollutants closer to the ground on cold winter days. He found out about atmospheric related coal burning emissions that contributed to climate change. That winter day face down on the cold street ice he could not think let alone learn.

He darted in to centre to check another boy and then back to the side to pick up the pass. Puck on his stick, he pushed in backwards and spun around to shoot. But just when he raised his stick for the thrill of a slap shot goal, he crashed face forward down onto the icy street in that face plant.

He recalls his first try at getting back up to keep playing. He had to make that shot on net. That never happened—he had flopped out and couldn't move. Terror swelled up from deep inside. He could not breathe! And when he tried to yell he couldn't even talk. Not able to so much as lift a hand to brush the snow powder off his face he could only stare shivering at that ridge of dirty ice in front of one eye.

The ambulance ride was a blur. Nothing but a struggle gasping into that oxygen mask the medics put on his face. One medic made the call to rush him to ER at the city hospital. That wasn't the first time he'd been taken gasping into an Emergency Room but always at their town hospital before, never to the city. And never before was he admitted. He knows most of the story by what Mom told him later. That's when she told him about that woman Minister's visit. Mom had a long serious chat with that other Minister back then.

His memories were all mingled in with Dad talking about Paris that winter, that Christmas of 2015. The talks over in Europe Dad kept saying were super important, to their planet and their atmosphere and everyone's changing climate. By everyone he meant everyone on the planet. Albert had listened close then. He understood all that so much better now, that COP21 international conference on a carbon emissions agreement. His second year class at the university had been specific to the binding international contract hammered out in Paris. The Paris +10 review would be out in a few months. Some even said the trickle down from Paris motivated that other Minister's new strategy. Her office communications had gone out searching for a human interest story to promote the Minister's conceived Energy of Tomorrow program. They came upon Albert and his emergency story at the city hospital. That's when the ten year phase out coal program started coming out in the news. Most city citizens supported the phase out when they knew the whole story. Like a hundred people dying every year and millions of dollars spent on medical bills. Mom talked to other mothers in his town. When they found out prevailing winds blew that power plant asthma air right into their neighbourhoods the spoke out loud and clear.

Had the cleaner air been Albert's gift? Or that he even walked back out of that hospital?

#

Minister Nick Teslo arrived in his e-limo and stepped out. Walking briskly up the steps beside another assistant he moved smiling along the line shaking hands with the other fellows first. When Albert looked he recognized now those two older guys. They both went through that steam operator retraining program the Minister wanted to profile. One's name was Hank. The Minister gave Albert a big nod and a wink as he grasped his hand firmly before stepping up to the podium and clearing his throat.

He began his speech on the carbon bubble. He went over the touchy idea that local oil and gas reserves though maybe proven were actually stranded assets never to be burned. That had been such a hard sell around here Albert knew. Yet, Minister Teslo emphasized, the booming geothermal potential had been proven local too and could replace coal as a primary energy source. Geothermal wells drilled with local rigs would supply the energy of tomorrow. Clean energy—better in many ways. Right here, right now he waved back at the power plant for the media to notice. Evident before their eyes today his department had successfully replaced coal burning for citizens' electricity needs.

Albert gazed out at the brown leaves blowing across the parking lot. Dad had always said politicians wanted their photo ops on beautiful weather days. This sure was one nice day for a bike ride.

The Minister went on about how his department was actively promoting a program of transition to geothermal energy based on oil and gas drilling technology. He rattled off the annual rig stats, those active and those scheduled to spud in for proposed geothermal wells. His office would maintain a controversial price on carbon as an economic incentive to this newer technology. Twenty-first century energy technology phasing out coal by strategically replacing the steam source for generating electricity was good policy. He put in some good words on wind and solar too.

Albert glanced down at his jPad as he stood half listening. Kali had a tweet burst going.

That rig Albert worked on last summer had come off a seven month foothills gas well. With little more modification than switching drill bits, the deep-hole rig had spudded in on a geothermal lease. The drilling engineer said the geothermal hole was a special twinning lease right next to a producing gas well. The drilling location was selected based on the existing well's temperature log and distance from the coal burning plant's steam turbine. The design trade off was piping distance versus subsurface temperature. You twinned a well based on bottom hole heat and the cool thing was you got a heat measure from your well's twin. That drilling engineer projected hitting the target heat zone at 6500 meters. Although that well wasn't completed until Albert was back in class, the next summer he helped design the piping to tie the well into surface facilities.

The basics of geothermal shown in diagrams hung on that office wall poster. He passed the thing every day. Geothermal energy was scalable, for a village or a large city or a jurisdictional power grid. The Minister could say that in his speech. You ideally produced water at 120 degrees or higher, the hotter and the more water the better. But there were plants running on lower temperature water. Maybe too technical for a politician. As long as they listen to their advisors Dad said and he knew it too. That Minister who came to the hospital had taken on the permitting process, outdated and convoluted. You couldn't even get a geothermal lease back then let alone a special twinning permit.

#

By the time they arrived at the hospital the ambulance medics were barking out silent chest to the ER nurses. Face down on the street ice he had waited for his wheezing to quieten down and then planned to at least stand up. But he learned later the silent chest of an asthma attack was a deadly sign of danger. When he couldn't keep even that familiar wheeze going things were not getting better. So little air was coming into his lungs they were going silent. They were giving up. They admitted him at ER passing in an out of consciousness. He'll never forget that back and forth, from the terror of impending doom when awake—no air, can't breathe—to the relaxing bliss of zonking out.

After that failed slap shot and his face hitting the ice, he vaguely remembers Duke's taunts turning into a hoarse yell as he ran to tell Mom. Mom told him later Duke came running in with tears streaming but he never mentioned that to Duke. In an unnaturally serious tone for Le Duke his brother told him later at home how Albert's lips had turned pure blue. Duke never treated him the same after the hospital. His brother stuck with sports through high school, but showed a lot more respect for how well Albert did in the classroom. And he never did call him by the T name again. So maybe that was Albert's gift.

#

The Minister talked on how he had worked hard to bring about government implemented clear regulations on geothermal energy and set up research grants that helped form into the fourth year option at Albert's university. He waved Albert's way when he mentioned that engineering program. Minister Teslo had been to the Paris +5 and Paris +8 conferences to keep well informed Albert knew. He and his friends felt a little excited about those updates on Paris. But scared too.

Other new training programs had come out. Duke would be challenging his third class steam ticket that fall. A practical field engineer—the brothers joked neither would be driving a train. Duke told Albert of guys who worked in the coal burning plant getting touch up training tickets as coal plants modified to geothermal. A lot of the same equipment had been upgraded but those guys knew the valves and gauges. Hank had been the First Class steam engineer who helped Minister Teslo's office talk to the plant employees about their new source of steam. The Minister waved over towards Hank. Minister Teslo had other programs for the coal miners. The initial feasibility study Albert knew showed conversion from coal to geothermal as a cost savings. That was a bonus! When you wanted people to act, money talked loud. The concept plan before had sifted through existing well logs around the coal plants searching for the optimal geothermal reservoir. Geothermal was so cheap when holes already drilled were reclassified as dual purpose exploration wells with a heat play as the target.

Resistance always arose to any change Dad would say. The Ministers said about the same but in different words. Albert's one friend had a great grandfather who homesteaded close to the coal excavations. His uncle kept the farm for years, always talking how the surface coal mining operation would expand and he'd be moving to Florida. That uncle would never be seen standing under any Energy of Tomorrow banner. He still had his case going in court over appraised land values. Traditional outlooks were one of the reasons people change slowly according to Dad. And politics move in slow unfair jolts. The renewable energy targets had come two Ministers ago, Albert knew and now Minister Teslo was celebrating the credit. He was honorably cool enough to mention that though. Albert had a Prof from Iceland who knew geothermal inside out. Yet he lectured on people and how the laws of physics didn't care much about people's diddling around or their reasons for doing anything or not. Albert told Minister Teslo about that law but the Minister's smile looked kinda vague. Politicians need good advisors. Natural laws don't negotiate, plain and simple. The Minister did mention that his energy experts projected continuing expansion of geothermal. If politicians listened to their scientists, good enough.

Albert felt the warm breeze on his face. The Minister was lucky on the weather for this podium speech. Dad said they strategically scheduled this ceremony for the calmer fall weather. That early snow dump last year again broke still green tree branches all over town. Albert and his classmates connected that one to the planet's weakened polar vortex and how that kind of weather was now kinda typical. The new normal was their normal. The Minister's office might have run numbers on the probability of a baseball hail storm in the summer and the unpredictable floods in the spring. Local extreme weather events here, Albert knew from Rawiri and Kali his social media friends, were happening globally.

Minister Teslo finished his speech and descended beaming at the media people ready to field questions. He kept that power plant in the camera background and Albert glanced back at the plant one more time. He read the sign—this last plant designed around coal had opened four years before his hospital trip. Yeah, he sighed. His life changed then, totally. He was glad to no longer be a boy withdrawn into reading books. He felt like he had grown up and he sometimes wondered about that in some adults. He checked his jPad as he shuffled down the steps towards his bike.

Kicking his way through the leaves Albert thought of the international school children networking that came out of the Paris talks. The Intergovernmental Panel on Climate Change in their fifth Assessment Report—their IPCC AR5 conclusion that global cooperation would be absolutely necessary had been reconfirmed at each Paris+. That was true no matter what older generations wanted, believed or remembered. Even back in junior high teachers started that connection with a web of global schools. Albert had researched the basics of the greenhouse gas effect of dirty coal in high school online with his friend in Warsaw. He aced that class. He made good friends with Rawiri in the South Pacific island country of Tonga. The guy had courageous Polynesian ancestors but he worried about rising sea levels. He had met a girl really good at high school math, Kalila who lived in the city of Chittagong in Bangladesh. She tweeted endlessly on their freaky situation. They all agreed true courage meant standing up to old beliefs. Fearlessness became tantamount to finding a global cooperative way forward. That came straight from Paris reminding Albert the Prof just might throw in a paragraph question like that on the midterm. He followed the canary hashtag in Chittagong and he talked face to face with Kali on 4D, what used to be Skype. He told her of their downpours and river floods, but knew they never matched her rising sea level threat. Rawiri lived a little higher above sea level but not much. Kali's river delta country for sure held the questionably desirable status of the climate change canary. Her tweet bursts to #Canary had helped Albert understand that bird from the archaic days of underground coal mines. A warning signal of bad air, something he certainly needed. They all did actually.

As young adults Albert and all his friends talked at length about the slow human response to climate action. They had all heard his hockey game nearly killed by coal story. Albert was glad his Dad had such a progressive outlook. His engineering student friends knew the risks of technology like carbon capture and storage, how that only kept coal or oil use going. Why not think out of the box? Like geothermal! Dad talked about that long ago politician who called some project back then a no brainer. The geothermal shift fit that easily. No matter what anyone thought, he and his friends knew they would be living through all the scary times of a late start energy transition.

He popped his carrier to retrieve his riding jacket. At the hospital he never had seen his body from above, or flown supersonic down any tunnel to meet an angel or the light. He had come so close to a permanent stay on the blissful side with a silent chest. He found that out when he was more grown. He only recalls coming to looking up at his mom's tear stained face. Life was a real gift she kept saying then. All life he thought and their planetary life support system.

He swung his leg over this e-bike seat and sat strapping his helmet under his chin.

Albert's engineering classmates and global social media friends were fully aware of climate change efforts people had yet to make happen. He had learned a lot about the pollution that had exacerbated his asthma attacks and came so close to knocking him off that street hockey day. The farmer kids back in school said their parents talked about the longer growing seasons and bumper crops. Drought hit too or they were hailed out other years. Two kids from that little neighbouring town were canoeing around their house last year of high school—they could almost paddle in the front door that spring. The big house people living on the golf course were totally swamped by that river flood. Others east of town watched from their hallway hideout as huge hail stones smashed through their front windows.

As he pulled out to head back to the city, he felt his highway bike ride elation coming on. People were finally talking openly about climate change...just kind of late. Maybe getting a chance to slowly repair the planet was Albert's best gift. He was excited about it...and scared. Making friends all over the world was so cool but they were scared too. They should be. That Polynesian boy maybe killed a shark, but Albert had other issues to challenge. It took real courage to speak out. The politicians needed to hear loud voices. And lots of voices. Doing something was better than doing nothing. The new transitional outlook towards clean energy sources would allow clean air and water for his future. A cooperating planet would give people young and old a happier healthier place to live. Yet still, there was so much more to do.

Next Door Data

Calvin noticed a new trailer in the campsite next door as he eased the family vehicle in beside their tent. After a great day at the beach they were sticky-hot and not a little worn. Leila looked over knowingly—that young couple tent camping out of their truck last night were gone. This trailer stretched out all along the gravel drive surrounded by a spillover of unloaded trappings and flashing a factory-fresh Spirit of the Wild logo. A 4-wheel-drive guarded the front, and squinting through the branches Calvin could glimpse mud-grabber tires below a full four-door cab.

They opened the doors of their Tes-2.

The noise reverberated hard and they froze. He sagged, glancing at his wife's deepening frown. They couldn't take off again—their daughters both needed a shower. The hot breeze wafted through, draining the last of the solar-cooled air from their e-car. At least the walk to the shower house would be through tree shade, and away from the noise. Yet, why should they be scheduling their time away from campsite? Leila told the girls what to take as they tumbled slowly out.

The hammering of more than one small engine resounded across the campground. Two others distinctly echoed in the distance, but this noise-maker was right next door. No birds, no children's laughter, all drowned out by the irritating drone of a power generator. Calvin stared hard—the trailer was sealed shut. The campers enclosed no doubt enjoyed a full range of electric devices, insulated from the outdoor racket they kept around back.

At first he tried ignoring the clamour, as he flung the towels over the line to dry. He could wait on that moment when peace would return. Wasn't that what people came camping for? Peace and quiet out in the soundscape of nature. He felt his jaw clench. Yet that family—he could see their juvenile bicycles—would be sitting about in conditioned air and any other home amenity they might have plugged in. Could be running a clothes dryer for Christ's sakes. A true wilderness experience. Why not bring your lawnmower out camping, and cut grass all day—the chatter in his head was incessant. He gritted his teeth.

As he lit the propane stove and threw burgers on to sizzle, ideas began lining up as they were wont to in his mind. He could be cutting firewood with his chainsaw, that howl might penetrate their camper wall. Wire cutters. Spray paint—a message on the trailer's side—Thanks for the racket, asshole! But, he had no spray bomb, or wire cutters, or chainsaw, they were all at home in the garage. Recall of the think tank cut in, reminding him to process the emotional first, to allow positive ideas to emerge. He forced a smile as he waved at his wife and daughters walking off down the trail. They would have a little respite over at the shower building— that was good. He watched other children riding by on bicycles, oblivious it seemed to the noise. Encultured, they would term that in social science. Was that good? Generators were for emergencies. Was this an emergency? It could certainly be associated. The emergency developing around his recent research. The impending climate change crisis.

He flipped the burgers.

These people were inefficiently generating power to support their back home lifestyle. As if unaware, as if uncaring at all of their own children. And at a campground where you and your children came out to experience nature. That kind of nonresponsive attitude combined with the lifestyle it denoted was what disproportionately caused climate change. Simply put, a lifestyle of higher consumption translated into a more changed climate. So he was stuck in awareness of a problem that no one wanted to talk about, even campers out here. He could not escape his research data now, and likely wouldn't for the rest of his life.

He fumed as they sat to eat, forcing jokes out for his daughters. He could laugh, but with effort. They chomped at their burgers like true burger-monsters, with monster ketchup and just a little mix of fairy pickles. The neighbour, thank god, hit the switch part way through their meal and their local soundscape found relief. The more distant generators kept running, but thankfully not as close.

After a marshmallow roast, he helped Leila tickle the two girls into their sleeping bags, and strap on their LED headlamps for undercover reading. His laugh relaxed, almost becoming genuine.

As the sun sank, the final generator fell silent and the last reverberation drained from his head. He looked at Leila across the picnic table, sighing. At long last! Official quiet hours she pointed at her watch. Ten PM, the sign said. So there were rules of sorts and at least people paid attention to those. Like laws, like regulations, like social agreements. The evening birds sang out clear, and a squirrel chattered from high in a tree as the air cooled ever so slightly with the sunset.

He sat musing, poking at the fire with a stick. Recent lifestyle research would not leave him alone now, how this way of living just could not continue—he was never free of these thoughts any more. He had come to realize he could no longer keep his analytical mind from seeing the data. Wherever he looked, all data. Never mind the changing weather events and his guesses at how extreme they rated. Right here he could estimate the planet consumed by each trailer, and each monster truck needed to pull that trailer. Those huge baby boomer motor homes were another noticeable artifact. His sustainability research had also filled him in on his daughters' future, and that future was looking bleaker as each year passed. Society continued to nonchalantly treat their world with a business as usual outlook. The belief in a limitless planet had been proven repeatedly to be so false. Which left him now so aware, so fully aware. An awareness he often wished he never had, one that brought along with anger alternating depression and fear. Hope filtered through, the odd time.

#

He awoke in a sweat. The sounds were pounding all around, a louder one closer and right overhead. The booming noise jackhammered right through his being. Almost like helicopters! He caught his breath, careful not to arouse the others. A distant loon call resonated across the lake, helping bring him back. He checked the time—2AM.

Calvin sat up. Goddamit.

The sounds that had taken over until midnight had been teenagers' voices playing hide and seek. The full moon evening had enhanced their game. That party had come to an end, but this bigger party had to end too. People could no longer be dumping carbon like empty candy wrappers and drink cans into the atmosphere. They had to make a change to keep a clean house planet as a viable life support. The global teenager had to grow up. The party had to end.

Generator thoughts returned. A shotgun blast through each machine flashed. He shuttered, struggling to slow his mixed up heartbeat. Think rationally. There was no shotgun, no shells, and no, no explosives. Yet pots and pans banging at their doorstep jumped out of the lineup next, early in the morning when he first arose. That should be as disquieting as their generator noise. God, now he was thinking like a teenager. A sign plastered on their window. A noticeable written warning. Pay attention to your children's future he would write.

He rested his chin on his knees.

He had tried writing warnings through his research, the science was clear and he had published what he knew. Just that nobody took notice, except other interested research scientists. Social science told him the average person did not act on rational information anyway or even good information. They decided in a large part based on the guy next door. And modern consumers were so filled with an almost drugged dependence and disjointed belief system. Someone else would take care of the big problems, the politicians or God. A hope built on by the billboards, showing them the monster trucks along with happy faces, their faces. That Spirit of the Wild trailer beside a splashy water scene, a summer dreamtime come true. Like living the pioneering life yet in aristocratic comfort. Pioneering truly was now only for the final frontier. Those astronauts preparing for the Mars mission grabbed the attention of the all the reality shows. There was little pioneering left to be accomplished on a fully occupied planet. Anyway people only paid attention to certain items. Space heroes, plane crashes ... or crime.

He raised his head, listening.

Now would be the time to act, under cover of darkness. A huge spray bomb screaming shotgun blast. Shit—he had to get out. He crawled from his bag, fumbling with the tent door zipper and walked stiffly off towards the washroom. The moon hung bright above, bringing an awesome middle of the night tranquility. The loons called again. As he scuffled along the trail to the washroom, he stared at those trailers half hidden by moon shadows. He could write a letter to the Minister of Parks, that would be a rational action. But, he realized, that Minister would be with the established government that was doing so close to nothing. And the generator noise wasn't the real problem anyway; the true issue was the lifestyle it symbolized.

What to do. What to do? He entered the tent again, crawling back into his sleeping bag and nodding off.

#

With morning came his sometimes deep emptiness. What was the point? People, him included, were an endless juvenile project. But his rage tagged along too, always there, smouldering. Combined, these feelings brought on other ideas—he could break rules, any rule. They sold firewood here, right? Leave the forest wood alone they said. Screw that. He walked out behind their campsite and picked up deadfall from the trees, smashing it to pieces with his ax. That felt good. He grabbed up a small dry log, feeling his two hands grasping it and then couldn't keep from walking defiantly towards that next door generator. But before he got too close, he smashed the log across a live spruce, breaking it into fire pit sizes pieces. That felt real good, to smash, to crash, to release the rage. These goddamn people, everywhere around him. Politicians were doing nothing and citizens kept voting them in. As more of the same lurked on the horizon.

He stomped off down the road away from their campsite, he had to. Leila would get breakfast for the girls. She had grown tolerant over the last years. He passed the campground edge and headed off to the lake. The helicopters in that dream ... choppers now flew over his favorite mountain hike, back close to the city. Ruining his peaceful hikes, and for no other reason than tourists wanting to go for a thrill seeking ride. This immature insanity was ubiquitous. He walked fast.

He had to take care of his own, his family he thought at times. Basic instinct came down to survival. His tribe. With all people thinking that way, what would come about? That's a sure sign of chaos setting in, when authority reverts to the more local. The historical downfall of previous civilizations revealed much. There was Easter Island and there had been the Anasazi at Mesa Verde. The collapse of the Roman Empire brought the feudal fiefdoms of European medieval times. No straight road was built for centuries. How to hide from the impending chaos, how to build a refuge to keep his daughters safe. A retreat from that backwards step. There had to be some way.

His thing had always been data. Data! He could collect evidential data, he knew how on that one. He would tour the campground, marking each generator on the campground map. Yes, that he could do. And take a shot at turning his thinking in some unknown direction. His wife had mentioned the campground was almost all trailers and motor homes, almost no tents. He could carry out a simple survey, by counting up this campground data. Everything needed for a situational infographic.

He wandered back to the campsite, driven to act.

He grabbed his jPad with its digital grounds map and walked, snapping an image of each license plate number at each site with an active generator. They were easy to find—the morning sound a give-away homing signal. And excellent on-the-ground survey data, the type of people science that had always fascinated him. As he followed his route, he noticed the data highly confirming his wife's observation. Trailers everywhere. He picked up on another interesting aside, tent campers tended to be younger but also more ethnically diverse—recent immigrants still climbing the consumer lifestyle ladder. The focus on data gathering at least brought on a level of calm.

They made their way to the beach later, grabbing a picnic table and setting out towels in the sand. Others arrived, and he stared when he saw that next door neighbour family in the crowd. Why not bring along a hedge-trimmer and wack the grass along the edges of their beach blanket? Four children he counted, Christ! Don't they know of the population pressure on the planet?

He stood, and started walking towards the guy. He would punch him square in the head ... that would get attention. But in front of his family? And attention to what? OK, he could instead shake hands and start a bullshit conversation. He stopped, glancing at his feet, then up again. OK, really, they probably didn't know. And they were following existing rules. He took a breath, relieved he hadn't had a spray bomb. He knew from other survey data, that family size was typically associated with one or another religious belief, and outdated teachings on procreation. That would be a hint of their mindset. Women mostly made decisions on childbearing. And housing, come to think of it, like the tent or trailer decision. What do you do with something like this? The trailer did bring the family more comfort in a better shelter. These parents were looking out for their children with good family values. These people. The voting masses of a democracy. They were ... yes, like milling constituents. Yet needing a new political speech.

All research told him the biggest barrier to action on climate change was political will. The coming election jumped into the ideas lineup. If he ran for office and got elected, then he would have a voice. Even a possible media voice if that voice was controversial. His anger certainly seemed to have a will of its own—he would campaign on a platform of outrage. A warning signal might catch attention—people paid attention to stories of danger. Bring science into politics. Speak the truth. The truth about generators, big trailers and how much life support was left in the planet. Raging around the campground snipping wires on generators would have little effect. And why should he voluntarily finance a Nikola aluminum oxide battery to share the unbelievably quiet auto experience only with his family? Any carbon he kept out of the atmosphere got dumped there by the average guy driving a monster truck to drag his mega-trailer around. His e-car lifestyle needed to be a media highlight. Regulation came from law makers, from political legislation. Bringing about policy change would have better, much bigger impact than a spray bomb. On his daughter's future.

He could talk to that professor on recent research he had seen. Theories on intentional cultural modification. Culture needs to be redesigned. Women having children, selecting housing and consumption, all that business of life. Biological evolution took way too long, that prof had stated, even if they had genetic engineering functional. A cultural shift could theoretically happen over a single generation. And that was barely available on the climate change schedule.

Yes, politics would be a good start. He would call that party office Monday. His fall campaign for office would translate into the story people needed to hear. And why not watch the campgrounds as a proxy for change? The first thing to go would be generator noise, highly restricted by new rules and replaced by birds and children's laughter. People needed to hear their children playing to the background of forest birds, not internal combustion engines dumping more climate altering damage into those children's lives. This next door noise needed to rapidly become a part of the unwanted past.

That evening they drove over to the e-car charge station along the highway for ice-cream. They had planned a little better that day, him scampering back to bring their propane stove and cooler to the beach side picnic table. Eating away from the campground had been a smart move. The Nikola charge gave a thousand kilometer range, but he knew charging when you could extended the battery life significantly. Care for your e-car and care for your planet while you enjoy an ice cream. Why not?

The campaign brochure and posters lined up in pictures in his mind. Beside the campground infographic, the image of a happy family enjoying time at the recharge station. As the baby boomers had once glamorized the drive through food bar back in their times, now people would cheer on a lifestyle image of a conserved planetary future. One he knew, and many constituents would soon know they so needed. To live a lifestyle not worst, just different.

Planetary Infraction

Wenzel glided his e-bike up the sunset lit back road, glancing at the screens bottom of his face shield. His drive-by satellite markup map showed the dead end ahead could double as their backdoor entrance, and their best exit point. Having scrutinized the country estate houses from the front, he needed go over this messaging job with Detroit.

"Site's got a class one layout, Dee." He spoke into his helmet mike. "How's our personnel list?"

"Narrowing that down. One confirmed." Detroit's voice came clear through Wenzel's helmet telecom. The guy lived off campus by choice and by strategy, somewhere around the city—best not to know exactly. "We got a self-proclaimed colors expert volunteering on composition—the guy rides too."

"We'd need a team of four for the late-night," Wenzel said. "Hazel might be good to ride." He could picture his woman's eyes, color like her hair matching her name. She did the insider psych track of people, and rode better than any.

"Yokay," Detroit said. "And Wenz...looks like we got us an empty house tomorrow."

"Excellent. Which one?"

Detroit moved a cursor to circle the house on Wenzel's face shield map. Back of the estates—he should see the place from the dead end. Site access looked even better.

"Whole weekend actually," Detroit said. "The family's off on a mountain vacation. To their kind of resort."

"Wilderness retreat," Wenzel said dryly. "Swimming pools and waterslides."

"Waterslides and chopper rides, site says," Detroit read. "Take a stroll in a mountaintop meadow."

Wenzel had trail ridden hover bike to a peak or two, and seen the high flying picnic sites. A helicopter ride for those with the finance wanting the last of the spectacular scenery not chewed by pine beetles and forest fires. Scenery they needed to learn to take in on a home screen, or back off on trashing at least.

"Who's the confirmed dude?"

"You met him once," Detroit said. "On that last paint ball run."

Wenzel glanced at the face image Detroit pulled out on his chin guard screen.

"Oh yeah...Marv."

"Guy's half out of it," Detroit said.

"We manage that, Dee. Another kind of rebel force."

Wenzel glimpsed alternating lights between the trees trunks flashing by as the estate house lighting winked on.

"Sure," Detroit said. "He gets us a heavy transport option— lined up this Picky Part buy a couple weeks back. No serial numbers, just a bucket of parts assembled into a van."

"Okay... so we go in the front as an upgrade crew," Wenzel said. "Window contract or something."

"Sure."

Wenzel back-braked to a stop at the dead end in the waning light. Entrance roads with estate numbers wound off in two directions through the trees to the left, gates open. Potential exit routes. To the right open field stretched across to the treeless country estates. Swinging his lanky leg over the seat, he sat sideways and slid his face shield up. Mini field glasses to eyes, he picked out the target house among the darkening building forms.

"How many jobs we done this season, Dee?"

"Two paint ball runs, Wenz, and two country estate jobs."

"Never urban."

"What for? Rural houses make for bigger targets. And you like the extra maneuver space."

"Yo."

"Still risky. Think Hummer job, dude."

Detroit and Wenzel first met junior year at EM High. When Detroit asked the science teacher a pointed carbon emissions question, and got no real answer, Wenzel repeated the inquiry. They talked later, and chatter turned to a bemusing carbon police idea, and their vigilante heroes. Do you speed up when you see flashing lights or slow down? Detroit knew a Hummer in his neighborhood, and Dee even rode bike that late night plaster-the-windshield carbon ticket. They learned caution on vehicle alarms then, how to structure their team and the thrill of watching real impact. Detroit best fit on the inside—he caught that Hummer owner reaction on video, texting Wenzel play by play next morning. Wenzel best worked the outside.

"We aborted that one estate job." Detroit's last minute info on who was coming home that time saved the day.

"Yo, so we did," Wenzel said. "We being tracked this time?"

"Looking clean so far," Detroit said. "You and me only to start, wiped the contact slate clean at level one."

"We gettin' paranoid Dee?"

"Strat game tactics, dude," Detroit said. Later high school gaming days they spent endless hours engaged in STRATegies. Weave together your world with care, maximize options gettin' outta there. Detroit figured out dirt boxes back then too; Quasimodo became his fave. Snooping others' business might be borderline wrong, but what difference from any overheard conversation? And what was crime anyway? They churned that conversation in the EM cafeteria.

"Misdemeanor, no more," Detroit said.

Vigilante police meant civil disobedience or a civil step or two past. Required, to get noticed. "Couple cases we know. Vandalism, or maybe trespassing. We're not in Texas, so we won't get shot. Worst case scenario a fine or a couple months." They'd talked this one to death since high school too. "Who best takes the fall?" Detroit asked.

"Guy like Marv fits," Wenzel said, lowering the glasses. "Depends. Couple months to plan—could be good for one of us."

"No thanks."

"Me then. How sure are we on the empty house?"

"We intercepted a business email string between target house and people next door," Detroit said. "They leave the neighbors an entrance pass code for emergencies while they're gone."

Local business around this western city led to typical planetary consumption behavior, Wenzel knew. The satt map showed a massive RV parked in the back. And a tennis court. And on top of the excess here at home, this family was splurging on a resort weekend, in their version of nature. Consuming what they had and could translated in a large part into emissions—consumption the politicians had finally put out in a public appeal. Well, this weekend will be one for this household to reconsider—their neighborhood lifestyle played well into a carefully calculated messaging plan.

"Alright," Wenzel said. "We need a day-job team by morning."

"Last risk analysis running on that colors dude's profile," Detroit said. "I'll get you that."

Wenzel stashed the field glasses in a side pouch. Pulling his face shield down, he headed back toward the city, thinking Hazel's dorm. College res was a good place to spend a night or two or bounce a living place quick. She whipped up great meals in the tiny kitchen, and told him flat out when his turn came up to cook. The girl's plain flower prints reminded him of home. He'd stay over if she invited him.

#

Next morning Wenzel mounted his bike in Hazel's campus back parking lot. Brushing his hair back between his fingers, he slid his helmet on, flipping the shield down. Hazel had left ahead of him; they'd meet at a coffee shop. He voiced Detroit's code.

"Okay," Detroit said. "We got this guy named Joge."

"Clean background?"

"Unless he's real clever." Detroit liked to talk of people as Homo callidus in place of Homo sapiens. Clever, not wise, in reference to much. "First contact came into our ideas bin. He gave colors feedback on the paint balls—how to splash a planet image at highway speed."

"Okay...Hazel's good to go for late-night," Wenzel said. "How's the house?"

"Listen Wenz, I followed up that city business chatter with the pass code neighbor," Detroit said. "Even slipped in a text edit, GeoChem house owner to the neighbors, adding in an extra line don't mind the windows guys. They'll never notice."

"Genius dude," Wenz said. "What's GeoChem?"

"Owner of the empty house shows a company logo named GeoChem. Site for GeoChem says business doing chemical contracts for big oil. Another source says family business. Bonus there, Wenz."

"GeoChem...right," Wenzel said. "Not the geoengineering in Africa guys?"

"I'll check. Maybe they got an overseas project, but the company owner's here, heading out on weekend vacation. Chatter with next door neighbor confirms whole household's going."

"Need a total green light," Wenzel said. "Go or no."

"Call you back."

Wenzel pulled out into morning traffic. Ever disgusted by the vehicles sharing the road, he cut between young men like him maybe not in university, but taught by advertising to glamorize the tough-boy four-wheel-drive trucks. Even more disgusting, the carbon spewing four door one tons. Biffy boys, he said, or schlocks Detroit called them. The carbon infraction tickets would be for the older ones, the old folks teachers, with their three ton RVs, and exotic vacations.

"Alright," Detroit said. "Quazi geolocates a cell phone registered to said business owner two hours out of city, moving at highway speed away from home."

"Excellent," Wenzel said. "Let's get a crew together," He pulled into the Javashop to meet Hazel. They could coordinate timing from there.

"Hey babe," Wenzel greeted Hazel. He pushed his helmet onto the table, brushing his dark mane back behind glaring blue eyes.

"Wenzie, I got you a large black," she smiled, pushing a coffee cup his way.

He leaned over to kiss her on the lips. "Thanks babe."

"So we enter the hive," Hazel looked over her coffee cup. "To sting the queen."

"Queen's taking time off, babe, so we leave her a simple clear message. She and her hive gotta learn how to count planets. Or biospheres."

"Anyone can count to one," she said. "Past one, there's no room for children's future."

"Absolutely," Wenzel said, grinning. "Kids would need space."

Her freckled high cheeks blushed a little, but her smile burst into a beam. They talked about children a lot, and their times ahead on a degraded planet. She liked to talk about family, like his mom had, but her generation held an alternate vision, and acceptance of past reality.

"What's our queen got for a count?" Hazel asked.

"Planet app says," Wenzel touched his jPad. "Eleven."

"So how many planets out of eleven would be carbon?"

"Take a head estimate, say...seven." Wenzel sipped his coffee. Seven planets worth of biocapacity to absorb their emissions. If everyone lived their lifestyle.

"God, I can imagine what goes through her head," Hazel said. "Like not much. Any kid in the sandbox could tell you we got no spare biosphere. Eleven!"

"So what drives them?" Wenzel said. "Or her?"

"Cognitive psych says people get stuck in a multigenerational rut." He gazed into those hazel eyes as she explained. "Belief systems evolve ever slowly, unless bumped along by a traumatic event. Punctuated psychological transition points."

"So, bigger's better. What's that from?"

Family business people attempt to replicate medieval aristocracy," Hazel said. "They gain and then believe in an aura of entitlement, and pass that down the generational tree."

"Talk about backwards."

"Prosperity can take many forms," she gave him a sly wink.

"No exceptions?" He caught her look. "The business families, I mean."

"Any deviation from the traditional business model could be a sign," she said. "Likely at a generational gap—the kid rebels with a new value system, and a new business plan."

"The business of life," Wenzel said. "We need kids talking about the climate like old folks talk about the weather."

Detroit buzzed his helmet, and he switched links to jPad on the table.

"Independent source confirms said person booked in at the Ridge Haven Inn, a five hour drive," Detroit said. "And

Wenz...yeah, some GeoChem department got that African cool the planet going. Outside their regular business of heavy oil pipeline chemicals."

"Deviating?" Wenzel looked to Hazel.

"What?" Detroit said.

"Tell you later, dude."

"Van and crew are assembled and mobile."

"Take them in through the front entrance," Wenzel said. "I'll be there in an hour." He touched Hazel's hand as he left the coffee shop.

#

Wenzel pulled up beside the parked van glancing over at the target estate on Wolverine Drive. Marv and the other guy had the total legit look, dressed in workman's clothes setting up scaffolding in the front like a dedicated on-the-job crew. Worst case scenario, they drive away arguing the office messed up on the address. That cathedral window stood out as the front page image space they'd need, a glass panel radiating their message.

The two in the crew walked up on his bike.

"Hey Marv," Wenzel said.

"Yo, boss," the guy half-giggled.

"Not your boss, Marv."

"Sting coordinator man."

No room for any superior position, but tight lips were important to secure an organization. Wenzel swung his leg over his seat to stand.

"You got our paint ball colors right," Wenzel said, looking at the other guy. "Joge right? How do you mix that seventy percent ocean blue with thirty percent forest green?"

"Inject a higher mass sticky green blob into a super size blue ball." The Joge guy looked at him bright eyed. "The blob weight gives a projectile spin to keep the colors separate."

"Worked on the last highway run," Wenzel said, slipping his helmet off to hang on the handlebar.

"Marv's been telling me," Joge said.

Wenzel looked at the Paint by Numbers image on the contractor van's side. Marv would never have pulled that off. He was talking to an artist—excellent for visual messaging. Just that, he felt a tingle of concern, big oil saw value in patronizing artists.

"We need explain a planet measure to these country estate people." Wenzel looked at Joge. "Our message needs to connect those paint ball dots." The paint ball count had to also be understood as number of biospheres consumed. "We want that cathedral window showing an eleven planet lifestyle."

"Zion paint," Joge said. "Adheres like your Sticky Backs."

"You can give us an infogram?"

"Oh yeah," Joge. "How many colors?"

"Blue, and green," Wenzel said. "Can you bring out invisible carbon with a third color?"

"I've done an image or two—yachts on trailers make targets. Like Hummers," Joge said, looking at him sideways. "That Zion paint eats right into boat windshields."

"You got a boat thing?" Wenzel watched his face.

Joge's look turned to a glare of near spastic rage, but then calmed.

"Had a friend who loved to swim across lakes," Joge spoke quietly. "Boat like that conked him."

Wenzel nodded. Lotta motivations out there. He followed the two over to the van, and grabbed scaffolding to carry to the house, walking beside Marv.

"You tell Joge what're wasps?"

"Rich bitches."

"Whatta we swat?"

"Wasps."

Close enough. One like Marv doesn't need the smarts. Wenzel discovered white Anglo-Saxons in junior high, but his juvenile site on protestant affiliation worn thin. The idea stuck—to sting or be stung. Wasps are wasps, people are people. If you wanted to support a wait and see policy, another wasp acronym, that now warranted you a sting ticket. The waspinator off the shelf sticks the feet and wings of pesky hornets and wasps tight 'til they die. Take the stickies into the country estates hive, where vehicles and estate houses were message billboards waiting to be plastered.

"You from a farm, Marv?"

"A cow pasture like this," Marv said, twirling his hand around his head. "Why would ya build a mansion where the cattle shit?"

"Sends a cultural signal," Wenzel said, smiling.

"A what?"

"A status thing, like I'm better, dude," Wenzel said. "We're sending a cultural modification signal—like no you're not, dude."

"Yeah," Marv smirked. "Like on the highway. Told Joge about that paint ball run. How we come in of the forestry service road outta the foothills. I'm ridin' my Snakefire."

"Sounds like quite the ride," Joge said, twisting a scaffold arm into place.

"Lotta congestion slowed traffic, hey Marv," Wenzel said. "Helped us weave in and out."

"Ratta-tat paint splatters." Marv shook his head wildly.

"We need a distinct hit rate. We keep planet icons spread out in a nice easy-to-count line across any RV," Wenzel told Joge, lifting a cross bracket up to him. "Six or seven for a heap like that." He waved at a huge classic Neptune motor home across the road. He could only picture it being drive by some white bearded businessman. In his traditional roll, with his traditional views. "Five for that Grey Wolf unit say." He waved further down.

"You don't wanna hit a moving windshield," Joge said. "Danger line."

"Naw," Marv said. "Rake'em from the side as you ride by."

Any RV rolling along the highway of indifference dumping carbon brought on an increasing future disruption danger, Wenzel mused. The real question was, how much danger lay in the wasp, wait and see policy during an escalating climate crisis?

"Cops?" Joge asked, climbing up to stand on the plank.

"By the time they get out there, we come to the river, eh Wenz?" Marv grinned. "We tear up river off road into the foothills and spread out."

"You thinking of a paint ball run?" Wenzel looked directly at Joge.

"Oh yeah."

"Fill in the request," Wenzel said. "Let's see how you ride tonight." Dedication and ridership counted a lot. "You ever bounce a fence?"

"Over sideways?" Joge said. "Yo, dude."

They walked back to the van for another load, and brought more bars and planks over beside the window. As a team, they put the bracing into place.

"We flash mobbin' Wenz?" Marv said.

"Kinda. Vigilante messengers talking through social media net," he said. They hung a sheet over the scaffolding to close out the light. The neighborhood message would come that night—all neighbors to know they had billboard windows and a planet count. "Call us a flash mob with a planetary purpose."

"Yo, dude," Marv said.

"They recently went public with carbon emission numbers," Wenzel told Joge. "You give an address, or a zip code, and Planet app converts to planets." The laggard politicians at least went public; they just needed some help with their messaging campaign. "You get biosphere?"

"Yeah," Joge nodded. "Cool."

"This neighborhood whines the most about their carbon tax," Wenzel went on. A few jurisdictions had taken on carbon taxes, while stubborn others had not. He looked directly at Joge. "Like someone put the burden on them, like they're not responsible in any way."

Joge nodded, flipping the paint cover sheet to step in under, and the others followed.

"This billboard window before us fronts a house ranking third among neighbors," Wenzel looked at his Planet app output. "Neighbors like to point fingers at a worst case scenario, so good enough." Doing one house would impact many houses. "

Joge pulled markers from a pocket, and set to work sketching an outline. Marv turned to stack the remaining braces and connectors.

"Alright." Wenzel flipped the cover sheet back. "You guys get the infraction notice on the window. But leave it covered—we want the whole neighborhood to know. I'll get you guys your time and place for tonight—we come in the back on hover bikes."

#

Wenzel sat tight up behind Hazel, focused on his face shield screen as she zagged their way in along one escape route out. His hover bike floated along in tow behind. The woman found her way through with no map reference—reverse this trip and they had a scouted exit. As she pulled out the entrance gate to the dead end he checked time—three AM on the nose.

"What's your take babe?" Wenzel said, as she flipped her face shield back. He caught her eye beneath her hair tied high under her helmet.

"This one's hidden," she said, dismounting to unhitch the hover biked towed behind. "The other way's straight, so faster."

Attentive to the headlights approaching, he watched the vehicle pull in at the dead end. The van good, and yes, Marv's crazy wave. Timing fit schedule and that telltale Paint by Numbers had disappeared. Wenzel slid up to the front of the bike seat, as Hazel hopped onto the detached bike. Waving Marv back, she directed him to park behind trees at the last field access. Watching her from behind, Wenzel felt a simmering confidence they'd planned well. Riding in on near silent hover bikes, their fat floater tire inserts would smooth out any rough terrain and give that needed elevation assist to bounce any fence.

"Listen up," Wenzel said, as Hazel led the other two up to hover facing him. "Hazel and I come in from the south, and veer down to keep along the tree line. That's a wire fence in the middle, so laser detectors on. You two stay north side of the fence," Wenzel directed Marv and Joge. "End of the fence you turn to catch Cougar Way."

A farm dog barked in the distance, echoing over the light hum of the bikes.

"You got your routes and named targets," Wenzel said. "We helmet talk—but any questions now?"

"We gonna bounce that fence?" Marv giggled.

"We bounce on the way in," Wenzel said. "You guys on the way out."

Marv shot a fist up in the air.

"What about alarms?" Joge said.

"Good question," Wenzel said, always recalling that Hummer night. "Do not touch any vehicle door handle. Leave anything looks remotely like a sports car—they got the sensi-sirens, and not worth tickets anyway. For an SUV, plaster the windshield but don't push any harder than a breeze or the police lifting a wiper blade. We trip anything, we got five minutes to finish up and abort," Wenzel said. "That happens, we ditch the van where it is and leave on bikes."

Marv sighed audibly, as if losing a darling possession.

"You guys circle back down Cougar Way—a boat on a trailer for you Joge—but get the Cyclone first." The RV name spoke of itself, once a wild adventure, but now a destructive ocean storm. Intensified by climate.

"We meet at the target house," Wenzel said. "And roll our final warning across their door."

Donning Sticky Back carry packs, they road off across the field following the edge of the trees.

"Wire fence starts here," Wenzel said. He fell in behind Hazel as she slowed to let the other two forge ahead. Then she gathered speed tight in along the fence line, bouncing fat tire to gain upward momentum. Wenzel segued in on her final high spot pick, and blasting hover jets to full rose up in the air. Stringing out the moment as long as he could behind Hazel, he skimmed the top wire with one boot until at the last moment as he felt momentum drag he swung past the fence to land on the other side. Wanting to let out a whoop, he beamed inside his helmet.

They turned to the right, splitting away from the others to swing in along the next tree line.

"Okay, you get the Arctic Fox RV, babe, and I'll plaster the Prevost TOUR." He'd tagged estates by recreational vehicle in the yard.

"Yes Wenzie."

Veering apart from his woman on his separate routes, Wenzel breathed in the cool night air as he slapped carbon ticket stickers on his target RV, and the trucks and RVs along the way. Coming to a stop finally at the house next door to the cathedral window cover, he imagined these to be the neighbors. Taking his last Wilderness Sticky Back, he rolled it gently across the SUV windshield, watching as it slapped into place. "We warned," He said quietly. "Be informed."

"Hey Wenz," Marv giggled through helmet telecom. "That Joge's lost."

"What?" Wenzel said. "Joge respond." He could see Joge's icon heading past the end of his route towards the far corner of the country estates. No response, the guy must have switched off.

Hovering the last few meters along Wolverine Drive, Wenzel pulled over at the cathedral window house. Looking up the street, he watched Hazel turn a corner and cut over towards him. Marv rode in off Cougar Way onto Wolverine Drive. Sitting silent for a moment, they waited a minute for Joge to pull in. Then the yattering started about what he did to the yacht, and Wenzel remembered that front road drive by, the huge boat on a trailer he'd seen. The guy must have had a moment.

With the other two watching, Wenzel grabbed Hazel's hand and they walked up to the target front door. Each holding an end, they rolled a custom Sticky Back out across the door like a banner. Your Party, Our Mess. He gave her the thumbs up and she kissed him on the cheek. The sticky clean up job would be horrendous, clinging in hopefully reformed minds. No one forgets an infraction ticket.

"Okay, nothing left," Wenzel said. "Reverse exit."

They split apart again, steering clear of streetlights. Wenzel checked the time, they were just within Detroit's forty minute limit.

At 4AM they looped back past each other on either side of the field. Together at the dead end, they split three ways. As the van headed down the road, Wenzel took the scouted escape route, and Hazel the fast lane. The distant siren howling could be anything, but if approaching here the cops would come in the front road first.

#

Late next morning Wenzel sat with Hazel—after a drowsy van ride home, they'd faded back to observational positions. Traditional news could cast the Wolverine Drive household as victims, as long as their warning came through clear. Social media trended not so much a sob story, but as a new world culture set in, a reminder to locals of the pathetic way things were and could no longer be. Taking a gulp of steaming coffee, Wenzel voiced Detroit's code to his device.

"How's it look?"

"Action started at sunrise," Detroit never slept much. "We leaked to that reporter wannabe journalist, and the ambitious boy got there first."

"And?"

"We got the neighborhood warned," Detroit said. "No question."

Detroit ran video clips of home owners gawking and talking to that reporter, torn between outrage at their own vehicle sticker mess, yet glad when they heard about the Wolverine Drive home. A windshield Wilderness Sticky Back slapped on any parked vehicle impressed chemically into the glass within minutes, leaving a light green subliminal message. A later surprise. Get rid of it by replacing the glass, or live with the reality check warning. Footprint stickers placed mid windshield stuck hard, a real chore to remove. Many were so pissed, but others spoke softly of their rage, mixed with fear.

"That's not all. That Geochem family came home this morning," Detroit said. "Heard the news."

Informed by those neighbours, Detroit said, and not just the pass code guys. The family matron from Wolverine Drive caught the spotlight. Her twit posts on the way home screamed disbelief, extreme distress, and a meltdown outrage. The GeoChem boss stayed silent. That reporter stood around Wolverine Drive like a casual bystander, but a city news crew showed up too with big cameras.

"Classic dude," Detroit said. "They pull up at their house to a crowd of neighbors coming and going, the news guys are there and a police car just pulls up. That backdrop and the Wolverine woman stole the show."

"Anything like the Hummer guy?"

"Check this clip," Detroit said. "Shows it all, dude."

The SUV door opened and with cameras taking from different angles the woman raged out across her front lawn, barking hard at the injustice and tearing down the cathedral window sheet. Shocked by the image, she fell to her knees among her flower beds, sobbing, screams subdued, as if having a conversion.

"She apologizing?" Wenzel said.

"No way, dude," Detroit said. "But that Joge portrait talks for her."

Whatever her take, the cover coming down—the clip slow motioned that part—revealed their eleven planets message in flaring drama. If she wasn't sorry, Joge's infogram stated the my bad for her with or without any promise to pay back the extra planets she had taken.

"Aww, man," Wenzel looked at Hazel. "Her dream home."

"She needs a new dream," Hazel said quietly. "Other people living like her do too."

"She can replace her glass," Detroit said. "Or she can advertise for us."

"That's our dream," Hazel smiled. "She joins us to become our conversion icon."

"That's like a stained glass remodelling job," Wenzel said. "House's big enough for a church—the church of the newly opened mind."

"Replacing the poisoned mind," Detroit said.

They watched the drama from another camera, the feed zooming in on the distress in the woman's face. Transforming...one could only guess now, and wait.

"All wasps melted back?" Wenzel said. "Marv and Joge like disappeared?"

"Yeah...got more on that Joge guy," Detroit said. "He's got artwork in the downtown oil towers."

"Ah shit," Wenzel said. "The guy's a excellent artist. Perfect message."

"Be careful," Hazel said.

"How do we wrap this one?" Wenzel asked Detroit. "We cut all ties?"

"Best option," Detroit said. "Wipe clean all communication links. You and me, level one again."

"Keep Marv?"

"He's got level two. He'll find us if he makes another cut."

"Joge?" Wenzel asked.

"Level three, tagged caution." Detroit spoke game strategy. "We take no chances. If he's gets paid by big oil, we take that infogram portrait as a financing gift. Like the fossil fuel guys paid a tiny bit of their infraction."

Storm Punchers

Staz flicked his dark hair to get that islander ma'on look as he stepped off the family jet to greet his cousin. "Hey Kai." Dozing on the early morning ocean crossing to Uncle Davey's mountain-top Caribbean manor, he'd wondered how to play it cool on this trip. His twin sister Larissa was dragging butt de-boarding, to avoid Kai, no doubt. She'd be finding little Jodie quick enough.

"Last time was that chopper ride." Kai gave him an up down fist bump. "Wave top touchin' over the Dead Barrier Reef."

"Used to be Great, not Dead," Staz said.

"Fuck that." Kai's lip curled into a sneer. "Remember the reef sharks?"

"Total fake." Staz added his scowl. They went swimming in the reef replica pool. "Those sharks sourced Zee-on archive video like any His-Tory game."

"His-Tory tells they actually flew those clunky choppers, not just on tours," Kai said. "You know?"

Staz looked up at his cousin. At seventeen, a year older than Staz, the guy had that intense red-freckled look under his curly blonde hair. Staz had been tasked with attention to the family leadership challenge, see what you see on this trip, and pay attention to the business end. Family future was hardwired into dad's brain. Staz would be advisor, but would Kai become leader?

"You always went for speed," Staz said.

"More than one kinda speed." Kai raised an eyebrow tapping at his front pocket. Staz wondered what kind of dope his cousin would dig out of his stash later.

"You play any Zee-on HighFly?" Staz shifted talk from the drugs.

"Screw gaming ma'on." Kai led them towards the mansion complex. "Wait 'till you see our sky-wasp. We're gonna go on a real life high fly."

"Yeah?" Staz looked back to Larissa. She fiddled with the baggage remote.

"How's the fortress?" Kai spoke back over his shoulder, directing the domestic Larissa's way. Their mountain island mansion back on old Hawaii poked a steel frame out of the mountain side to the front balconies. No bullet proof hurricane doors like this mountaintop. Nor the high volt wire running between Uncle Davey's automated gun-towers keeping those living below out. Staz's dad selected a mid-ocean island for a place, choosing family protection by isolation.

"Our home you mean?" Larissa answered question with question, and then poked in a vague Kai teaser. "Mom always says they're spoiled rotten."

"Who?" Kai took the bait.

"Chucky and Davey." She sing-songed. "Our daddy, your daddy."

Staz sensed Kai stiffen. His sister never submitted to Kai's directives, mostly with taunting resistance. She called him shit box Kai...only Jodie kept her coming on any visit. Cool kid that Jodie was, Staz knew he'd never become the one in charge. Kai had an Uncle Davey's leadership style, one that Larissa could not stand.

Kai kept his poise, turning back. "Go get Krithi." He pointed at a stone arched side door. "Tell her to have Jodie's butt in the wasp by ten sharp."

"Yes sir." Larissa mimicked his voice, mocking a salute. Staz caught his sister's indifferent eye as she turned up the stone path, baggage obediently tracking behind. She'd get her Jodie time and he could role play advising a leader like Kai, on business or whatever came up.

"Gonna be Jodie's first time," Kai said. "Little shit's gonna be a man."

"He is your brother Kai," Staz said. Following down the stairs he wondered if Jodie was a teenage yet. The kid was hard to read, so in his own world and Larissa talked only vaguely about him.

"Little schanker! He'll make friendly with some clinger kid," Kai said. "Can you believe it?"

"Friendly gives diplomatic advantage..." Staz let that hang, then smoothed it out with a simple question. "What's a clinger?"

"Yeah, you'll see," Kai said. "Storming ma'on!"

Staz followed as Kai walked into Uncle Davey's cliff side launch pad. His cousin strolled up to the sky-wasp—a mid-sized rec-jet perched on vertical launch legs, glimmering blue. Swinging one leg first over the side Kai rolled into the cockpit, looking back at Staz. "You put a reef chopper next to a wasp like this—that's same as an F-16 drag racin' a biplane." Kai plopped himself into the pilot seat, and Staz stepped in to take the co-pilot seat. The cockpit felt like a limo sports car...you walked right around the upfront buckets. Or, Staz glanced behind, to a cushy backseat bench. Kai pointed out the retractable roof that sensed when you unbuckled to stand.

"Cool." Staz raised an eyebrow perusing the controls. The aeronautics part of Kai he liked. "What's that side panel?"

"Ahh, duplicate controls like for a body shield suit," Kai said. "You need the Davey family mansion code for that."

"Whoa, you guys got secrets."

"Whatever. Hey, this wasp makes top-o-the-air in two minutes flat," Kai went on. "Edge of space—then we go where we want. A total blast!"

"No shit." Staz felt his breathe quicken.

"You don't get no Stage 7 at old Hawai'i."

"Mid Pacific's calm," Staz said, bright-eyed. "You guys live in hurricane alley dad says."

"Uncle Chucky knows," Kai said. "Da-dee wants us stayin' close to business."

Staz thought quick, wanting to pick up on the touchy family enterprise talk.

But Kai cut in first. "Old folks partying at the Knob?" His voice taunted. "Talking that business talk." Family adults met regular to dine at that jungle restaurant on Cocos. His parents took a skim boat all the way across the Pacific but Uncle Davey had to lift out of water and fly over the dangers of the Central American canal passages.

"Couple weeks back." Staz nodded, then cast in an everyday parallel to guide Kai on topic. "Climate's still a stock market. Chucky predicts, Davey invests." He shifted his eyes sideways, feeling his cousin's intense stare.

"Davey pays his Uncle Chucky fees." Kai lifted his chin.

"All family." Staz shrugged. "All cool, ma'on."

"Sure," Kai said. Staz listened attentively. "So the Old Man got into islands when your dad figured out those mainland coastal properties. Don't know what this island cost back then. Use to be the country of St. Lucia for Christ's sakes."

"Uncle Davey raked in the business billions."

"We marketed Chucky's strategies," Kai said. "Now we live on our fortress island—manufacture on the others. Got lots of clinger kids workin'."

"Clinger? Ma'on, what's that?"

"You'll see," Kai said. "Old man stays off mainland now—crazy there. Especially the latest coastal cities."

"Been there?"

"Kinda sorta." Kai brightened. He caught Staz's eye with a forceful look. "We gotta go."

The thrill of business and the business of thrills, Staz thought, as the conversation drifted to girls. Staz asked about his cousin's girlfriend. Krithi might be from below their Mount Gimie gun towers but she loved to get out there, Kai told him, anywhere. She was cool!

"How's the chick scene on old Hawai'i?" Kai asked. "You gettin' any?"

"Maybe." Staz met his cousin's eye. "You?"

"Oh yeah." Kai grinned, nodding his head at the bench seat behind the pilot chairs. "Krithi likes getting in the back on any storm punching ride."

They heard the girls coming down the stairs, and Staz caught Kai's hard look as he switched talk back to the impressive topic of business. When they came in with sad-eyed little Jodie in tow, Kai took on a CEO-hears-report stance.

"So what're projections on Adaptation Strategies, the Coastal Fund?" Kai asked, speaking with his adult voice on investments.

"We're projecting lost markets," Staz answered squarely. "Accounting for the latest human cost factor."

Kai played for a CEO type business report so Staz went into detail. Real estate risk depended on past storm wave action before and after the slosh, Staz explained. Storm waves ripped out foundations so never before hit, you marketed the building as artificial island refuge status and the land value held. Foundations deep in calm waters held firm, like after the slosh if no storms hit before. If your foundations were ripped loose by wave action during sea level rise your investment risk went up.

"Excellent." Kai nodded. "Smart guy, Uncle Chucky."

"Like Staz." Jodie chimed in from the cushy seat.

Kai turned and glared, pointing a finger straight at his younger brother. The boy cringed instinctively, but Larissa wrapped a protective arm around him and glared right back at Kai. Staz knew his twin and Kai were different types—like opposing administrative material. Maybe she could be the family top dog. Girls knew better on a lotta things but as Krithi dug her nail file from her bag, not everything, Staz decided. As the moment passed Kai stood, swaggering to the front and turned to face his assembled crew.

"How many storms we punched?" Kai asked Krithi.

"Lost count babe." Krithi flashed a flirty smile. "Not enough."

Having their attention, Kai filled the crew in on the real thrill of storming. Whether you drift into the storm or ram hard out of the quiet eye, you let the howling funnel winds spin you any which way. You get peak rush when they spit you out anywhere. "How many doubles?" Two runs in one day happened regular and one time Kai and Krithi did a triple. Staz caught his cousin's meaningful wink as he powered up the sky wasp.

"Check out Zelda." Kai pointed at the satellite weather image. "She's a Stage 7 storm and we're goin' deep into her. Like us, babe!"

"Oh babe." Krithi looked at him sideways. "Let's do it."

Larissa rolled her eyes as she brushed Jodie's hair to the side. She told Staz before about Krithi—hard to tell how serious she was. The girl played out issues in her own complicated way. Seemingly submissive to men and to her man but, Larissa said, she could play the sly manipulation game. Jodie raised his eyes from the floor to Larissa, snuggling in as she whispered comfort into his ear.

"Now ladies," Kai said, eying them up and down. "Strap your curvy butts into position."

"Yes babe," Krithi said.

"Piss off Kai."

Staz noticed the smirk on Kai's face—he'd scored one big on Larissa. She hated that, he knew. Totally ignoring the back seat Kai turned to the sky-wasp controls. When it came to flight situations, Kai shifted to his bring-it-on commander-in-control attitude. The jet fighter hero type of leadership, dad called it, like his brother Uncle Davey.

"Storm punchin' ma'on," Kai said, pointing to Zelda on screen. "Let's do it!"

Lifting off the launch pad, Kai guided them out of the wasp hive. From a free hover he blasted the craft into a steeply ascending arc through the sky-high wisps of cloud. Staz felt the Gs as his body squashed back into his seat, and his cheeks flattened back until he couldn't speak a word. Struggling to do anything let alone talk, Staz felt the momentum squeeze even the tiniest thought to the back of his brain.

#

By the time they decelerated minutes later, the sky had taken on a clear shadowy look, near midnight black. Staz could pick out stars along the planet's curving away edge as he felt his thinking brain reorganize to normal. With the G-force subsided, he gasped at the stunning view, until he was finally able to choke out first words.

"Woahh, ma'on Kai." His voice resonated with the weirdest hollow rhyming sound. "You see through it all up here." He caught his giddy almost-giggle.

"Top-o-the stratosphere, dude. We fly way above any weather." Kai seemed unaffected. "You could never breathe up here, air's way too thin." He winked at Staz, nodding back at the bench seat behind. "And cold ... gotta get your heat somewhere."

Staz barely heard as he stared down at the ocean blue, loosely framed by billowing white cloud formations. His gaze zeroed in on the distant oblique white spiral disc of Zelda. With Kai tapping at the controls, the wasp zoomed in a smooth arc towards the eye of their target storm. This flight felt totally like being inside a Zee-on game, only five times better. The hurricane fingers spiralled out wide on the open ocean side, but squashed in tight touching formless green islands toward the continental mainland.

"Looks like a blaster, ma'on." Kai grinned.

Staz glanced back and forth between the real storm clouds below and the screen marked NAV tracking their wasp in a vertical view. Goose bumps rose up the back of his neck as he realized the old satellite weather trackers must still be functional. When dad talked about GPS satellites and land surveys, the business risk question always came up on how much longer government satellites would last—and the disorganized global replacement plans.

"See that?" Kai pointed at the NAV map. "That line of building icons marks the old coast line. When we get closer, you see those towers poking out of the ocean like piers around a harbour."

"Coastal cities before the Antarctic slosh," Staz said. "We classed that as high risk real estate."

"Based on?" Kai took on the adult tone.

"Distance from the waterline and elevation above sea level, current and projected," Staz said. "Compounded by the latest anticipated storm intensity."

"Buy and sell." Kai snickered. "Buy and hold. Heard it all ma'on."

"Risk of holding depends on location, location, location," Staz added.

"Life's a risk," Kai said. "You live, you die."

Staz looked at his cousin. "You the philosopher's stone now?"

"Stoned philosopher." Kai beamed, tapping his pocket.

Staz ignored Kai, turning back to the euphoric view. He could hear the talk he grew up around on big weather events and their real estate impact. After the Antarctic slosh—Dad anticipated that risk factor years before the event occurred—everything changed. Kai slowed the wasp into a hover position directly over the storm center.

"A'right you flying squirrels," Kai said. "Get ready to glide."

Before Staz could entertain another thought Kai plunged them into a top-of-the-rollercoaster power dive. Staring straight into Zelda's eye, Staz felt his body lift up to sway and float freely in his harness, light as the most genetically modified feather. Kai grinned wildly, glancing in the mirror back at Krithi on the bench. Staz watched the circle of dark ocean expand until Kai reverse arced them hard out of the dive to the sound of Krithi's fingernails-deep-in-your-skin screams. Jolting to a final abrupt stop, Kai released his buckle to let the roof extend and then popped the full wasp top. The last of Krithi's high pitched screaming escaped out over the quiet ocean waters. Kai stood, and with hand on one hip he waved out at the wall of storm cloud surrounding them in a tight definition below the blue sky circle directly above.

"A moment of peace," Kai said. "Before the storm." Grinning like a Zee-on Crazy-Dude, he reached into his front pocket, and cracking a vial threw a handful of greenies into his mouth. "Shady 80s for all." He tossed the bottle to Krithi, sneering at Jodie. "Except you." He pointed hard.

Krithi slipped her glittering fingernails over the youngest cousin's shoulders, crowding Larissa's arm off, and snuggling in close. "Ohh...my little man." She spoke softly into Jodie's ear, dangling the crystal vial of green tablets before his face.

"Krithi," Kai barked. "Front and centre."

Smirking as she came to her feet, she stepped up to stand next to him.

"Pick babe." Kai slipped his arm in around her waist.

Krithi absently traced a finger along the spiral arm stretching furthest out from the storm centre, stringing a winding path back towards mid ocean. Arms draped over Kai's shoulders she flirty-eyed Staz dangling the vial before him. Staz eyed her—his sister might keep clean with her Kai distance, but Krithi now focused her penetrating look on Staz and the vial. He casually took the pill bottle, and poured a heap higher than Kai's into one hand.

"That's like back to old Europe." Staz pointed at the NAV.

"Middle of the ocean's for you and me babe," Kai said, whacking Krithi's butt for attention. As she shifted her melting look back to Kai, Staz tossed a few 80s into his mouth, and dropped the rest into his pocket.

"Crew like this needs clingers," Kai said. "Pick again."

Krithi shifted her wavering fingernail to a second storm arm on the mainland side of the hurricane. Squeezing her butt in approval, Kai turned his attention to the wasp controls. Zelda would flush them out somewhere along the looming continent.

As the wasp top closed and the roof retracted, Staz recoiled as Kai's grin flashed at the corners into a distorted clown face. He gasped at the speed of the painless sillies rising inside—had the greenie handful been too high? Kai reached to his captain controls, turning their sky-wasp into a driving penetration of the wall of cloud. A surge of hysterical giggles broke out in the cockpit.

#

With all visual reference lost in an incoherent cloud-and-brain swirl, Staz struggled for focus on orientation. As they punctured the mist beyond Zelda's eye, he zoned in on their craft icon on the NAV map, and the tremors he felt in the wasp. Kai searched for a sonic wind-howl zone. Peeking again at his captain cousin through mounting euphoria, Staz caught real or unreal flaming red orbs pulsing below yellow fire hair, energy intense. For a second Krithi transformed into a wasp queen, huge octagonal eyes leering over her drone man deep into the storm. Staz stuck his fingers under his legs to keep them from turning into insect spikes, grasping to hold any clear brain moment. As his heart pumped wild, bringing on thoughts powerful and fleetingly perfect, he recoiled at the tiniest demon bubbles stabbed those visions, always unexpected.

The storm ride intensified as they burst into a clear zone between cloud spirals where Kai went feral slipping them in and out of the howling. Then he picked a spiral, dove them in and cut all power to take them on a total tumble, before half way through grabbing back control with a confident grin. Wheeling the sky puncher jet directly back to taunt the hurricane's power, he inched hard into the storm's face before arching off to let Zelda have her way.

"Speed's such a rush," Kai said as they slipped into the calm of an extra wide clear zone. "But we need people action." They were reaching the storm's outer edge and he pointed at the approaching line of oversized harbour piers. "Clingers!"

A high speed skim over the gap between storm and coastline brought their wasp to a line of high-rise towers poking out of the ocean. The main storm was still building at what once had been a coastal city. Staz grasped to form a thinking sentence, brain grappling with that clinger word while the hurricane intensity approached behind. The sonic speed roller coaster tumble left them dizzy, disoriented yet peaking.

Kai, having lost no fervor jumped their sky-wasp building to building, skipping from one sheltered out-of-the-howl side to a hover in the next sheltered wind-hole. As if he had been here before. Signs of habitation could be seen on many towers, rafts moored at the waterline, clothes lines between windows and plots of grey-green plants on the roofs.

"Woahh, lots of these apartments are so gone babe." Kai giggled at Krithi. "All fall down." He slipped into the sounds of a sarcastic kindergarten child reciting verse, then broke into a pitched dog moon yowl.

"Look at this one lean." He swerved tight into the lee side of a building, half protected from the wind's growing power. "Let's grapple here."

"Grapple." Staz could at least repeat the word.

"We walk right in and through," he said. "We be the landlord inspectors."

"Look." Larissa pointed at empty window panels. Torn clothed kids pointed back over the edge of smashed glass. "Children."

"Let's talk to them," Jodie said in a hopeful voice.

"Yes! We stop and chat," Larissa said in a firm tone. "There are things we can do."

"Give it a break." Kai's voice carried adult cynicism. "I mean, check out these clingers. They cling to their toppled buildings, they cling to their feeble lives."

Staz stared at Kai, brain half defogging. Had his cousin become the lamenting poet? Would a leader lead all...or better the select few? Only those with advantage, and the wherewithal to carry on.

"How can people live like that?" Kai snickered. "Why don't they get a mountain island? And a sky-wasp to get around?"

"They can't." Larissa spoke loud, her harsh face glaring at Kai. "You're so fucking ignorant Kai."

A woman with older raggedy children tugged at a boat moored half inside a broken window at water level. Fishing might be a primary food source, Staz thought, their main family survival strategy. These buildings could be loose at the bottom he knew—depended what kind of storms hit as the sea level rose. Once deep, the bottom turned calm as breakers shrank into rollers. But when the waves crashed, the foundations could be ripped bare—his dad knew all that.

"Let them eat fish." Kai gave the emperor's hand wave.

"Globally warmed water depletes fish stocks," Larissa said.

"Overfishing's not exactly a factor anymore." Staz gave his sister a look.

A moment of near sanity set in as cockpit giggles wore thin. Like they all were left brooding in the long seconds of reality, stoned straight. Staz saw Kai absently touch at his front pocket, but his hand fell to his side.

"We figured out a way to keep these type buildings occupied," Staz said. "With floating service lines you abandon one floor at a time."

"Three floors rental," Kai said. "Our one time slosh loss."

"Are these our tenants?" Staz asked.

"Doubt it—Da-dee sells before they stop paying," Kai said. "These clingers don't look like they're paid up."

"This tower might be still in the shallows," Staz said. All luck of the draw, and unless wealthy and mobile, your luck depended on your home local climate impact.

"Coastal real estate's good business," Kai said. "When you got risk analysis in your family blood."

"That's why your mom married your dad," Larissa said.

"Shut up."

"We caused this," Larissa said. "You guys know that?"

"Who?" Kai bit.

"Whoever had the wealth." Larissa set the hook. "The more money anyone spent pre-solar dumped more climate change carbon into the air. This air we breathe, our common air. It didn't matter if it was business or personal shopping in the old fossil fuel economy."

"Bullshit," Kai said.

"Excess consumption—that's us. More billions you got—more devil slaps on the wrist you get." Kai eyed her like a naughty child, rubbing at his wrist. Staz watched the interchange in disbelief as they met eye to eye. Was it the greenies, or a miracle? A tear rolled down Larissa's cheek as she looked up at Kai. "I tell you it's true." She spoke softly.

"Same that dad says sometimes," Staz said. "When he's had enough bourbon."

With a twitching lip Kai walked back to Jodie, embracing him with a brotherly knuckle rub to the head. "C'mon Jodie, talk to me brother."

The wild energy that erupted in Jodie's struggle for release said he'd missed the moment and Staz was sure he'd be punching hard into his big brother's face if he could. Kai let Jodie go abruptly, walking back to his seat.

"He'll get over it ma'on." Kai chuckled at Staz. "A couple more times in the quiet storm's eye—my little bro' will get the reality feel."

"Not fair." Jodie came to his feet, yanking his brother's hair.

Kai swirled around. "Fuck, you little shit did you see how those fuckers live?" Big brother flashed into his own rage. "The place smells like you stuck your head in the toilet."

"Leave him alone," Larissa screamed at Kai. "We did all this, you moron."

"We did." Kai eyes near softened for a second. "Or did we?"

Kai turned back to controls, speaking quietly to no one. "Fuck it all." A commander confronted, Staz thought, processing options. That waver in Kai's demeanour revealed a part of his cousin Staz had never known. Could the hint of a softer inner core be hidden behind that intense red face, a leader for one and all?

"The thing is, that we does not include us." Kai went on in a calm young adult voice. "Young people follow adults, and there's nothing any kid could ever have done or could ever do now."

"Kai!" Krithi yelled, pointing out the cockpit front shield.

They all stared past her fingernail, Staz gaping. The mounting storm was twisting the building before them into a creaking, bowing lean. Kai moved instantly to punch the grapple release, and backed the wasp away hard to avoid the slow motion collapse. Children dove in freeze frame and adults jumped from the windows escaping briefly into their familiar harbour pool. But the building followed them, crashing over further, vomiting shattered glass into the churning waters below. The last of the lee side pool flushed away as the storm waves crashed around the sinking building sides, to leave the luckier swimming above their sunken home.

Kai's twisted grimace transformed into a look of enlightened on-task lunacy. Popping the latch on the observation port, he poked his head out into the howling storm. Muffled fragments of his raging voice bounced back into the cockpit as he pulled his vaporizer pistol. Where a little girl in a red dress swam bravely across a high wave to snatch at a flotation device, he sizzled the life preserver into a puff of steam. And Kai didn't stop, evaporating any piece of debris floating, and the only empty boat adults were striving towards from the waves. Staz felt totally in a Zee-on game as his cousin kept blasting into the ocean swells even when only those who could swim were left afloat. With his gun empty, Kai descended into the cockpit.

"No way to live," he said calmly. "As our families have brought their lives to this, my cousins, so we keep them in their misery."

"You fucking asshole," Larissa screamed. "We need to help that little girl. They could all help themselves so much better without us."

Kai looked straight through Larissa, not seeing her, and not responding. Turning to the controls he skip-jumped the wasp into the lee of the next building, setting the grapple hook again.

Staz sat frozen, his brain calculating dictator image or tough decision-making by a benevolent monarch. The faintest turbulent giggle escaped Krithi behind and in that hollow background he heard whispers begin. What words might be passing from Larissa into Jodie's ear now? He turned away from Kai to see his twin squeezing Jodie close and murmuring on as the boy stared hard and enraged into the floor.

Staz turned back to front as Kai dug deep into his front pocket. Pulling out a blue patch, he slapped the skin pad onto his bare arm passing another to Staz. With new chaos in his eye Kai spoke firmly to his crew. "We find the streets of a dry land city." He released their grapple and tore away from Zelda towards the mainland.

Kai sat silent as he accelerated the wasp, staring straight ahead.

Staz slipped the blue patch in with his greenies, not looking at his cousin.

#

Sitting in a stunned brain-scatter, Staz could only stare as Kai skimmed the wasp over a watery corridor in harsh silence. The word-squeeze in Staz's brain didn't come from G-forces now and he could only listen to Krithi's suppressed giggles and Larissa's whispers from behind. As they skirted along half sunken buildings, the ocean bottom emerged from shallow rolling breakers into a rusty shoreline. An interstate took form beyond, strewn with a long dead grid lock. Lifting the wasp higher, Kai tracked the divided thoroughfare into the calm beyond the coastal hurricane zone.

An urban development poked a skyline among distant forested hills. Rounding a final curve, Kai piloted the wasp up to a jumble of broken buildings strewn along the cracked streets of an inland city. Skimming down, he pulled them away from the interstate to find a market street. The ocean storm far behind diminished, and Staz felt they had reached Zelda's other calm eye. Habitation spread around, from rooftop tents to broken corners and children playing on crumbling curbs. People below noticed the wasp shadow and pointed up. Around here they might notice the odd jet high in the sky. Or, Staz wondered, would they look like extraterrestrial visitors this close?

Kai pulled into a hover, turning to face them all.

"We come in peace." Larissa spoke directly to Kai.

Ignoring Larissa completely, he barked an order at Krithi. "Take the controls." He reached into a storage compartment to pull a shield suit. "Anyone who wants can go next but I go first. Alone."

Kai strapped on the helmet, clicked on voice and tested the transmission.

"You don't leave the wasp." Kai pointed at Jodie. "One of you can stay with him next."

Krithi came to her feet and walked up to Kai. Putting her arm seductively on his shoulder, she leaned in to him. "Babe, you can count on me." She'd hold his arm walking down any street or aisle. Staz heard her whisper. Kai turned to him and his twin sister. Gathering strength Staz acted out a punch to his twin sister's shoulder, saying he would go next. Kai nodded, like good enough.

"Fly behind me." Kai directed Krithi. "Keep close."

Hovering the wasp down just above the street, Kai checked his vaporizer pistol for load. The raggedy people outside approached hesitant, but some stopped and many kept hidden. He popped the floor hatch, stepped down and ducked to walk ahead out from under the wasp. Krithi waited for a full view of her man before gliding the craft along behind. More residents became apparent. Children played with the hovering wasp as if accepting the craft into their game. A distinct bearded face appeared at one window, staring their way.

Kai ambled past a city bus now occupied as an apartment. Boys at street-side played a war game around a dead vehicle turned playground. They turned their wooden sticks to point at Kai and he stopped breaking into a fanatical grin. Waving back at the wasp, he pointed his pistol shot finger over at the boys.

"He's a shit box show off," Larissa said.

"We should talk to those kids," Jodie said. Larissa squeezed his shoulder, pressing her lips together hard. Staz watched her face for any sign of a leader's choice but he could read nothing.

"We broke this." Kai's voice transmitted. "So we fix it."

Kai pulled the vaporizer pistol, plinking back at the boys. A boy in a blue shirt—a leader—turned to face him.

In Kai's glance back at the wasp, Staz saw another spark of that deeper inner look, flashing through the game-playing stance written across his cousin's face. Maybe Kai was not leader material at all and maybe he had no desire to be leader. Staz could become his sister's advisor.

"These kids are fine," Staz said under his breath. "Not drowning Kai."

But Kai's face convulsed as he slid his pistol setting to full vaporize, and he atomized the leader boy.

"Jesus, Kai no!" Staz groaned.

"No Kai." Krithi spoke loud. "No babe."

Kai took a carful aim at the rest of the boys and their war game. They paused in their game, a lead gone, and then all turned in unison pointing back.

"No!" Larissa screamed louder than Krithi had on the thrill ride. Staz could feel his silent internal scream join in with his twin like when they were little kids.

Kai calmly pulled the trigger. The automobile shell playground with the litter of war game boys shone brilliant for a flickering final moment before falling into a wisp of ashen powder to the ground.

"Fuuuuuuck," Larissa groaned. She bent over forward, pressing her face into her hands. Jodie now wrapped his arm over her shoulders.

Staz stepped up beside Krithi in the pilot's seat.

Kai broke into a run, skipping lightly along the street picking off any other child he spotted. The young kids joined in the action of the game as if life were a fantasy world where all could be reset. Then Staz glimpsed movement at the bearded man's window— knowing adults would be watching, the boys' fathers and their older brothers. The sound of plinking on the wasp outside began and as Staz watched Kai flinch he could almost feel the thud of the return fire impacting his cousin's shield suit.

"Adjust your suit, babe," Krithi said.

"Old percussion bullets," Kai transmitted, altering his shield proof to layered capture.

"Unbelievable," Staz said. "Our technology and theirs."

Kai ran straight down the street towards the bearded man's window and the gun fire. The impact of a stream of bullets slowed him but only slightly. Leading the charge as a Zee-on commander, he picked up the pace racing towards the enemy.

Until Kai stopped abruptly.

"Jesus ma'on." Kai's voice sounded loud, urgent. He hammered as his suit settings. "My shield suit! Malfunction!" He turned to stare at the wasp, fear glimmering in his eyes. "Come get me Krithi."

A single shot from the bearded man's window hit Kai, penetrating the suit. A startled look came over his face.

Staz turned to the suit settings side panel, looking to Jodie for the Davey code. But Jodie stood at the panel and Staz could only gape, any advice lost. Jodie held his finger hard on the deactivate button, Larissa standing beside, arm around his shoulders. She pulled his head tight to her chest, fingers squeezed into the back of his head. Little Jodie began humming.

"Not fair." Larissa's muffled whisper drifted over to Staz.

Krithi gasped, peeking through her fingernails. Staz could only follow her look as a burst of shells ripped through Kai's deactivated shield suit spraying pieces of his cousin into a red mist behind. The deep pleading of torn decision came out on Kai's face. As Staz stared, stunned, his cousin's stalled leader's role ended with a burst of gunfire blowing the rest of his head off.

Eco History Exam 2052

She double checks the name of the essay final exam - Global Environmental History 302, complete with her student ID number and the date, 23 May 2052. Deciding to use voice and gesture interface for input and edit, she feels ready. She thinks OK, Shazi, just keep it organized. Think chronologically and prioritize events by importance. She knows it was a series of crises and sometimes chaotic attempts at resolution, at times accompanied by the influence of previously initiated trends and general circumstance. She watches the time on the screen switch the last minute to 11:00 hours and she takes a deep breath. The entry screen changes color and the exam voice invites her to begin.

The first decade and before: Before the economically pivotal year of 2008, global citizens had gradually become aware of sustainability, but they and their governments had taken very little significant action. The primary global environmental predicament was climate change which overlapped with population, biodiversity loss, the soil nitrogen cycle and a host of other issues. Various measurements of sustainability had been developed in the late 20th century, including the ecological footprint (EF) published in 1996, with the carbon footprint as one subcomponent. Back calculated EF data showed that while only half a planet worth of resources was used in 1960, the significant one planet mark of resource use was crossed by the early 1980's and resource use was up to a completely unsustainable 1.52 planets by 2012 according to the World Wildlife Fund's report. That report showed an ongoing upward trend into the future highlighting and summarizing the global environmental crisis at that time. With one student interest theme in human geography, her favourite sustainability measure is the EF as it can be measured in global hectares as well as planet earths, hectares lending themselves well to display on a map and both units intuitively understood by people in general. She recalls the paper she wrote profiling the footprint, but she knows she needs to stick to the broader picture for this exam. Primary contributors to the dilemma included some cultural; running beliefs in unending increases in material living standards on a finite planet and consumerism viewed as the basis of cultural status and success, some economic; a traditional outlook supporting a growth economy with a finite resource base, a market driven influence over the general populace based on advertizing and controlled media as well as support for corporations as the basis of employment creation and some political; traditional partisan political systems in democracies based on mutual criticism and faultfinding and the major problem of a focus on short-term goals.

The second decade: The downturn in traditional economic terms of 2008 was only the beginning of what has historically come to be known as the social/economic rollercoaster of the next decade. Traditional players in the global economy made ongoing attempts to kick start the economy as it had been defined for centuries, the growth model. But previously predicted peak oil, now known to have actually arrived in 2017, as well as the obvious situation of peak planet (the EF measure is so right there) contributed to the ongoing economic crisis. Each time the economy was able to begin to "recover", speculative investment would begin, petroleum prices would leap again as they had in 2008 and the economy would "crash" again. In parallel with peak petroleum, the global economy was becoming more and more directly impacted by the effects of climate change, droughts, floods, wild fires and major weather events. The resulting drastically increased food price market signals led to social unrest including repeated food riots in developing countries which also contributed to the increasingly unstable global economy. One positive outcome of this circumstance in developed countries, fueled largely by the price at the pumps, was a strong movement towards finding cheaper sources of energy than hydrocarbons. There was a significant move beginning in Europe towards the deserts, where the algae lipids source of biofuel, grown in the sunshine of the Sahara became a rapidly increasing source of liquid energy and extensive solar arrays in the African deserts were also connected to the European power grid. The same pattern developed later in the southern deserts of North American, along with parallel development of geothermal heat sourcing at an industrial level. The destruction of rainforest for palm oil tree plantations ended when European tax incentives were adjusted to significantly reduce the use of any biofuel based on a forest or food crop source. This decade is referred to by many sources as the first transition, the social/economic transition.

The third decade: Then in the late summer of 2023, the North Pole became briefly ice free for the first time. Hollywood environmental activist film stars travelled there for a swimming photo op - images of some in dry or wet suits and some not appeared across magazine covers and screens around the globe. This event, symbolic and noteworthy for political activists, triggered considerable popular dialogue that would continue throughout the 20's. In the same years, frustrated by the lack of action by the countries most responsible for carbon pollution and the resulting climate change, a group of countries came together to form High Impact Climate Change Countries (HICCC), those concerned and effected most by desertification, rising sea levels and major weather events. Bangladesh was hit by storm surges from two cyclones in 2024 and the Maldives was forced to initiate moves to abandon several islands the next year. When in 2027, HICCC disclosed its plan to carry out a geoengineering project that would reduce the global temperature by their estimate of 2 degrees C by releasing sulfur dioxide into the upper atmosphere, the global reaction was calamitous. Though China was not officially an HICCC member nation, the advance of the Gobi desert was seen by some to have motivated their silence. Her mom sometimes talks about all the fear at the time, like the cold war of the twentieth century, but also about all the global awareness it helped bring about. The popular community was aware by then through a very well known set of drama movies of the dangers of such a onetime attempt to adjust a system as complex as the earth's climate. This was referred to as the political crisis and sometimes as the second transition happening mostly in the 20's.

Throughout the teens and 20's, two trends were having noteworthy impacts; the inclination towards Green party power in democracies and an increase in the sway of women in politics. As democratically elected governments grew in number worldwide, with increasing youth support, they one by one voted in Green parties as majorities or as parts of coalitions to include their policy drives for a Green economy. Some political leaders still came to power through coups or were democratically elected based on radical right platforms and several regional military conflicts broke out. In spite of this, many Green party members were able to educate populations on the benefits of a reduced economy. By the late 20's, reduce became the logo word from the token expression of the four R's – reduce, reuse, recycle and recover. After a grass roots campaign to randomly sticker label any gas guzzling vehicle in North America, bans were put in place on all recreational vehicles; the image of the Rambo man in his bush crashing truck and the high profile SUV driving consumer became an image of the past. Biodiversity was seen as protected by images of threatened species beside those of small efficient personal transportation units. Major efforts to sequester carbon back in to soils and forests, partially in response to the HICCC threat and partially due to popular demand, were financially supported by carbon taxes and cap and trade policies that were by then in wide use globally. Another North American grass roots campaign began to encourage reduction in animal protein consumption, looking towards Asian traditions where meat is often consumed as a condiment. The ecological footprint, which easily shows personal reduction of animal protein consumption results in a significant reduction in footprint, made the news at that time. She laughs at one of the jokes that came out about the dog tax then, when the animal protein tax on pet food made it clear how much the have-a-large-pet lifestyle was contributing to the demise of the pet owner's family future.

For almost two years overlapping 2027 and 2028, three countries out of the G8 had simultaneous women heads of state who came to be known as the W3 and were sometimes compared to Ghandi, Mandela and Martin Luther King and then in 2029, the long term global trend of women getting involved in politics reached the 50% mark in spite of major regional variation. This was seen to have had an important influence on the positive negotiations between HICCC and the G8 and OECD. As well, with this equal gender representation came educational campaigns speaking to the benefits to all of equity in education, income, health care and a recognized voice on care of the common biosphere and children's future. The ecological footprint had become a standard measure by then, known to each European and North American household through real estate transactions as well as property tax forms and to each individual through income tax returns from national statistics departments. Also, there was a major shift to redistribution of paid work hours and a reduction in formally recognized weekly work hours. Her mother had served three terms on their regional council and is now sitting on several committees. The human population was mined globally for human capital searching for naturally occurring intelligence, leadership potential, traditional beliefs on sustainability and traditional methods of conflict resolution. A drastic reduction in spending on the military was carried out, recognizing this huge resource waste when acknowledging that security comes from the ability to cooperate with and help out neighbours. Many female political figures and especially the W3 spoke out about and financed global education of girls and planned parenthood. This was also the beginning of the G8 cultural exchange program, first voluntary but now mandatory, where the selection of places available for exchange included Kerala in India, Costa Rica, Bhutan, Tuvalu, Maldives as well as Iceland, New Zealand, Norway, Samso island in Denmark and British Columbia in Canada.

The fourth decade: By the early 30's, the class action lawsuits against the major oil companies for their record of advertising and contribution to the climate crisis were in full swing. Many precedents had been set in previous lawsuits including those against tobacco companies, many by Canadian provincial governments responsible for health care. In 2034, the case of five western American states vs. Exxon Mobil was the classic, bringing forward everything from crop losses, wildfire damage, rising sea level surge tide damage and flash floods damage due to the now common heavy precipitation events. The carbon footprint had been used extensively as measurement evidence in this case. Mention was even made of Standard Oil's historical purchase of streetcar systems with the business objective of promoting travel by automobile. This was referred to as the third transition, the legal crisis. But this time period was also known as the decade of peaks. The ecological footprint was first to peak having reached 1.84 planets by 2032.Then in 2038, the important global population peaked at 8.73 billion, lower than projected and highly influenced by women in political positions. Finally, in 2039, the carbon pollution in the atmosphere was shown to have peaked for the first time at 465 ppm C02e. Global concern over potential climate change tipping points being reached were still a serious item of discussion and debate. The global focus on cleaning up the problems created in the past came to prevail as a global awareness came to be clearly focused on the self interest for all in maintaining a healthy biosphere.

The fifth decade: By the 2040's post partisan democracy was coming into play where democratic governments were becoming much more local and the idea of council and consensus decision making was rapidly replacing that of president or one person making decisions for any community. This system was found to work naturally especially for women council members. A council of nine became typical, though initially still including a sub-council of three with extra executive power including a secretary who could override council decisions or take on single person decisions at his or her own risk. Over the late 40s' and the first year and a half of the 50's, the use of the executive decision making by the secretary had been decreasing, going the way of the monarchies and dictatorships of the distant past. Local governments made most community decisions while the far off federal body was responsible for global security cooperation, national services and management of the currency. The global EF is now almost down to the one planet mark again, but still with significant regional variation.

She is reminded by voice she has 5 minutes remaining, and reads the essay over quickly, correcting a couple minor discrepancies. When the screen fades back to its original color, she acknowledges the submission request, sending her exam in for grading. She has a good feeling about this exam, quite confident it will keep in line with her honors level grades.

She relaxes and thinks about this afternoon when she will schedule her six month community engagement term, mandatory yet flexible. Her choice is to directly experience, observe and learn in an alternate cultural and sustainability outlook setting – everything from studying how their local council makes decisions, cultural traditions that have been determined to be valuable and their societal outlook on the earth's biosphere and its value to current and future human generations. She really looks forward to attending regional council meetings to observe how they come to resolution, another primary interest of hers. Through previous research, she has chosen Costa Rica, for its advanced methods developed over decades being the first nation state globally to attain a carbon neutral status, its influence in assisting neighbouring Central American countries to achieve carbon neutrality, as well as its progressive positive cultural model. Two days on the Pan American bullet train will get her there. Her evaluation and written thesis on the benefits of the learned lifestyle and their application in her home country will be credited towards her education and will also be seen as on her c.v. as highly beneficial towards her future career.

SPIRIT OF HUMANITY

The Matter of Love

Chris opened the door to the all-too-familiar office. In this last session he would but go through the motions. Gently rubbing at the apple in his suit jacket pocket, he stepped in. Letters lay written on the bureau, one to his wife and apologetic attempts at explaining human love, or lack thereof, to each for his two children. Once and for all he'd prove by action he could step outside the cage of rational thought. City traffic hummed faintly up from the streets through the window.

"Hello Professor Shuman."

He grunted, almost inaudibly.

"Please." Counsellor Jamal looked up, motioning. "Have a seat."

He took his place in the wooden chair, running his finger along the familiar bumpy underside of one armrest to find that protruding staple, keeping his other hand in his pocket. Days had dragged out lately into an interminable struggle for any positive thought. If there was no God, no god, no higher good, he saw no purpose. Rational understanding of a cold world...what for? His look penetrated deep into the floor.

"First thoughts." The counsellor intoned from behind his desk screen. "What runs through your mind at the moment?"

Suppressing the rage against a chancellor's directive to be here, he could find among his many thoughts none carrying value. Life had turned into a marketplace of empty shelves, and those few shelves stocked, full of items mislabelled—nothing held true to that advertized. He would expose his inner battle subtly he had promised himself.

With twitching eyes he half raised his head.

"Ohh...been reading."

The counsellor kept his eyes on screen, nodding.

"Research papers?"

His biologist's mind had noticed that bird along the walk that morning chirping with all its heart. So uplifting. Yet with the sword in his mind he'd sliced the invasive tweet to ribbons. The twitching notes remaining he powered upward with a rolling wave to pound through the razor edged sands on his beach of despair. Silence. As the moment dragged on, Chris rubbed his finger harder each time along the sharp metal staple. If one could not love one's own children, those who heard story, why go on?

"Snow White died." He shuffled in his seat, touching thumb to wounded finger. "That idyllic sleep version of the magic potion was written into a soft modern edition." A fairy tale shifted all to one's own childhood; to a person's deepest inner issues of trust or life's delusion, he knew enough about psychology. What he did not want the counsellor to know.

"Ummhmm," the counsellor droned.

"Misinformation, and deceit abound in our world." Chris scanned the front of Jamal's desk, fingering the pin prick in his pocket apple. A medieval herb woman might have a wide selection from her forest, but modern science availed one lab chemicals. "The witch and the princess held mismatched individual interests," he said. "The nature of any human engagement typically plays out through conflicting values." A characteristic human trait revealed a clever rational witch tricking the naive princess, all to the witch's gain. If pure evil abounded or even existed, why cast a princess character at all?

"How's your research Chris?" He could feel the counsellor's eyes fixed on him. "You do enjoy math, you always did." This counsellor favoured topic diversion in his psycho analytical tactics—diverting attention quick to gain insight.

"The latest analyses confirm the new theory." Chris lifted his look to the desk edge. "The old social evolution theory will die, but slowly." Given a choice, why would anyone want a slow death? Snow White's demise had been quick, even if not by her choice.

"Inclusive Fitness will fade away?" Jamal asked. "Or was it the Kin Selection theory?"

"One and the same, yes," he said. "The Kin Selection theory as a model explains the evolution of social behaviors or traits."

"Well professor, I've been doing my reading on the topic."

"Then you should know Hamilton gained wide recognition by proving out his theory mathematically." His indifferent tone disturbed, Chris heard the semblance of a student assignment completed, and felt drawn into his professor shoes as in a lecture hall. "Via indirect offspring and based on other than current data."

Shifting uncomfortably, he decided to ritualize now, to kill time.

He went on. "But in the interim, further eusocial species have been catalogued and they don't fit well. The probability of sharing an altruistic gene based on kinship has weakened. Many phenomena in eusocial species can no longer be explained. People cooperate with strangers of no genetic relation—people they will never encounter again." The witch certainly hadn't. "They pay-it-forward in popular jargon. Kin Selection could not explain this, nor other patterns." He paused, as he would to allow any lecture hall inquiry. How could any a loving god power allow existence of such a foul woman? Atoms existed, void of love, nothing more.

"Eusocial means highly social?"

"Yes, the eu suffix denotes gentle or pleasant."

"How does altruism fit?"

"Altruism stands as a primary signature denoting benevolence or affection." His lecturing professor life had been near fascinating as his research. Half entranced, he continued. "A eusocial species evolves into a state of truly social organization. Humans have evolved into one such species, and theoretically they can evolve further. Once the eusocial bundle of traits is acquired, the species dominates. The eusocial have dominated the Earth's biosphere for millions of years."

The biosphere, and human degradation of their ecosystem though climate change, and biodiversity destruction had caught his recent attention.

"Termites first, then ants, bees and wasps. Ants experienced additional evolution—harvester ants live as cooperative farmers, engineers and architects in air conditioned mounds, comparable in many ways to human cities. If you argue for domination, you can estimate the total weight of all living individuals, that being their biomass. Insects, though tiny as individuals, win hands down—ants measure half the biomass in certain ecosystems. Much larger humans are unique coming much later in evolutionary time and taking on a pinnacle role among the eusocial species."

He almost felt a tinge of the old excitement, but his new sword sliced through that.

"What causes eusocial evolution?"

The counsellor played his questioning student role. A strategy, Chris sensed, but he had strategy too and would piss this time away repeating this lecture by rote. Soon he and the apple would be alone, and one. Old moments of pondering came at him as arrows now, from all sides. Yet each avenue of investigation has turned to anguish, stretching out to point with crooked finger at but one resolution—the Snow White ticket out.

He must lecture.

"The key requisite for eusocial turns out to be what science refers to as a nest...or for homo sapiens a campfire." He felt that familiar absorption, as he flowed with the concepts. "Among the vast majority of species the young leave the nest and that leaving trait remains genetically prevalent. So a crucial step in becoming eusocial occurs at that evolutionary moment when the young linger, and assist in defending their nest, their den, their campfire."

The moment of magic, that fit into any story of wonder.

"At that crucial point, a final evolutionary step has occurred and the nest becomes multi-generational. In the case of a campfire, the site became a place to raise the young that could be defended by some while others went off foraging and returned with food for all. Evening collection in firelight safety allowed telling of the day's events, and the trait of storytelling developed."

His eyes flickered, glancing even to the counsellor's face. The sword would soon carve this moment into strips, but he could live in elation for this brief time. His audience of one skimmed that screen, as students do. He sensed a list of challenges coming.

"Dogs." Jamal said. "They defend the campfire."

"Analysis of symbiotic domestic animals remains an independent study," Chris said. "Science classifies dogs, and chimps as well, as species that have attained a threshold status. African wild dogs have evolved to a near-eusocial species," Chris said. "The altruistic traits of a truly eusocial species remain exceptionally rare. They evolve only under exceptional circumstances."

"Ahh, yes, borderline miraculous," Jamal said. "Altruism then."

Chris winced. In apologetic metaphors he had explained his position in his letters to family as best he could. In his effort to explain the human limitations, his limitation, his deduced inability to truly love. When it came to any love he analogized that family dog name from times past. People spend with dogs, getting what they can't from each other, he had theorized.

"Step back to another species. To define an act of altruism, a suitable social object must be available," Chris said. "A ground squirrel emits a warning whistle at a predator's approach. That act gives away the squirrel's location yet allows other squirrels to live. We could classify that whistle as an altruistic act." Like that kiss of the true, what returned that princess to life. He hesitated, toying with what words to use. "A true sign of intra-species affection, love, you might say."

The counsellor glanced his way and they locked eyes briefly. Counsellor Jamal certainly knew of Chris's ability to slip sarcasm into midsentence, so he stopped, freezing his look. Has he slipped, from sarcastic tone to any inkling of hope? He carefully shifted his gaze away and back down. The counsellor adeptly complied by switching topics but again.

"How's climate science?"

Was Jamal seeking to retain the mood? This was another lecture, but somewhat associated.

"Science has genetically coded Monarch butterflies now listed as extinct in the wild." He clearly emphasized sarcasm now as he spoke in a flash of bitter resolution. "Some among the oh so clever people act in the future interests of all. People cause climate change which compounds biodiversity loss. And our global tribe has chosen climate silence—denial in psychological terms. Effective towards major natural events for those around the campfire, but no longer. And yes, social evolution helps us understand our refusal to abandon our tribe."

"Frustrating," Jamal said. "And culture?"

"Our cultural models have the best potential for adjustment. Yet rational argument has no impact—people hear friends, neighbours and family, their tribal anecdotes, not reason."

"No one?"

"As per the Monarch analogy some... but only a few." Lecture topics fading Chris slipped into a personal rant. "You tell the Christians Jesus was Aramaic and they scoff. He had dark skin, black curly hair, no way they say, he had blue eyes. People are hard core tribal and to support their tribe they turn away, they don't want to hear a version that interferes with... well, say their childhood stories." The conversations in the church they attended when the children were young.

"What about those few?"

He half smiled, knowing he would talk his way through this one. "Now, and back then—okay, tribal commitment might be fluid but resistance to change will be strong. One of the first guys to shift support to Jesus after the nail-up-on-the-stick day was stoned to death – Stephen – people committed to tribe just don't want their core beliefs challenged. Jewish leaders gnashed their teeth. Especially a faith based tribe—that group highly resists anything new. Human nature. People join groups, and having joined, they cheer on their group as superior to competing groups."

'Today's scientists?"

"Take climate change. Overwhelming scientific evidence remains ignored. The Middle Eastern wars were sparked by droughts, a climate change influenced food shortage! Take the Syrian conflict. But the majority hear only of droughts and refugees, the familiar, instinctively ignoring the underlying cause."

The counsellor started to speak, then hesitated.

"You just added proof to the theory." Chris said. "Your pause supports climate silence."

"True," Jamal admitted.

"So what's the point? People will fizzle out, self-destruct, wipe themselves off the planet like that last cluster of Monarchs." He felt the rant gain energy. "They trash their life support system and say oh poor me. Then they adapt to the chaos and lash out at the government they elected. Or alternately at the country they pick that day as the opposing tribal enemy. The new player on the eusocial stage, the human species remains maladapted to survive at a planetary scale."

Chris sagged as his sword shredded any bird song. That morning, finished writing letters and secure in knowing no higher love, he mixed that vial of salts into solution and injected the required cyanide milligrams. Her having no syringe, he sympathized for a cynical moment with the witch's method. What a European witch might have done to access white oleander tea he had mused.

"Could altruism be energy alone? Or a structured fabric?"

"What?"

"Just reading here." Jamal looked up. "You are familiar with this superseding theory."

Chris sighed. His time here would soon be fulfilled; he could present final lecture part two.

"The latest theory of virtue. Multi-level group selection—a process where evolution progresses towards sacrificially collaborative traits, no longer based on kinship but due to highly cooperative communities beating out poorly cooperating communities. Supporting evidence is based on population genetics applied to multiple levels of natural selection and evolutionary game theory. Analysis compares individual and family selection to community selection with a big tribal instinct dividing line there."

"I see," The counsellor said, glancing at his screen. "First name makes the author primary?" Chris nodded. "So this paper under Winston writes to the general public... for someone like me. He mentions the creation theory."

"He'll never get that published in a journal." Chris met Winston at a conference. As known leader on group selection, his Shuman authored research reiterated and emphasizing human origin through random chance—no god influence.

"Maybe not in academic literature," Jamal said. "That's all you read?"

"And the odd fairy tale." The universe was so structured, so mathematical, but only in the realm of physics. What did it matter now?

"Any proof yet?" The counsellor ignored him. "That no god exists?"

"Definitive proof, no," Chris hesitated. To improve the world, moral values held value. The creation theory mindset carried him through his youth. "Kin selection theorists agree with the new theory on that issue—human existence came about totally by chance." Chris drew his finger across his thumbnail. As droves of scientists dropped off any believer list, claiming no god, no God, he followed as one of the last.

"People do love each other, Winston writes," Jamal said. "Protection and nurturing of the young creates a people wired for compassion."

"Mammalian instinct." As a theoretical biologist Chris had endlessly searched the data for a greater good signature. Among kin, family love varied but a mother's love for her children stood out. That now sank into the mire of theoretical oblivion as the Kin theory died.

"God was imagined?"

"Tribal instinct," Chris said. "A creation story bonds a tribe and that bonded tribe survives."

The homo sapiens species, uncreated, evolved over millions of years by genetic chance on the plains of Africa, with luck and many tries. Or were they tries, if no one was trying? The equation of love remained elusive, non-existent and Chris had no further tick of enthusiasm to search.

"Religion doesn't fit the new theory?"

Religious stories are so full of holes. He had discounted any second coming along with creation theory. Long term survival counts on intelligent self-understanding based on greater independence of thought and he knew where that type of thinking certainly would not originate.

"Religions will never coalesce with science," Chris said. "How can they when each teaching has a different creation story, all necessarily based on ignorance of what really happened in the past." He grimaced. "The nature of humans and tribalism leave humanity with conflicting beliefs each claiming to be the absolute truth."

Jamal's eyes appeared to be skimming in a moment of silence. "Did you ever read that search for meaning book?" He spoke almost absently.

"So the Nazi inmate survives within his own mind, no matter what his circumstance. My problem is within my own mind—that's where I have doubt. No guidance."

"And you need guidance?"

He hesitated. "Look, I need more than what I find in people. Look at the market system we maintain, driven by fear and greed. That inherent fear we have, that's of each other." He looked squarely at Jamal. "The fear of them by us comes from good cause. In any past village, or empire, in any war, any recent homicide. Though shalt not kill but we are a species that kills...each other."

"Could climate justice become social justice? In the villages, in the new market place you allude to people needing? Climate change could be an opportunity. For those aware, like you Chris."

Chris looked to the window. "Our inherent nature rings hollow," he said in a tedious tone. "We need outside guidance, and an amiable guidance. To design a market model past fear. That requires faith, a faith that I don't have."

"Scientists have theory faith," the counsellor said. "You told me that."

"I find no viable creation story." He could feel his voice become loud, and consciously shifted back to lecture hall calm. "Like all people, I need that."

"And something to care for you," Jamal added. "Otherwise, what's the point?"

"Yes," Chris felt his tired eyes soften. "Like any child."

"You need a personal understanding of a God power."

"That's more or less true..." Chris took a breath.

The counsellor paused. "Does science not tell a story of creation?"

"Yes it does," Chris said. "But...all based on random chance. Probability."

"How about this?" The counsellor looked at his screen, speaking carefully. "Your latest social evolution theory postulates a new universal definition."

"Oh yeah, that we are permanently unstable and permanently conflicted," Chris said. "Into this state our nature has evolved and will so remain forevermore. Permanently destined to be torn, we struggle between acting in our own interests, our sin, and acting on our virtuous community interests, our virtues."

"Yet friendly communities survive the struggle better than communities of the selfish."

"That's being shown," Chris said. "But without any caring signature...it's all crap."

"Is it?"

"Absolutely!"

"Has it always been?" Jamal asked. "For you Christopher Shuman?"

"When I was a kid it was easy." Chris stared. "Jesus loves me this I know. On other days I hear story of the wicked witch. Pick your tale. At this stage of my life there's no more heaven than happily ever after."

"What's heaven?"

Chris remained silent.

"Could it be an alternate concept? Love only?"

"Take historical Jesus and science." Chris shook his head. "Take Christmas. C'mon, gift exchange fits any model of human survival instinct. And the late December winter solstice was a universal celebration at high latitudes. Isaac Newton was born Dec 25, not our historical Savior."

"What about Jesus' main message?"

Chris felt a once meaningful flicker, but that faded. "The Kinship theory can haunt any adult hope. Within families we measure significant altruistic behavior. Love appears there on the edge, but social instinct explanations can be made. Unless one questions the deeper origins of love."

"God?"

"Or some version thereof."

"Where is deeper love then?"

Chris pressed his lips together. Feeling the hanging weight in his pocket, he half smiled. Soon he would know. He could play or play along now. You found appeal—beauty—in your own species. Everyone deeply desires that someone feels for them. Yes. That a higher love exists is certainly an inner desire across humanity, past the social instincts. Even past the strongest human love. What rings in children's laughter? More than our instinctive fear of being alone, our innate loneliness for social contact. The inexplicable perception of beauty in the sky, in the face of youth often came out in song. In any evolutionary tribal past you could feel the beat of the drum on the African plains.

"Music connects with the internal yearning of all people."

"Where then?"

"Love is…in the raindrops, on the rooftops," Chris to Jamal. "Another song says deep within or in the stars above."

"Could it be both?" Jamal challenged. "Winston argues here for an up in the stars community selection."

"What, in outer space?" He half laughed. Was he about to be tricked by psycho-analytics? He no longer cared; he would go with any tune, and bite any apple. Scant minutes remained here. "Tell me what he says."

"He makes a case for the moral outlook of interplanetary ET."

"We've no proof of extraterrestrial life."

"Nor, he states, did we once have proof of planets beyond our solar system," Jamal said. "Now, the exoplanet count grows by leaps and bounds."

His mind wandered; his wife and children had often challenged his know-it-all attitude. The curse of intelligence.

"Space once was made up only of stars and galaxies, all visible to the human eye," Jamal took the lecture podium. "Now space has dark matter everywhere, more dark matter than light matter. And dark energy. Winston principally argues we have yet to definitely detect the fabric of love, though we have the theory based on our own social structure."

Chris felt a flicker rise. "A living community beyond human?"

"Winston argues ET would possess high level social intelligence."

"That's not an academic paper?"

"No, but by a well published academic scientist. The rational goes that an extrapolation of our terrestrial nature into a star wars mindset would not pass the evolutionary test. With a warlike outlook and advanced technology, a species would self-destruct before venturing far past its own solar system. An alien race out to colonize interstellar planets would be unlikely to succeed. Development of universal care, affection and benevolence would come about Winston postulates and he finds no more appropriate known analogy than human love."

"Ahhh." Who was he to claim discovery finished? He had challenged many a student. The princess explained?

"He argues humanity will develop in one of two ways— towards universal love or extinction," Jamal said. "Based on that multi level group theory, affiliations of altruistic planets would beat out empires of warring colonizing planets. As historical facts have a record of being detected over time, so he poses the idea that the true energy, and matter of love have yet to be found. A theory for any scientist."

"Any proposal on the fabric composition?" Chris placed both hands on the armrests.

"Emotional...possibly a super conscience."

Chris felt his inner flicker spark, and unbelievably into low-flame re-ignition. A sense of relief washed over him, growing in profundity—there still could be a god. If he could not love his own children, a proposed extraterrestrial complex could. "The brain has never been definitively connected with emotion," he spoke almost to himself. "Science finds implied association only." His mind ran wild as in years before. The laws of physics could simply be a stage setting where emotive guidance came out independent of physics. All the world's a stage, and we the players on it. The learning of love, onstage, as the play. People make their exits and entrances yet play many rolls in building that higher love. The unfeeling laws of physics would originate from some other source.

"Winston claims the theory of dark matter in the universe to be synonymous," Jamal said. "The supplementing theory of unlit energy explains potential. His speculations better explain altruistic evidence he claims."

"Ahhh," Chris spoke as the counsellor had. For how long was humanity ignorant of the link between energy and physical matter...so elegantly revealed by Einstein's relativity equation. The fabric, the matter of love, why not? Simply put, God or god constitutes love. Not a new idea, simply a modern viable explanation. And that universal higher love could be helping little cousin planet Earth grow in love.

"We suspect love energy through altruistic acts," Chris read slowly. "People of faith find deep satisfaction in their cultural religious teachings."

The purely evil witch fell in status to a background footnote. People had yet to conclude their inherent quest on the matter of love. What of night time mind wanderings? An angelic network could be linked through a network of dreams—religious teachings are rift with dream connections—all those angel versus devil confrontations in the Abrahamic faith. Intuition too required a deeper conscious source, and, he'd always wondered about the purer mind states of children. What the universal brothers developed out there could be shared with people in ways they have yet to understand.

Could not struggling civilizations, with competition and hate combined with cooperation and compassion and intermittent acts of true love have grown on many planets scattered among sextillion stars? And grown into a universal web of higher love? The idea so amazed him, he could picture a prophet starting a new religion...they almost needed one to translate the climate crisis into brotherly cooperation. Worship paid to their life support system, to Mother Earth would go a long way. Subsequent to the Big Bang the new scripture would teach of an organic Presence taking on form of love science. Look not for terms of endearment in the cold creation of physics, but find affection developed independently into a compassionate Being. Join in caring for self, for planet and gain interest in the social wellbeing of your own species.

He stood excitedly.

"Thank you so much counsellor."

"Until next session Professor."

As he walked out, Chris felt the bulge in his pocket bang against his side. That apple—he had almost forgotten. Waiting for the elevator, he pulled out the witch's trick, and hesitating but for a second dropped it into the waste bin. With a new theory and research to do, he would lecture on the path to that time when a grown up humanity could reach out into the universe in a mature way—not in war, but with a wisely outstretched hand.

Orion Ang0157

where every step I took in faith betrayed me
and led me from my home
... are you an angel
Sarah McLachlan

The Request

He held his hand to his code tag, mind recall percolating through his existence in human form. A spiritual being having a human experience he'd heard on the planet, though rarely. Roused from a blank inward stare, he focused his eyes when the voice behind the desk spoke. Standing on a bridge between nothing and tomorrow, he steadied his resolve.

"You are requesting an assignment termination." The galaxy supervisor peered over scanner specs. "Once again."

"Yes," he said, determined, yet unable to hold in his misting eyes.

"The beings in this dimension refer to linear time," the supervisor said. "We'll speak in those terms if that works."

"Sure."

This administrator would be managing all missions in Spiral Arm OHO44, locally known as the Orion Arm of the Milky Way galaxy. Tasks such as reviewing any updates, progress reports and modification petitions. A petition to abort an assignment, such as his, needed clearance at this level before final decision.

"The request states you feel a longing."

"Yes." He shuffled in the chair. "For home."

"You carry an evaluation assignment," the supervisor said. "In the realm of sentient beings who seek out and believe in angels. You are scheduled for at least two more decades in local linear time."

Home, he repeated under his breath. *I just wanna come home.*

"Another assignment might work," he said. Any place better than this. "I did check off the transfer box."

"A review, then," the supervisor said. "We'll need the latest."

His hand fell from his name code, youthful human need to pretend abandoned for now. The supervisor glow-scanned his badge, capturing all recent and yet to be submitted data. Any mistake on his part would be known, minor and that haunting major. All his chips were down, his truth laid bare.

"Zero one five seven, Ang code, yes...you are on this third planet from the star unit...okay, we're bringing up the life form class."

As an Orion Ang child he went by Fifty Seven, or Sev among those he knew.

"Let's see...you are posted among an upright water based life form. A eusocial mammal, a humanoid." The supervisor looked over the specs with a penetrating intensity. "These types often develop quite successfully, albeit over the long term."

He didn't say a word.

"Why don't we carry out a spot check, first impression?" Exposed, having no choice he felt the scanner specs evaluate his disposition. Transmitters tingled, and he sighed, fully submitting. As a human, he'd learned much on the art of deception, but here he knew full well the worthlessness of any restraint.

Taking in a shuttering breath, he glared upward. "I hate it here." His watery eyes flooded over. "I've always hated it here." A moment of childhood's first awareness flashed over him. Under the family Christmas tree, he found material gifts in place of any oh-so-desired early life hug. What love? At the school grounds he confronted children learning to berate and degrade. Negative love. As a child, he could name the bullies who sought out and harassed him.

"Thank you," the supervisor said. "That response record will assist immensely in our evaluation. Now, I need to probe your mental processes with a question."

"Sure." He forced an adult smile, covering any youthful desire to hide his bad. Later in life, lost in the wonder churn of young adults discovering themselves, drinking at bad days, drugging to enhance the good, he laughed along with social interaction rules underlain by tactful distrust. Lies, deception and manipulation—all part of the human condition.

"You challenge portions of the evolutionary path required for your species' nature, human nature in this case, to fit into the progressive model of assisting with universal love."

"Absolutely." That distorted young adult outlook had crashed, hard, with no clear escape avenue. He'd wandered church to spiritual group, seeking out any confirming support for his assignment. He even filled out application for astronaut, longing for the spiritual awakenings reported by those viewing the living planet below. That lineup was far too long, clogged with adventure seekers and jet fighter pilots.

"Such as?" the supervisor said. "First to mind."

"This species wars upon itself," he said. "With premeditated intent to kill."

"A problem, yes."

"A huge problem." He forced his voice to stay even. "They agree to punish for everyday killing but all rules shift for war—a killing in many cases for religious beliefs."

"The record shows you have never killed." The specs turned to him. "Do you think of it?"

"As a human, one cannot help but think this way," he said. "This activity developed as an evolutionary survival requirement among the species. Thus, an inherent residual sits ingrained within human nature."

"You know and I know Creation requires emissaries," the supervisor said. "To bring in experiential data—your design specialty."

He waited, silent.

"So...your last request to drop the assignment came after you submitted a *trim* proposal."

He knew they'd bring up last time.

"Cull the herd," Sev said easily. "A local domestication expression."

"As in? Kill off the select few?"

"More like the select many." Perhaps spawned during youthful drinking, the idea had resonated with him over time. "They cull themselves at certain levels. Those most undesirable—criminals—they execute based on whatever select values of the day. Witch burnings at one time—religious teachings of a sort then. So simply expand that definition—bring school bullies into the equation and an abrupt set of alternate values."

"We turned that one down," the supervisor said. "The concept contradicts our ethics directive on multiple levels."

"They might just get it though." Better maybe than his other proposal, the one admin did accept it turned out. "Humans breed animals for desired qualities, and they're aware of improvements in their stock. At the nice story end pets match the temperament of individuals, satisfying affective social needs. Unavailable from each other, I might add. At the not so nice end, they remain omnivorous, and choose yet to gain nutrition from once living animal flesh."

He could tell reviving the proposal would go nowhere—the specs' interest shifted.

"I want to make a request," the supervisor said.

"Sure." Sev sighed.

"Your project termination rationale runs long," the supervisor said. "Your first to mind was intra-species killing…can you express another species proxy, to symbolize your overall evaluation?"

"They pay lip service to assisting the weak and vulnerable," he stated emphatically. "Yet not only do they allow, but flat out glamorize the famed lifestyle of the rich and powerful. Excess riches in the hands of a few serves the many no real purpose, yet they worship at the feet of these few."

"I see…thank you."

"A question on my part." He felt emboldened. And if he could keep the conversation going, maybe they *would* overlook his big bad. No matter how juvenile the strategy.

"Yes?"

"Why not communicate directly?" he said. A rhetorical question, yet one often wandering into his stream of human conscience. "Why not directly engage humanity?"

The supervisor peered over the specs.

"Why send one like me?" Sev went on. "You get huge interference with any reporting ability I can supply as a participant observer. Hormonal drives distort and emotional reactions run wild. I feel disgusted at most times, and sidetracked at others. Just reveal yourself."

"Do humans respond well to voices in their heads, to dreams even?" The supervisor looked up from the reports, directly at him. "Do they listen to any prophet? Or stand long around anyone proclaiming from a box in the street of once being lost and now found? Any of our other past messengers."

"They've got a story about a being cast as the *Son*, another named a *Prophet*," he said. "Speaking of being born again, or talking to angels on higher love awareness." He hesitated, but then added. "The *Son* checked out at a much young age than my term so far."

"Were those successful?" the supervisor said. "The teachings of the *Son*? Or the *Prophet*?"

"For some, maybe..." he shrugged. "Others quibble over differences, even calling on war."

"Enough on that then," the supervisor said. "We need talk on the proposal we did implement."

He paused, shaken, then broke out into rational babble. "Self-observation has run its course, and provides no further useful data. Beyond genetic modification, and adjustment of the original creation material, I find this personality I experience contains defects that will not modify."

He took a deep breath. Distraction would go nowhere. He and his truth were on the block.

"That was a mistake." He switched unconsciously to youthful language, those idealistic times when the idea came about. "Totally, my bad."

"Yes?" The supervisor looked at him expectantly.

"Look, at that time, I petitioned a binding force." He fell into explanation. "A common cause—a problem for all to join hands in solving. As it turns out, this global biosphere issue—their very life support system on the line does not budge them. With a threat to their nest, their home, to their very existence, well, they refuse to cooperate. They resist profusely, clinging to finger pointing or denial or worn out beliefs. I believe I was mistaken in this request. The risk was too high—my bad," he said again. Even as scientists chat about their survival chances in the universe, they argue back.

The supervisor silently glanced across his desk to that latest update, listening.

"They would so benefit from a human conscious awakening, and I did think they had that at a subconscious love level." Sev went on. "When they hear climate change, most clam up. Most don't talk about it, most just whistle in the wind like the juvenile boy children of their species. At this point in their evolution, definitely too early." Everything around the beings required change, and quickly, with self-interest transitioning to other caring, mutually felt. But that it turned out was a huge ask.

"If we chose not to terminate your task?" The supervisor shifted talk back to business.

"You see value in my continuing to walk in circles, screaming at the walls?" Sev argued, playing a trump card. "Spitting on my own reflection in the mirror?"

The supervisor looked over the specs, unfettered.

"Look, this species often ends its own biological life by conscious choice," he said bluntly. "The human life form developed long ago to the self-aware knowing of self-termination."

"I see," the supervisor said. "And you have thought of taking your own life."

"Of course," he said. Both in early youth, and later as an adult he had experientially come close. "A conscious choice to pull the plug on a ridiculous situation, an existence with no purpose. Look, why not simply assign another?"

"We do at times…"

"Consider this," Sev stated firmly. "The reason on record for pulling me from this assignment would be my mistake. A major error on my part cannot be overlooked. Climate change carries an existential threat to the species and they are clearly not evolved enough to face the challenge. I screwed up—you pull me, all's good."

The supervisor held his silence.

"If you don't want a return by protocol," he added softly. "You can deal with my return by choice—I will simply pull the plug."

The look in the supervisor's eyes told him his request had gained serious consideration.

The Review

Through the opening door came the singing of euphoric voices. Glancing over at the desk, Sev leaned forward in the chair as a wave of home washed in around the edges of the room. His true home.

"I've invited Aurora to attend," the supervisor said. "I hope you don't mind."

Resonating with the all-knowing, the unknown, greeting in whispered echoes her *hello* emanated out from all corners at once. He felt her slight-touch presence, yet no more than half-heard the aw-tingling female voice reverberate across the room. Reminiscence of human dreams, and moments of deeply inspired conscious thought flowed through his being.

"If we could begin," the supervisor said, grounding the session. "We will first review your report addressing our universal development target." His pragmatic tone continued. "To be clear, our objective remains focused on expanding a love inspired and amiable universe. What your species refers to as God could be equated to love in its purest form."

Sev trembled, thoughts swirling into a cauldron of soul stir. "Sure." God is love...he'd heard the words, but thought more like...love is god. The toil of love learned, and toil it was, builds or can build a loving god. Only with motivation...

"For Aurora—your reports," the supervisor said. "Can you summarize?"

"Sure," he said, resolved on his decision no matter what. If he could get through this, it just might get him a ticket home. "Any progress toward that target on this assignment, as per my observations, weighs in as minimal. And I have been hopeful, so generous, at times."

"Can you take us to an experiential scenario, to allow Aurora a sense?"

He stared, building up for what they requested. First response energy burst out in a childhood wail. "I just don't want to play," he sobbed openly. Rational adult overwhelmed him next. "In ancient times they buried girl babies in the sand, for cultural survival reasons of powerful men. In near recent times, the matchstick girl dies in the city streets of hunger and cold, to preserve the excessive wealth of powerful men. Today girl children still die to bombs and hunger." God of war—god of power. Zero love.

He held the fist of youth stuck out before him, angrily judging, thumb down.

"Excellent," the supervisor said. "Another please, oriented to your termination request."

"Right," he said, hanging on to that taste of the rational. "Okay, self-observation informs my negative human traits are worsening with age, not improving. This decaying body's becoming not better at, but less and less capable of doing as I could back home. Back here. In the end, this human body serves as nothing more than a life support system for what we truly are, locally a mind and soul."

"Yes," the supervisor said. "Occupational hazards, no? Yet we truly anticipate the wise mature voice developing in association."

"I rage," Sev emphasized, ignoring the interest. "More than I raged as a child, more than I raged knowing I would be born into this state." Those human moments flaring into wrath contrasted so with others times, moments sublime, bathed in pools of languid compassion. How to harvest the second, to be kept and stored, while leaving the evolutionary needs of the first behind. Impossible.

"That maturing mind soul phase has become useful to us," the supervisor repeated. "We have an increasing interest."

He said nothing.

"Alright, we engage Aurora," the supervisor said. "First reviewing the knowings."

This will be intense, he knew. Aurora's presence flooded in from the edges, flowing throughout the room with a powerful taste of a just creation's desire. He near lost himself in the moment, yet focused on what he knew, how these ideals were only ever the slightest part of humanity.

Her voice stitched a trail through the air, weaving the flowing energy among atoms into a comfort to his being. Her evaluation swirled in among his rational thoughts. *The human species has evolved wired for compassion, for attachment.* Yet authenticity versus attachment remained unresolved, resulting in problematic acting out, he thought replied, having read that somewhere. *Especially pertaining to protection and nurturing of the young.* His daughter—she's like an inner app. Theory had it not having these traits would have long ago precluded this species from getting to first base so to speak. Simply put, authenticity awareness results in likely survival. He'd heard that in some academic discussion, among the wiser ones.

Waves of the heavenly flowed from Aurora's presence as she absorbed his mind patterns.

The barriers to social inclusion spring out in a million ways, typically due to fears, and mistrust, he thought further. He supported his input projecting experiential knowings. Devious thought and resultant behavior has been advantageous to survival in intra-species struggles. Patterns remained, creating distortions in the species.

The essential self, what is always there, a part of us that loves us more than anything else. Aurora's energy washed over him. *This essential self can be detected within all.*

But, conscious awareness comes only in a very few he thought replied. Those most connected socially remain the most content and aware, while those extra disconnected cause huge problems for all. They drag the species in a negative direction—human science knows this but presents no solution.

Potential abounds...

He knew of her final desire to hear him speak, and sensed a need to do so in a poetic voice, leaving the pragmatic behind.

"Among these beings, the chime of love rings oh so hollow tones," he spoke rhythmically. "Unspoken, but in dreamy verse of inner desire." Aurora touched his being at the deepest, and he felt such an urge to meld with her.

People have a unique opportunity now, Aurora swirled softly. *Your input helps confirm that we best allow them this.*

And she was gone.

"She'll be taking that to Upper Floor," the supervisor said.

"I estimate the chances of this life form, this species, progressing any further at low to medium." Sev had wanted to add.

"Got that," the supervisor said. "I'll forward that up...now we chat a little more."

"Fine," he said, resigned. "But before we go on, can we simply consider the situation? My request has that transfer box checked off, and I would suggest reassignment to a more progressive life force. Less tied to instinct, with a higher level of potential—I don't want to waste any more of this linear time. I see no real further observations to be made, and do not have high hopes for progress on this file. I'm pissing away effort, assigned to save a world that doesn't want to be saved. Or, more truly spoken, doesn't want to participate in the actions required in growing up enough to save itself."

"Anything else?" the supervisor said. "On your part."

"Yes, in fact." A chance to get in a long held peeve, finally. "Based on the lax performance I've observed, I conclude I've been conscripted. I *never* would have volunteered for this one."

"Interesting speculation," the supervisor said. "Records say you gave up conditional access to that information. So you couldn't actually know that, one way or the other."

And he wouldn't be informed now either, he knew that. "I would also suggest whoever you get to continue on this file needs assistance. Higher love type assistance, cause humans don't really love all that much. They talk obsessively about love, they want to *be* loved—they sing about it endlessly—but they aren't much capable of giving what they seek."

"Yes, although..." the supervisor hesitated. "Aurora seemed to indicate otherwise."

"Overly optimistic in my opinion," Sev said. "Replace me, I say and send more help."

"More on self-termination," the supervisor said, switching topic.

"I was fully aware at age six or seven of the defective ways humans have of treating each other, a few signs of love development, but a highly significant level of non-loving acts and thoughts," he said. "By age twelve, I was out of there." Random events had precluded his short term desired outcome.

"Why would you consider such action?" the supervisor added.

Sev could almost sense the *precious feeling of life* as it might emanate from Aurora. But the hollow space often associated, that feeling of utter despair, reverberated through him in reminder that it lurked around every corner. *'Fuck I hate life'*, had resonated through his mind, and at times embarrassed mouth, from youthful times until now, this middle age. The biological sneezes that set in at the slightest cool breeze, an allergic reaction to the daily, were not too different than his disdain for the species. Contained by one genetic trap, his, this one human existence with all character and body traits set firm, unmoving, he felt allergic to the world. A world where each lives in a myopic box of self-indulgent beliefs, refusing otherwise, unless driven by the dire.

"A conclusion reached through rational thought," he said. "No more."

"You report random events I see," the supervisor mentioned, looking to his records, and then back over the specs. "Upper Floor does intervene from time to time although they don't release details."

He stared, taken aback, not saying a thing. Totally unpredictable events had come up, a phone call, an invitation that turned into a distraction, and...so easy to forget at that age. Random he had been convinced in his pull the plug moments. But now, how would he know absolutely? Serendipitous events, spiritual groups talked of, like walking on water for others.

"Another evaluation question," the supervisor said.

"Sure."

"Aside from any intervention or assistance Upper Floor might provide, what else might keep you on mission?" the supervisor said. "All else aside, what's your highest hope for humanity?"

"My daughter," he said, unhesitating. "And other children."

No question. The times when he knew she faced the same school ground he had, he was right there with his school yard moments. In deep compassionate despair. At other moments, the only hope he knew came from the purity in his daughter, and children like her. Her snuggling in with a fuzzy at bedtime. That, he at times dreamed might lead the evolutionary process to an improved world, significant enough to be worth the effort. But other children were not that way, and adults much less. What he saw among people either enhanced or devastated his dream. Encountering a little girl moving out of his way along a city street, not a trace of smile on her face, he felt like one big tear drop splattering on the pavement. The answer could so be in that humble being, but, she had no voice among those who decided.

"And worst?" The supervisor tapped the glass of his reverie. "What's the worst of the assignment?"

"How about instinctive cruelty," he said. "Or crushed emotional hopes." Little girls grew into young women, finding crystal blue dreams crushed by a not so Valentino power driven male ego. One gender dominating the other. Tainted love. Early human nature needed animal drives to reproduce and to survive. That may have fit in with getting the species this far, the struggle against nature, but those drives no longer assist with any vision of a universal loving future.

"Personal experience?"

"Human love mixes hard with lust, and sexual urges take on the role of an endless cycle," he said vaguely. "For me? Brief peaks of *pleasure* driven by demanding bio-hormones, and then endless time spans—hours—of disgust, frustration, despair. To me, this brings on the feeling as these beings would say, of gross."

Sev hoped not to hear another comes-with-the-territory quip, and was grateful when the supervisor seemed distracted.

"I'm getting input from Upper Floor," the supervisor said. "Having recommended a species wide global challenge, climate change in this case, as a motivator to cooperate in action that correlates with love, well, they wonder if you have any other proposals."

"Sure, I've got a list stored in an unrecorded source," Sev said. "But not for you, not for them."

"They do want to hear," the supervisor said. "They see you as a valid source."

"Look, I cheered on a faster paced climate change—science calls that a higher climate sensitivity—and I was wrong, totally wrong," he said. "So maybe I cast that vote out of my own human self-interest, allowing me an exciting career saving the world." Climate change sprouted up out of his youthful idealism, what at the time seemed like a way to bring on brotherly love. All would grow up, together, holding hands as the singers sang. But the brothers with influence, those dominant, decided no on that potential, dragging all humanity along in a high risk charge in the direction opposite. Immature, totally, but they didn't notice, wouldn't care. Would a boy laughing at a well-dramatized Ice Age story realize the destructive forces associated, only opposite in temperature direction with global warming?

"Duly noted," the supervisor said.

"So, you still wanna hear?" He felt like that boy, giving a youthful sideward glance.

"Upper Floor expresses specific interest in knowing what might supplement this growth opportunity," the supervisor said. "Your familiarity with what humans respond to makes you a practiced source. Based on experience cooperatively taking care of a mutual nest, in this case early campfire like instincts, Upper Floor predicts a certain probability of success. Combining your reports with eusocial theory puts high weight on the ingrained instinct to gather about a mutually protective life giving source. So…yes, please."

Sev took a guarded breath.

"Right, okay look, many people revile the idea of climate change as a moral judgement. My intent had more to do with a focus on opportunity, a tough task yes, but not much different than any teenager growing up. The primary purpose of a global issue, climate change, is for humanity to grow. A huge focus on Aurora's *potential…opportunity* I say. To grow up." Like astronauts looking down at the planet, and their conscious growth moments.

"Yet you believe it's backfiring."

"Just check the list of the species' negatives," he said adamantly. "They can be delusional, often irresponsible in an immature party 'till the music stops way. They flaunt themselves as highly intelligence, yet that depends on comparison. They're self-inflated and self-overrated on many issues. So, they participate only at the bare minimal level of cooperation—only that required, and often with underlying self-interest. At this time, far from that original campfire, they participate in and support highly dysfunctional political economic systems that only exacerbate their climate change challenge."

"This is background?" the supervisor said. "A review?"

"I know, I know...but you guys should be fully aware of all this."

"Upper Floor wants alternatives. Do you have one?"

A modifying life support system, their biosphere fell in on a long list of issues associated—due mostly to an economic system driven by less desirable traits. Traits the species acknowledged. Greed, they often mentioned and reviled. Stupidity might not fit into polite conversation, but what purpose does politeness serve when it overlaps so greatly with mistruths, lies really? And...survival.

He could feel the specs turned directly his way, waiting expectantly.

"Okay, how about a climate hero, an astronaut or political leader," he said. He took human history in school, and knew of the tendency to know of the great—humans follow well and even worship the Winston Churchill type. That man, though often intoxicated, led them in a struggle tantamount to the size of effort needed to address climate change. He took geography too. "That hero could be a nation leading to a lauded cultural model. Models existed in several tiny countries. Tiny, like fairy heroes or a faraway kingdom. Costa Rica or Cuba could fit." One quaint, the other politically offensive to the big West. Not the same as a wartime hero, as war was inherent in their nature. But maybe.

"A faraway kingdom," the supervisor said, specs nodding.

"Look, at a real level I need to let that go," Sev said. "Much too dreamy—faraway kingdoms get my old ideals fired up...but, that stuff connects us to children." He learned a little psychology and had come to know children go through stages, pre-cognitive thinking, when certain mixes of awareness might be expanded to evolve into an improved being. Teach the children...not a new concept.

"So next on the list: induce a heightened awareness among children," he said. "What you teach children becomes your society—now that has potential." Often, boys in the bodies of men competed over who could make the going conversation more stupid, or more immature. Girls, in the guise of women, dressed to catch the eye of the prince, and gain delusional princess access to castle security. Behind all that, could the child's mind contain the answer? Does that age of development, known to be synchronized with evolutionary stages have potential to inspire? Humanity needs a boost in trust level, trust of each other—what comes innately to children. Blocking trust, a high level of deceit had historically been useful in their evolutionary path. As tribes, the *us* versus *them* mentality allowed progress for the stronger, what may now be the primary force destroying their life support system. A deceitful non-trusting tribal outlook. Did not the *Son* tell the people let the children come to him?

"Matches your highest hope," the supervisor said.

He glanced straight at the specs, squinting, but then went on.

"Third on the list...assign them an Apollo 13 astronaut-type situation," he said fervently. "Allow them a significant crisis." They responded to crises with gusto like the calamitous moon mission, or the Churchill hero time. Promising and even acting differently after...post world war many statements came out about never again. As if they had learned something. Yet, they forgot and currently seemed set on self-destruction, including destruction of their future. They risked the wellbeing of their own offspring—children who in practice they do love so much—rather than simply forsaking older ways, even when those older ways brought them minimal satisfaction.

"You don't find that one so appealing."

"They would respond, but again, war? Okay, how about modify their mating needs," he said. "Their sex drives are distorted, dysfunctional. Allude to anything sexual among a gathering of responsible adults, and an easy to predict round of tittering giggles will come forth. Little advanced over a junior high party. These decide leadership through democratic voting. The whole mating design needs a complete redesign as I have proposed in more than one report."

"Anything else?"

"Alright, last on my list, how about a new religious figure, the return of one like the *Son*," he said. When those who believe in angels hear proclamations of the second coming—they might listen. "Give them a cell phone video of a laws-of-physics defying walk on the water miracle—that would go viral. So people wake up one morning looking for a friend rather than an enemy. Or a fear, or a terrorist." All the spiritual teachings, those made available for a least two millennia by the time count of Earth years would have an opportunity to come into play. Now, will be the time to apply these teachings. Traditional angels would need shift from medieval paintings into the world of science—feathered wings transformed into wireless devices, detected by other than human perception. As a mode of engaging, of communicating, these must become interactive. An angel app.

"Alright, I'm feeding that all back to Upper Floor." The supervisor asked.

"Do what you can," Sev said, resolute.

"Alright then, Orion Angel 0157, we appreciate you bringing this request forward," the supervisor said. "If you can wait on deliberation, I'll be back with a decision soon."

He could wait. He'd been waiting forever already.

The Decision

Sitting before the supervisor's desk Sev thought a bunch in that human processing manner. He decided to accept not knowing whether he'd chosen or been assigned to this species. That set him free. And, if he simply allowed humanity to have its own way, truly not at all wanting to grow up or grow in love, well that could be just fine. The hollow feeling of failure wasn't worse than any other bad day in the human world. The emptiness one knows should be expected, seeking love within a species barely able to give. Processing allows this conclusion, and by extension, acceptance of the inevitable allows him personal release. Supposing he chose to remain, god forbid...why *would* he even think that, yet he could be free of responsibility. Aurora had insinuated that in her energy flow. Detached acceptance allowed people to choose their own path, even if they chose, crazy as it was, to revert to lesser ways. A career astronaut could never allow expectation of space flight, keeping that desire only as a back of mind bonus.

"We checked with Upper Floor." The supervisor broke the silence. "They say again they found your last report and now these latest updates highly informative."

"Don't you guys know all this all from day one?" he said, wearily. "Destiny, and pre-design."

"No," the supervisor looked over the specs. "We don't."

"Whatever."

"And, they still conclude the human future has potential," the supervisor said. "In their view the mission's worth continuing."

"I, conversely, do not," Sev said. "We clearly are at odds."

"Yes, well in anticipation of your views they've come up with a counter proposal," the supervisor said. "Would you like to hear it?"

"No," he said. "Not at all."

"I see...look, there's a note here on an initiative they already have going." The look came over those specs. "In case you do go back they say watch out for a programmer, a smart girl app...watch your daughter, and other children. Watch close, they say."

His heart skipped a beat—would the send in a child hero? He stared back over those specs.

"Okay," he said. "I'm listening...what else?"

"You commit to the remainder of your term." The supervisor paused, switching specs to full scan. "With a decadal review, so we talk again ten linear local years from now. And you don't worry at all about the climate change issue—Upper Floor takes care of all the details on that one. They ran the risk analysis, they decided to implement, so they take any concern off your plate."

He hesitated, fumbling on the inside in such a human way. What a relief, yet then what? "Two more decades give or take," he mused. "That makes me a senior."

"They anticipate quality data from those decades," the supervisor said. "Think of yourself as an active elder. They encourage discipline and maintenance of your human body—go jogging or something as they highly value a maturing mind body soul connection."

He knew his inner response was being scanned, recorded, and he let it all go.

"Look," the supervisor gave a peering look over the specs. "You weren't the only one. I'll tell you now, and I okayed this with Aurora, not Upper Floor, because we wouldn't normally declassify this. But, in your suggestion for a common task—

climate change or any other—you're not the only one in Orion making that call."

He wasn't alone in cheering on a higher risk…Sev added that to his acceptance process.

"So I do another ten years," he said, eyes intense. "You guys take on all climate crisis details."

"Yes," the supervisor said.

He took a deep breath, near overwhelmed processing it all. Raising his head, looking directly back, he blew the breath out slowly until gone. "Sure," he said. "I'll go back."

Think about it, there must be higher love
Down in the heart or hidden in the stars above
Steve Winwood

The Church of Kâhkâkiw

The girls stretch-stepped across the high school yard. With Friday afternoon teacher class cancelled, and little motivation to attend remote sphere, they weren't going to spend forever standing around the empty bus bench. Tricia dashed laughing out ahead, tossing her brown hair into the hot spring sun. She turned about-face, hands on hips, giving her two friends the what-we-gonna-do girls look. But behind them, her eye caught that dark bird.

"Check it out," Tricia said pointing. "Following us. Again."

"Just one of those crows," Xia said.

"Raven," Salina corrected. "Elders say ancient eyes."

"Yeah right," Xia said.

Tricia turned to the side, beginning the circle step of their talking churn, and the other two fell in. As they curved around, Salina at least peered across at the jet black raven perched on a street pole, midnight feathers rustling.

"Watching us," Tricia said, squeezing her lips.

"He tells you what your ancestors knew, your family before," Salina said. "Elders say he's Creator's messenger."

"Oh yeah?" Tricia said. "Translate caw caw."

"He's got something to tell you, Tricia," Salina said. "Listen to Napi."

"To tell us maybe," Tricia said, looking hard at the other two. "And how do you know he's a he?"

"I don't," Salina said. "Grandmother might say woman's whisper—from Mother Earth."

"She then," Tricia said. "She makes the weirdest sounds—not like any whisper. Not like a bird at all."

"She's not a song bird," Salina said.

"It's like...a chortle."

"The tongue of the ancients." Salina poked two fingers at her eyes. "Look into her, deep."

"How?" Tricia said. "She only came close once."

"Okay native girl, and white woman." Xia, having had enough broke circle ranks first. "Let's take a downtown tour; see what's shakin.'" For a Chinese girl, she'd picked up well on the western lingo. She led them off the school grounds, and across the street.

"Boring week," Salina said. "Except Ms. Ojnee's project."

"We need a cultural topic," Tricia said. She had an idea or two, but wanted to hear her friends first.

"Birds' influence on people," Xia said.

"Sure," Tricia said. "Could be good."

"I look up your raven bird." Thumbing a quick search into her genius phone, Xia popped an image in sphere and pointed. "Wūyā, how you say raven in Mandarin."

"Yes...we research," Tricia said, joining in the quest on her device. As they walked along the broken sidewalk, swerving over towards the town hall clock tower, sphere bubbles hovering before each of them led the way.

"A member of the corvid family," Tricia read. "Birds with brains, like smart birds. These Indonesian corvids actually make and use tools." Her sphere hologram presented a black bird clip, first shaping a stick and then digging a grub out of a log.

"Must be European expression—birdbrain as insult," Xia said. "More like Asian intelligence."

"White people," Salina said, shaking her head.

Tricia nodded absently.

"Listen, Brân, that's the Welsh word for raven," Tricia said. "A Welsh king had his head buried on the grounds."

"Legal grounds?" Xia played challenge.

"No," Tricia said, eyeing Xia. "At the Tower of London grounds." She wide-eyed her Asian friend, pointing down. "Like in the ground, ground."

"Where's that tower?"

"London," Tricia said. "In England. Look at the spin globe." Her sphere spun their blue planet, zooming across the ocean and in on the city on the Thames.

"Your ancestors come from there," Salina said. "They'd know those tower ravens."

"My name is Scottish," Tricia informed. "You know that...Moon Water."

"Now you call me by my given name," Salina shook her head. "White people, all one tribe."

Tricia brushed off the remarks like she would in any churn circle. "Listen," she said. "They've got a raven master who clips their wings so they can't fly far. And here's a connection to your ancient, Salina—a European legend. The story goes," her voice dropped to a hoarse whisper, "should the ravens leave the Tower of London, the tower will crumble and fall--and the kingdom with it."

"You Europeans and your fairy tale kingdoms," Salina said. "No respect—a bird was meant to fly. Our raven turns a bear white—to remind the people."

"C'mon, stay connected," Tricia said. "So, remind the people of what?"

"Our legend tells how the raven turns every ninth bear white—the spirit bear—to remind people of the time when the earth was all ice and snow."

"The Ice Age," Xia said in ominous tones. "More like the Frying Egg Age now."

"Xia's right," Tricia said. "The raven's story's gotta change—no more ice and snow memory, more like a heat's too high warning. We need a flame colored bear."

"Grandmother dreams of new legends," Salina said.

"How about other stories?" Xia said. "My parents hear the preacher's talk in the church." Her parents emigrated when Xia started elementary school, and hadn't picked up on the lingo as well.

"Bible stories, Xia, "Tricia said. "Not legends."

"Explains Western history, and customs," Xia said. "Simpler than Buddhism, or teachings of Confucius."

"Hey Asian cousin," Salina said. "We gotta get these white people back in their place."

"Yes, my genetic relative."

"Whatever," Tricia said, squinting one eyed at the other two.

"Kid-ding, girl," Salina said, slipping her arm over Tricia's shoulder.

Her so confident friends could be totally up front. But that's what Tricia liked about them, sometimes—good in any churn. They always got lit again after any crash, Salina consoling Xia's sometimes blunt talk.

"Hey girls, we need music on a Friday." Salina broke the tension. "Let's check out the Den."

"I dunno," Tricia said. "Things at home...I can't get in any trouble."

"Bus will be another hour," Xia said.

"We're not old enough," Tricia said. "They'll never let us in."

"Ancient rules," Salina gave her, and then Xia the totally look. "My cousin Geri will be working, okay? Maybe he'll get us a drink."

"Workin' in a bar," Xia said.

"Hey, Gerri's gonna be a land harmony advisor soon," Salina said. "At the RO."

Tricia's shaking head turned slowly into an acquiescing shrug. She'd make her own decisions, no matter where the situation got to. And maybe she'd find out more on the RO for back home.

They cut across the cracked main street pavement to The Den under a dangling wooden sign. Tricia followed last behind Salina squeezing through the slot between buildings. As they snuck out at the alley door, and ducked down under the half stairs, Tricia heard a sudden whoosh. She whirled about. The raven swooped in close, and at the last second veered off to leave a black feather in a drifting down-spin. Squeezing her lips tight, she hesitated but then caught the feather before turning to rush through the door.

Down a short hall, the dank smell of an underground cavern flooded the air. Tricia felt her way barely following Salina's voice, until fleeting shadows melded into a softer aroma. Kinda like one of dad's cracked beers after work. As their eyes adjusted, they fumbled their way around the bar, and tossed school bags into a corner.

"Hey Gerri, play us a song," Salina called out. "And bring us a beer."

"Who you wanna hear?" Gerri's laid-back voice came from behind the bar. "And no way."

"He's a good guy," Salina whispered.

Tricia relaxed, even glancing at Xia.

"Four Non-blondes," Salina said. "You need to dye yours darker, Tricia. And sunglass those hazel eyes. Otherwise, that's us."

"Count Salina," Xia said. "One, two, three of us."

"Technical issue," Salina said.

"Our raven's not blonde." Tricia revealed the black feather, waving a pattern before their eyes. "That's four."

"Problem solved," Salina said, elbowing Xia.

The old surround speakers crackled to life.

"What's up, that's the song," Salina said. "You guys know it?"

Trailing Salina's lead, Tricia edged out behind the others feeling her soft shoes sliding across the scuffed wooden dance floor. Salina flipped her braids back, framing her cute pressed nose against high cheekbones, while Xia tossed her short black hair back. They did look like cousins Tricia noticed, but she wove the feather in wing flaps waves to the flow of the beat.

"And so I wake in the morning, and I step outside..." Salina intoned.

"Knowing nothin's goin' right 'cause the man done lied," Xia sang out.

"Shut up Xia," Salina said. "That's not the words." She searched for the beat again. "I take a deep breath!"

As the song took them into emoji world, the three wish-washed like waves across the floor, shifting and swaying one direction against the other, still ever immersed as one. When the final chorus came, even Xia joined in raising hands on high and singing the eternal question in bonding inward tones. "What's going on?"

"What's going on?" Xia said loudly. "Re-colonization. My parents talk to the relatives in Hangzhou. They say Salina and I are DNA relatives."

Tricia stared, the mood broken and her mind raced over the information they were getting at home. People from Asia arriving in droves at the coastal city, to make status claims. She told herself again that she decided, and she would face life's problems by keeping an open mind.

"Hey girls," Gerri called out. "Nice dancing."

"Just ignore him," Salina said. "Another song, Gerri."

Tricia took a determined breath.

"History lesson for you school girls," Salina's cousin said. "Black Velvet's comin' up. First rock'n roll singer ever, this guy."

"Whatever, Gerri," Salina said. "Just play it."

Tricia, feather in hand, wove defiant images up in the air seeking escape into the feel of the moment. Moving with the new tempo, she found the flow between the riffs, and as she mini stepped into the growing beat let her mind engage with this latest song.

"A new religion..." blared out of the speakers.

The girls acted out the tune, improvising the words as they sang. Tricia led a lyrical rephrase of little boy's smile into big girl's, pushing her voice loud to emphasize girl. She could so feel that coming from deep inside. As the song came to a close they fell to their knees facing each other across the dance floor centre.

"What's going on?" Tricia said. She stuck the black feather into her hair, looking to catch her friends' eyes. "Forget re-colonization. Our future, girls, will be a new belief. A new church."

"What, the Black Feather Faith?" Xia said.

"Girls, think about it, yes!" Tricia said. "We post a social media invite, a girl god belief. You write the app code, Xia."

"Ms. Ojnee might like," Salina said.

Xia pointed at the time and, looking at each other, they rushed to grab their bags.

Following her friends' scurry out the door, and along behind their rush back to catch the bus, Tricia felt that feather stirring her hair in the wind. She pushed her mind into drift mode, letting thoughts flow back to the ancient. Girl god, goddess, yes. People needed a belief, she'd always suspected that, and especially lately like at home. Something rebellious, devious, yet still close tuned to the heart.

#

Tricia sat at the no-spheres-allowed dinner table across from her little brother Ben. She quietly thumbed a text into her genius phone. Of course not!! Why would she tell her parents about The Den? Xia might get the lingo, but she just didn't get a lot of other things.

Family laughter had recently turned to the totally serious, and she knew there'd be a no-smiles conversation tonight. Re-colonization, god, she felt so disoriented with that. But, she had learned to be a part of dealing with the moments at home. She sent Xia a quick later message.

When that last notice informed them of no seeding this spring, Dad wavered back and forth from rotten crop luck to a held in fuming at the unfair. And mom, of course, always followed his mood. The latest letter arrived just that day, official, from the RO, with the certified Repatriation Office logo.

Dad looked extra pissed.

"What do they say Malcolm?" Tricia's mom asked, carrying another load of dishes to the sink. Tricia knew her role queue, to get in there and talk at the right moment. If she could.

"Starts with that treaty crap Darlene," Dad said. "Listen, acknowledging we are on treaty 7 territory."

Mom started washing the dishes, losing herself in the sound of running tap water.

"We are dad," Tricia said quietly. "On treaty territory."

"I never signed any f'ing treaty." He took a swig of beer, peering at her with indignant blue eyes under his light brown hair.

"No dad," Tricia said. Ben stared silently at the table. "But remember when I did our family tree for school? Your great grandpa Craig McIntyre. You remember Dad?"

Dad's look drifted up to the sword hanging on the wall, there above his rifle. Grandpa McIntyre's family sword. Tricia had explained before how in Scotland, swords symbolized honor. Dad kind of heard—she knew he had a big heart underneath. Honor solves the problem, not a sword fight; she said that more than once at home and emphasized the idea in her school report on modern life. She dreamed a search for peace had motivated Grandpa McIntyre to journey across the ocean to over here. He did bring along that sword, but also the symbolism in the McIntyre name—

meaning son of the carpenter. Maybe some peace loving genetics in Dad.

"The treaty was signed for grandpa McIntyre," Tricia said. "So he could settle the land, our land now." Up until now, anyway. What once was Salina's people's land. And now they said Salina's people came from where Xia's people lived, like Asia. That had to be back in ancient times. The Crowfoot buffalo people learned to make pemmican to keep away winter hunger, and out east other natives farmed corn. Salina's grandmother said the people lived a lifestyle in harmony with the land, not perfect others said—torture and warfare, but at least they never killed off all the buffalo. Like Europeans did when they showed up.

"All lands west of the river so far east of here," Dad grumbled. "Who could ever own that big of a piece of land? Treaty my ass!"

That would be insane—to destroy your own source of life, like Ms. Ojnee talked at school now about their global biosphere. Miss Ojnee talked too on cultural differences, like ownership wasn't part of the native language when it came to land. But Tricia knew enough she had to focus on the current issue, right here, right now. She could only get so many other ideas in.

"So dad." Tricia kept her voice adult calm as she looked over the letter. "We go to the office tomorrow and find out the status of our land."

"What status?" Dad growled. "That's our goddam land that we farm every goddam year. Case closed."

Tricia gave a try tuning her voice tone down to as little girl as possible, and spoke plainly to what she knew. "The natives hunted buffalo every year," she said. "Before us."

"Salina's crowd can eat hamburgers," Dad growled. "Any time they want."

His voice came out less harsh, maybe affected by the beer. How would a girl goddess speak? She felt room for another angle.

"Xia says we'll still be able to eat hamburgers."

"F'ing Chinese," Dad said under his breath. "Bill says that's where all the First Nations legal funds are getting their 'anonymous' donations. From China, Darlene."

"Yes dear."

"China's one country in Asia, Dad," Tricia said. "The Asian Alliance has others too."

Dad had made so much progress talking on First Nations. Some of his friends still called them Indians, or worst, those who lived on and belonged on reserves. Like Xia's family, maybe ethnically Mandarin Chinese, but with relatives from Indonesia arriving to line up at land claims offices on the coast. Enough, she held her thoughts; Dad could only handle so much.

"The Warrens are talking on moving north," Dad said.

"Do you want to move dear?"

"Bill says that's like losing a war," Dad said. "Forced to move."

That one time Tricia followed the #NAbrothers #Asiancousins hashtags, they trended to a total spike late one night, and not long ago. One decision she'd made was to not to take in any conspiracy thoughts.

"Who wants to pioneer a life up in the bush?" Dad said. "You can't farm up there without breaking a lot of land. Crap land, lotta rocks."

"The letter says," Tricia chimed in, voice light, "there's a new strategy on how to care for the land."

Salina's grandmother talked about how natives lit fires, and Europeans put them out. That's partly why the pine beetles had such a feast in the lands of the Ktunaxa the first valley over the western mountains. Different concepts on land use there, no question. That valley tribe had been forced by the long ago Indian Act to move onto reserve and build a house and settle. The soldiers at Fort Steele made sure that happened.

"We might get some good ideas," Tricia said, pushing a smile. "Tomorrow, when we go in."

When she got herself to listen close, Tricia heard Xia saying Asia had a plan to settle the land European settlers didn't use. In Asian eyes, she'd say, a lot of land remained empty, or wasn't used properly. Properly, that was the key word, open to interpretation.

"We take good care of the land," Dad said. Tricia knew of Dad's passion for being a good farmer. He was a handy guy too, helping out neighbours, and caring deeply for farm and family.

"Yes Dad," Tricia said. "They want us to come in tomorrow. To the RO."

"We got us one smart girl, Darlene," Dad said, sliding his beer bottle across the table.

Tricia looked at her father's jaw, judging how settled that Scottish highlander conviction might be on the inside. God, not the one that picked up the sword of combat, she hoped. Sensing a good moment to bow out, and braving a smile, Tricia rose to head up to her room.

As she sat at her study desk looking out her window, twiddling the black feather, Tricia pictured that raven out there in the evening air. The bird had first showed up on a Sunday evening, like weeks ago, when she vaguely noticed a dark feathery shape approaching in the distance. Circling in closer, the bird eventually took the sandwich bread she tossed, but never again came so close. Having established contact, the bird made it clear something other than food to be the reason.

Tricia first told Salina that Monday, and her friend told her how ravens often sat on treetops looking over the world. Crows gathered in flocks, cawing a lot, Salina said, while ravens hung out in quieter pairs. Or all alone like this one.

She let her head drop to the desk to rest on her hands. Now, Salina talked on wisdom and that spirit bear legend. She rested, figuring, and waiting on any inspiration that might come racing in.

Why would Salina's grandmother, an elder, be looking to the youth for leadership? Like, the ancient wisdom totally shifting. These days. Like, how could Tricia ever get any more of what she knew through to Dad? She'd seen that bird turn completely over in the air once, showing how a feathered creature could navigate air currents on clever wings. Could the message be about the atmosphere? Ms. Ojnee's biosphere.

She popped her head back up from the desk and clicked her genius to bubble sphere. Checking for Xia or Salina, she wondered if she'd ever truly be able to look into those ancient bird eyes.

#

The McIntyre family minus mom pulled up in the gravel parking space in front of the RO. Tricia slid her toe down, feeling for that step her daddy welded on when she was six. The work truck was so high, she still needed that step. Her father's work ethic, embossed in that paint chipped Malcolm McIntyre Welding decal, blazed out from the vehicle's side. Ben piled out of his reserved front seat, and Tricia tactfully followed in after the men.

A friendly faced attendant nodded as they entered. "Please, one minute." This guy could have been Xia's cousin. Or Salina's. Tricia quick checked her father's jaw.

"I think we take a number, Dad," Tricia pulled a dispenser ticket, and glanced at the LED board. Kind of overboard for a small town.

Officially with one to wait, they took seats. Tricia's eyes drifted across the script of tacked up wall posters. Land changes people, people don't change the land. Feather icons outlined the text, all black—what might hang from a native Band Office wall. When Salina talked as Moon Water, the girl told of days when their Piikani chief met a Scottish colonel under a tent awning at Blackfoot Crossing. To sign the treaty. Today almost felt like time travel, that past to this future and back again.

As Tricia's mind wandered, her ears tuned in to the counter conversation. A young couple with a DNA result...found the test showed no Asian ancestry. Assigned to a pure European classification, they needed help understanding the land rights implications.

Land on her mind, Tricia glanced back at the wall. As a farm girl, she'd forever been hearing Dad talk about crop land and the fallow land and the part-broken back quarter. Moon Water once said if you thought people change the land, you're seriously mistaken. What a switch, buffalo hunting to farming. Those elders said if we don't take care of nature, nature won't take care of us. Their native language didn't even have a word for their people, except human being. Like, everyone's in that us. She read another poster; Your breath is the wind. Native beliefs...they needed a second coming, not another colonization.

"Next," the attendant said.

"C'mon dad, that's us."

They stepped up to the counter as the young couple shuffled out, distorted looks on their faces.

"Picture ID please." The Asian attendant beamed.

Dad passed his driver's license over, jaw set on a face hard and silent.

"Current address?"

Dad shifted, nodding.

"Mr. Malcolm McIntyre." Xia's could-be-cousin looked directly at dad for face recognition. "Did you arrive in a vehicle Mr. McIntyre?"

"Yup," Dad spoke, thumb poking back over his shoulder. "Work truck." Tricia took a breath, not sure how the pride in his voice would go over here.

The attendant glanced out the window at the welding truck.

"I'm afraid we will require adjustments to your mode of transportation," the attendant said.

"What?" Dad's voice hardened.

"Our technician can look and you can apply for a vehicle evaluation but we have seen others like yours. You will likely have carbon back taxes of higher value than the market value of your vehicle. That's my at-a-glance evaluation, but you are free to fill out the paperwork."

"I don't know what you're talkin' about," Dad said, staring.

"We need your registration please." The attendant went on, undeterred.

"Glove box Ben." Dad pointed to the door and Tricia's brother scurried out.

"Okay, Mr. McIntyre." The attendant took on a practiced calm voice. "Along with your vehicle, we need to discuss land and living arrangements."

Tricia could almost feel her father's heart hammering below his totally solid set jaw. Keep breathing she told herself.

"You will realize the Asian Alliance does not recognize your land ownership system—that has been explained in our letters," the attendant said. "We wish to assist your transition to our improved system. We have literature to read—here is a pamphlet you can look over to consider your options." Dad totally ignored the folded glossy paper. "Or, if you wish to speak to someone, we have a land harmony advisor with whom you might discuss western grain farming practices."

Judging the moment, Tricia gently put her hand on her father's shoulder, and piped in. "Could we have the most pertinent pamphlets?"

"Here you are young lady." She reached for the paper prints. "Our Manila office analyses show the land here to be best utilized for food and bio fuel crops, to be optimized at a new scale." The guy rattled off more Dad's way. "Huge fields are very inefficient when we have so many people. Grain field production has been deemed critical, and will be nationalized..."

The first title in Tricia's hand read The Smaller Plots of Land Plan and flipping to the next she read Soil Revitalization Program. Glancing over itemized sections, she saw mention of biochar, soil health and negative carbon emissions.

"Do you have any questions Mr. McIntyre?"

"My land." Dad's voice came out loud. "What about my land?"

"Our agricultural head office in Bangkok wishes to see agricultural productivity go up, energy available go up and carbon emissions go down."

"What about my land?" Dad banged his finger to his chest. "Bought and paid for."

"Ahh, Mr. McIntyre." The attendant's practiced smile widened. "Here is a question to consider. Did your ancestors apply for or obtain a migrant permit vis-à-vis the original Asian residents?"

"What the f... what are you talkin' about?" Dad's neck bristled.

"Did your ancestors ask permission, Mr. McIntyre, in any way from whom you call Native Americans to enter the lands you now occupy? Your previous government may have failed to do so, but we now recognize all signed treaty rights de facto."

Tricia's mind raced as she scanned through the pamphlets— emphasizing the huge western farming fields seen as vacant by modern day Asians. Like vast buffalo pastures were once seen to be by Europeans.

"I need to feed my family." Dad's voice cracked. What would Moon Water's ancestors have felt, coming out of that treaty tent?

Tricia touched Dad's shoulder again.

"We wish to assist you in repaying your carbon debt," the attendant said. "We have ways you can do so. You will be allowed to stay in your current residence, but only if you pay the adjusted taxes."

"What taxes?" Dad boomed out. "I pay all my taxes."

"Unfortunately, your previous government was very lax in accounting carbon emissions," the attendant said. "The true cost required to offset carbon emissions has been left out."

"F...ing taxes," Dad growled, shaking his head.

"If taxes are not paid by the default date," the smiling Asian said, "we will be subdividing your many gongmu, your acres, into plots for the many coming."

"I can't pay tax," Dad said, gripping the counter, "unless I seed the fields this spring."

"Due to transition requirements, that will not be an option. However you can move to a smaller house. If you move to the special designated area, you will pay smaller tax." The attendant pointed to a map on the counter. "We encourage you to integrate your family into the new arrangement."

"Those plots can't be two...three acres!" Dad said. "Like a vegetable garden."

"We revitalize the soil, to make the land more productive." The attendant started another spiel. "You may wish to work your back taxes off in the Soil Revitalization Program, the SRP. You attend land harmony classes—the minimum required, where your Treaty 7 First Nations people qualify as teachers. Upon completion, you apply for work at the SRP in several capacities. SRP has 9 billion ton negative emissions target over the next five years based on biochar techniques."

"Any welding work?" Tricia asked, sensing Dad's frustration reaching a peak. "Dad's got a pressure ticket." With the old oil and gas industry fading fast, Tricia knew Dad might adapt his welding work.

"That may be possible," the attendant said. "The biochar burners require maintenance repairs."

"Could be good, Dad."

"Listen to your daughter, Mr. McIntyre. We invite you to continue farming—but learn a new way. Check out biochar." The attendant smiled, as if noticing his own local lingo.

"Army's gonna march in from the south." Dad blustered out. "Jet fighters are gonna be flying over any day now."

"Ahh, Mr. McIntyre. Your southern neighbours' system allows inadequate leaders to be chosen." The attendant smiled. "As yours did. They are no longer in a position to interfere. We have an agreement across your southern border."

"Dad, we can plant a big garden this spring," Tricia said. "We'll have lots to eat. We can take Mom to check out that new little house. Please."

"I am required to inform you of an item on living arrangements, Mr. McIntyre. If you wish, you can initiate a land claim case. You to take that first to the local band council for initial evaluation. You live on Treaty 7 land and all treaties your ancestors signed are now recognized by the Asian Alliance," the attendant said. "All legal fees will be taken on by yourself. We have sample cases and their outcomes; I would suggest you refer to this pamphlet."

The attendant slid another piece of paper across the counter.

Dad tapped his fist harder and harder on the counter, ignoring the pamphlet and staring at the attendant.

"We refer you to treaty 7." The attendant patiently tapped at the pamphlet, continuing undeterred. "European people signed treaty 7 in 1877 with the Piikani people, our genetic cousins. You can appeal your claim to court, and any decision will be reviewed."

Dad's fist stopped pounding.

"We do want to help you Mr. McIntyre." The Asian's voice lowered. "For your personal reference, I would suggest a court case in Bangkok or Manila, not Beijing."

The door banged open and Ben came bouncing back in. Tricia stepped between her brother and the counter, taking the registration papers to hand directly to the attendant.

"Hey Dad, they got e-bikes out there," Ben spouted. "Josh got an e-bike—super fast."

"Yes, we have a record of your vehicle," the attendant said, glancing at his screen. "Mr. McIntyre, we cannot allow you to leave driving a vehicle such as that."

Tricia ignored the tension her mind rushing at warp speed. She had to divert Dad's attention from the moment, and get him thinking past his welding rig truck.

She turned to her brother, picking up on his energy.

"So cool, hey Ben," Tricia said. "You know HOV boards?"

"Course I do," Ben said. "C'mon, check them out."

"Thank you Mr. McIntyre," he said. "Please leave your vehicle keys in this tray."

Dad wrapped his arm over Ben's shoulder as he dropped the truck keys not looking in the plastic box. As her father turned from the counter without a word, Tricia heaved a sigh of relief as she followed the other two out.

#

That afternoon, the whole family went over to check out the smaller house. Ben's enthusiasm had held long enough for Tricia to talk Dad into showing Mom. Walking through the place gave Tricia a whiff of the totally new room that would be hers, kinda squashed, but kinda cushy. No more hidden off by the back quarter, here she wouldn't be last off the bus anymore. Instead, she'd be right in this rural village living close to her friends. She could walk over to Xia's or Salina's right now even. She closed her door and followed the short hallway back to the front room.

"Forget spring seeding, Bill." Dad paced the kitchen floor, bubble sphere tracking in front of him. "The crops we took off last fall are the goddam last. What's that leave us?"

Tricia could hear the other male voice barking back. "They're subdividing my fields into trash little shit gardens, Malcolm." She could see the other gruff half bearded face pulling at his ball cap, waving at a map of his land.

"Yeah, and last time I had a pressure weld was a repair job," Dad said. He switched voice to personal, on headphone listener. Dad could be handy with the latest tech when he put his mind to it. "On that tank up Longway Road."

Tricia sat down at the table and flicked her phone to bubble sphere.

"Abandoned, huh" Dad spoke quietly. "How about torch cutting for scrap?" Dad listened. "Uh huh." Tricia glanced to see her father's jaw tense up.

The sphere tracked in on her two friends together, close and outside. She had to get out of there, and she clicking walk find, she quietly stepped out the front. Turning right down the path, she clicked the sphere off when she spotted Salina's braids, right there. How could everything be so close? She headed directly over.

"Hey guys." She walked up to the outside plaza table.

"Ciao," Xia waved.

"New neighbour," Salina said. "Yes?"

Tricia shrugged.

"You ever live on reserve Salina?" she asked.

"Born in town, been here a couple years," Salina said. "Reserve's emptying out now, like town."

She circled the table, slowly, inviting the other two to join a churn.

"What you guys been into?" Tricia sort of sang. "Like, what's going on?"

"That Indonesian bird, the corvid that uses tools, that's a crow," Xia said. "Not a raven."

"Alright," Tricia said. "That's rad."

"Bird brilliance," Xia said. "Equals Asian genius."

"Cool." Tricia said. "I checked out the Blackfoot Confederacy, and before. So like the Avonlea people were the first to use bow and arrow on the plains. Before that the Clovis natives first invasion lived with the mammoths."

"The people were put here by Old Man Napi," Salina said. "Thousands of years ago."

"But how far back do you go?"

"Niitsittapi. You just say the original people," Salina said. "My grandmother's been tellin' me about this Piikani girl, who became a buffalo runner. Pretty cool for a girl back then. At the buffalo jump Silent Wind could mimic the calf cry, to draw the herd. The boys would do the wolf chase and stalk behind buffalo. 'Cause buffalo have lousy eyes, but a good sense of smell and sound."

"Me and this native girl got kinship genes." Xia shifted talk topic. "The Alliance says so."

"You guys could be like cousins." Tricia said, going along, staring and comparing the other two. "You know?"

The two stopped walking, and spoke in unison, wrapping arms over each other's shoulder.

"Hey girl, we band together," Salina said to Xia. "We take our turn."

"You Europeans are gonna be reclassified," Xia said.

"We'll give you a reserve, white woman, don't worry," Salina looked at Tricia.

"No reserve," Xia said. "We keep her as a pet."

They all fell silent.

"You really want to do that?" Tricia eyed the two. They looked at each other, all eyes meeting.

"Okay, we all live together here in this village," Salina said. "We're all cousins."

"We take this apart for social science," Xia said. "Asia colonizes the Americas, then and now."

No way. Better the girl goddess. But Tricia knew that would take tactics.

"Hey Salina," Tricia shifted talk back. "What's that mean 'dog days'?" She suspected the phrase came from pre-contact times.

"People had to get around before horses," Salina said. "The horses you Europeans lost got to us before your explorer guys."

"And..." Tricia said.

"Back before horses, the people took pups blind out of the den, and never even let the children play with them. 'Cause they were working dogs—they pulled the travois. Long before grandmother's day, back when the people took medicine bundles to Napi the Creator who made the earth. Those were the dog days, before horses."

"Cool. C'mon girls," Tricia said. "Now we churn. I'll take you both on—you take re-colonization Xia, obviously, and new church me. Salina, you play arbitrator and side with Xia."

"Okay."

"Sure."

"First challenge to you Xia, like how did the natives first put a claim on this land?" Tricia challenged the conventional directly. "Your ancient ancestors from Asia you say."

"Short and simple, DNA," Xia said. "Science proves strong genetic links between native Americans, North and South, and Asia. Who shows up first gets first claim."

"Okay."

"First challenge back to you Tricia, like how legal is the European colonial claim? Showing up second."

"Europeans came as explorers," Tricia said. "Take Peter Fidler in 1792; he was the first known Euro contact with the Ktunaxa, the Kootenay Indians."

"Explorers, yeah, nice word," Xia said. "More like invaders, a military scouting for conquest."

"European farmers came after, and signed treaties with the natives," Tricia said. "Treaties supplied food, education and offered an improved lifestyle."

"Assimilation!" Xia said. "Aggressive assimilation equals cultural annihilation, cultural genocide."

"And," Tricia said. "Does the Asian Alliance plan the same?"

Tricia had her going. Strategically backing down, she listened hoping to hear an underlying belief.

"European expansion was aberration in the destiny of humanity's true story," Xia said. "Most people always lived in Asia over times historical. First moves into New World were real long term manifest destiny—the natives. The space here now remains as 'empty' for Asian density as Europeans claimed when they colonized. Now Europe and her unethical empires fade further into background of global story."

Tricia glanced to Salina, but kept listening.

"Second challenge white woman: Were European treaties ever recognized?" Xia said. "Natives were moved onto their designated reserves, taking away their land and their lifeblood. Until Asian Alliance, native claims on their land and their true heritage, remained unresolved."

"Cede," Tricia said. She nodded carefully, choosing to smile.

"Fun fact on DNA: Everyone will be brown skinned in the future," Xia said. "Blue eyes, like yours Tricia, are recessive gene."

"Salina, oh Water Moon," Tricia said. "Participate."

"My ancestors' children were ripped from their homes by the Europeans," Salina said. "We were called heathens, pagans, savages—all noted in the Truth and Reconciliation report."

"Not so fun fact," Xia said. "Thousands of native children died in residential schools. You Europeans have lousy record."

"My great grandmother went to St. Eugene Missions School," Salina said, nodding. "She survived, with stories to tell."

"Cede," Tricia said, nodding, lips tight. "Anything else?"

"When Europeans colonized, they brought backwards ways with them," Xia said. "Conquering, taking."

"Partying like the crazy Tolome boys," Salina said.

"They brought lower moral standards," Xia said. "Maybe explaining reasons for colonizing. Admiral Zheng He in the Ming dynasty, at the time of your Columbus, sailed ocean going junks on seven voyages bearing gifts for any he encountered. Next Emperor kept those ships in harbour, but now, Asian Alliance comes for other reasons. Offering gifts of global organization."

"We need to get lit, Xia," Tricia said. "How?"

"The Alliance understands evolution, cultural evolution too, and forgives these past acts," Xia said. "Asia expects appreciation for gifts at this time. People here are offered not 'residential schools', but opportunity to learn from the land people how to better live in harmony with the biosphere. Confucius way."

"Really?" Tricia said. "Final comment allowed?"

The other two both nodded.

"Now, here, today, how do we get trust?" Tricia said. Maybe we can do better. "Does repetition of the past bring on a solution? Like, if everyone talks recolonization. No. How about a totally new idea? Like…a new belief...in Mother Earth?"

"Same churn org?"

"Yes."

"First challenge," Xia said. "You need a prophet guy. They keep saying in the church the main guy's coming back, but that hasn't happened for thousands of years. How you gonna get that to happen?"

"Another problem is the guy part," Tricia said. "We like need a girl."

"We research," Salina prompted. "Like, what search?"

"Ancient beliefs." Tricia popped sphere and joined Salina. "You know, I saw this image, boy and girl bull jumpers, by the horns, yeah, Mycenaeans or Minoans. Look for that."

"Minoans," Salina said. "They lived on this island in the Mediterranean, named Crete."

"Yes, them!" Tricia said. "Before the traditional boy god Greeks. They had oodles of goddesses. A girl bull-jumped with the boys back then."

"What ever happened to them?" Salina asked.

"Thera volcano erupted, and hit them hard," Tricia looked into Moon Water's eyes softly. "Then, the mainland Greeks colonized."

"So, you have history," Xia said. "Chinese talk of Confucius, land harmony, for thousand years."

"We'd need a sign," Salina said. "From any girl goddess."

Maybe not for school, but for any more than that they would need a real sign. "Yes," Tricia admitted. They'd need some water into wine moment, or a walk on the water. A bird might kinda walk on water, skimming low over the surface. But they needed what a girl could do.

"Salina, how do you call raven in native language?" Tricia said. "And how come you never told us?"

"Just for you white girl, I'll tell you Kâhkâkiw," Salina said. "My people don't often say raven in our language, 'cause that talks to the spirit bear. Kâhkâkiw, Tricia."

"How about the revised spirit of Kâhkâkiw for a sign?" Tricia said. "Messenger of a girl goddess."

"Churn wind down girls," Salina said. "Final comments?"

"My relatives arrive at West Coast tomorrow," Xia said. "Asian office says they can make land claims here if they don't want city life. Do they learn church songs? Or bird talk?"

"We have to learn harmony," Salina said. "Learn to honor the land, like grandmother says."

"Our land, our life-blood, our biosphere," Tricia said. "We need a girl goddess as our teacher."

"Churn over," Salina said.

"Okay girls, Ms. Ojnee's project, I say," Tricia said. And totally more too she thought. "We've got to decide."

#

Tricia nudged the farm home door opened, that familiar twilight gleam of the setting sun catching the worn brass knob. A pin dropping might resonate off the walls around her parents sitting under the kitchen lighting. Mom's hands rested unmoving on the knitting in her lap. At the table, Dad sat before an empty hovering sphere, an RO pamphlet flopping in one hand.

Ben must be in bed, she figured walking in carefully and pulling out a chair to form a silent triangle with her parents.

Glancing at the pamphlet, Tricia recognized what she'd left on the table hoping Dad would see. This RO transition could turn out so cool for farming, and great for the community. Everyone having a piece of land gave everyone who wanted a garden and local food. Fields the Asian Alliance planned on keeping for grain could ensure bread on every table as the biochar program revitalized the soil. As long as there was trust; a common belief. The SRP took carbon out of the atmosphere, the pamphlet emphasized, as people adapted to an Anthropocene world.

Tricia looked to her father's eyes, but his face remained frozen, not one tiny muscle twitching. His eyes bored through the tabletop, his jaw set hard. He refused to glance up.

She began a gentle sentence, but before two words were out he sprang to life. Exploding to his feet, Dad walked away from the pamphlet flat fallen where it lay. Without a word he crossed the room, not looking to either of them and reached up to grab his rifle off the rack.

The moment he hesitated at the door Tricia felt an urge to have her hand on his shoulder again. But, she could only watch wide-eyed as her father reached back to the key rack, grabbed the spare truck keys and dropping them into his side pocket stormed out.

Mom let out an moan, unnatural even for her.

Scattered, Tricia leaped up first towards the door, but hand frozen on the knob she stopped, and stepped instead to the window. Staring out, she picked out her father's jagged shadow tracking his form off into the dim light. Would he go on foot all the way to the RO, miles off down the darkening road?

Taking a cautious breath, Tricia turned back to Mom.

"Mama." She found her voice as she sat. "Do you believe in anything mama?"

Her mother's mouth twitched at one corner, and a slight glimmer rose in her eye. Raising one hand from the knitting, she formed one finger into a pointer, stabbing lightly Tricia's direction. Breathing as gently as she could, Tricia took her mother's hand and pressed it in a tight squeeze to her chest, lips pressed firm.

What could she do? Wait?

In the silence she could have sworn she heard a feather rustling—like a girl losing all sense of reality. Keeping it together, Tricia left her mother with a fumbled hug and made her way to her room. Collapsing head down on her study desk, almost against her will, she struggled to figure what might bring a man like her father to his knees. Or new senses? Some kind of miracle, or shift to stir acceptance in with pride.

Eyes closed her mind lost touch, scattering to the edges of space. To a place where all rules crumbled, to the realm of gods, or ancient eyes.

The raven veered into her inner plane of vision, behind her fatigued eyelids, as if flying through her window to flap about her inner room. Her walls shifted, melding into the outside as she gained wings, swooping along behind the black bird. A silent scream escaped her trembling lips as they dove steeply, then careered back up to circle the midnight air. Half believing this to be nothing but dreamland, she made an effort to lift her head. But unable to even find her human form she gave up and lost herself in the flight. Breath caught again, she found herself skimming tree tops. Then, realizing the raven to be distant, she found that she could choose her own flight path.

What to do?

Of course, determined, she would find her father's road and track down the man and his frustration. She needed get into his mind, hand in hand with Grandpa McIntyre speaking Scottish ancestry into a mix with the ancient, and help his transition. Whooshing in, she would drop him a black faith feather.

But, would he get it? Help, she let her call drift deep into the world of whispers.

Staring hard, grasping to find orientation she came face to face with those raven eyes. Dark, universal, the eyes penetrated her soul until she became one with them and she was looking out from within. Through those eyes she saw further, and she saw through the mysterious dark. Soaring upward she let go in a total release, wondering what next. Kâhkâkiw took her as if from the nest, steering her flight skyward, up beyond where even a bird might go. At the edge of the sky the moon beamed into the form of a white bear, curled up in a ball with orange flames licking at all sides. And from the flame's glow she peered down at the big blue marble, the Goldilocks planet, the third rock from the sun. A rush overwhelmed her, as if that of the whole of life, and as if she was one with it.

God, what next? Staring hard into those eyes one last time, she whispered her thanks, now determined it be known she was on task.

And she was free.

Plummeting back down towards the trees, she picked out a spec moving along a darkened road, tiny at first. Yet as she approached the spec became a person, walking, and she knew the ball cap. She read a desperate fury in her father's racing walk, and an overwhelming urge to lash out with the weapon at his side. He felt so familiar, yet not, so ancient, yet totally now, of today.

As she swooped in, the ball cap slowed to a less hurried pace. As if he knew of what was above, as if he could hear something, though she made no sound. She sensed his concern, fear in the night, but worry of so much more. Fear for her, his daughter and for his son and wife. He came to an abrupt stop, and then, in an instance whirled about, whipping his rifle upward to point into the baffling darkness.

Taking in all his turmoil, she felt filled with a burst of knowing, like a year of school all in one bundle. A child's smile broke over her, like a girl watching her daddy weld a step onto his accomplishment pride. A wave of pure energy took her over, flowing that child's smile into her father's being. In a flash of starlight, she dived down into his arms. Dad...daddy. Singing to her father's heart she offered a musical flow like the lullaby of angels.

All time stopped, for who knew how long.

Then, as a bird, she flapped her wings, flew out ahead of him, and soared up in an ever expanding circle. The raucous chortling of a raven called out from her, or the other she was in, sounding but once as they drifted off into the beyond, and then apart.

And time returned.

The front door banging open, Tricia lifted her aching head from the desk. She rushed out down the hall to find her father entering. Totally calm, completely unaware of her presence, he leaned his rifle into the corner. Walking over to the couch he crashed softly down, his snoring beginning before his head came to a deep rest on the cushion.

Half in a trance, Tricia turned slowly back to her room to snuggle in under her covers. What had happened, she could totally not ever guess. Drifting off, she clung to all she could. She knew she wasn't the girl, for sure not like a prophet after days in the desert and certainly not any goddess, and that there never would be any the girl. Any girl could be the one to stretch out to what she knew, to know her talk. She so needed a churn with her friends. Tomorrow.

#

Tricia half skipped about her room, ready for a Monday morning bus ride to school. They had tiptoed around Dad's gentle snoring all day Sunday on the couch. And after churn talking all day, and then late into the night with the girls on bubble sphere, she felt totally rad-a-tad-tad.

"Dad came home way after midnight." Tricia told them. "So, like my grandfather kept his sword in the sheath, Dad never pulled the trigger either."

She fumbled any words on the raven story, slipping into a half conversant whispering, at times until her friends could coax her back. They talked forever about the ancient eyes and what a girl goddess meant.

"Moon bear," Salina drew the words out, extending the awe.

"On fire," Xia dragged her back. "No ice."

Tricia had danced around their circle waving the black feather as if in ritual. Raven brought the woman's whisper to the inner goddess of any girl, she told them when speaking clearly. Xia challenged black as a feminine color, but the black velvet tune helped smooth that out. Black held rebellious overtones, which they needed, and, any church needed a dark side. To contrast with the answer woven elsewhere into the fabric of belief.

Convinced they'd take the faith of a feather on for school, she talked on and on about how they could fit that onto re-colonization.

"We code this into an app, right?" She told Xia. "We pass it around."

She had smiled when she got a nod from Xia.

Bursting into the front room she found Dad talking excited to his buddy in the sphere. Glancing to the coat rack, she saw the ball cap missing, replaced by an e-bike safety helmet hanging on the peg. A box of rifle shells lay tossed up by the garbage bin, and the gun had been fitted back in its rack by the Scottish sword.

"They call it pyrolysis, Bill," Tricia's father wacked a pamphlet on this knee. "You elevate the temperature with no oxygen. Like a low oxy torch. A permanent process, you get charcoal or they got this other word biochar. You match it to your soil. Kind of a fertilizer, but more like it holds your nutrients and your moisture in the soil. You do it right, you really boost your crop."

Dad grinned Tricia's way, giving a solid thumbs up. Holding his hand to block the sphere, he gave her a loud whisper. "Your dad's got a birdbrain, this bird squawky walkin' around in his head."

"Chortling?" Tricia said.

"Yeah," Dad said. He laughed, jaw totally relaxed.

Made in the USA
Charleston, SC
22 December 2016